The Artifacts
A Flint Hills Story

Eric T. Reynolds

A Spec Historical Novel

To Kansas Friends

ACKNOWLEDGMENTS

Special thanks goes to my first reader, Nancy Reynolds. She makes everything in life better. And thanks to my editors, Megan Lucas, Claire Nuti, Alex Shine, and Rose Reynolds.

I also appreciate the encouragement from my friends, Sherry Stapleford, Kathy L. Murphy, Heidi Surber Teichgraeber, Jody Stephens, Barbara Jean Clopton, Debi Carbaugh Robinson, Terri-Lynne DeFino, Tom & Terry Denner, Jeanette Carter, Jill Bailey, Judy Fugett-Gaines, Teri Heyl, Sue Flowers, SueEllen Bodenhamer, Laura Reynolds, Matthew Reynolds, Tricia Beavin, Kathy Pierron Chartrand, and I know I've missed many for which I hang my head in shame. (And those whose names I've misspelled.)

And to my original hometown of Eureka, Kansas, on which Sycamore Falls is based.

Photo © Michalakis Ppalis | Dreamstime.com

Unto the hills where dreams live lift your eyes;
Though grim clouds burst, hold close your paradise.
—Serena Truman Robinson

PROLOGUE

THE GIRL HOPPED ONTO THE BANK OF THE CREEK and waited for the boy. He skipped across the same exposed rocks and landed next to her. "Toss me the pack," he said, then flung it over his shoulder and started up through a grove of trees toward the top.

Reaching an outcrop, he grabbed an exposed root above, found footing on a small tree just below, and hauled himself onto the ledge.

He called to the girl down by the creek, "Hey, I'm almost there!"

"I'm not going up that way—what about snakes!"

"Go around this and I'll see you up at the top!"

He hiked up through the last of the trees and emerged onto a level grassy area. When he got there, she was already standing on a large rock, shielding her eyes, looking out at the vista. He went to her and took in the view. A sea of green hills rippled to the horizon beneath the big sky, the land broken by an occasional silo and cattle dotting some of the slopes. Distant oil wells continued their perpetual seesaw almost in sync along the side of one hill.

"Look how far you can see," she said, her hair flying out in the breeze. "This is one of the highest hills here. There's an eight hundred foot rise in elevation from Mound Grove to here."

"I want to bring my easel up here and paint this," he said.

"You should!"

He pointed to a neighboring hill. The roof of a house poked up from behind the hill's summit.

"Look, an old house," he said. "Let's go."

They hiked downhill, around outcrops and over a row of square-ish rocks that ringed the hill. They reached the edge of some woods on the other hill and ran toward the house. The boy tripped over something along the woods and fell flat on his face.

"You okay?" she said, rushing to him.

He caught his breath. "No broken skin."

She pulled him up.

He pointed at the old house. "Let's go in!"

"What if somebody lives there?"

"In that dump?"

They headed to the back porch and climbed up rotting steps.

"Back door's open," he said.

"We can't go in there," she said.

He grabbed the doorknob. "Come on!"

They stepped in and wandered around the mostly empty rooms for a few minutes, then found a more intriguing room.

"Hey," he said, pointing into the room.

She grabbed his wrist to discourage him from going in. He shook free and went over to the shelves.

* * *

A few minutes later. . .

"Getting dark in here," she said. "Let's go."

"Okay, just a sec."

"Hey, put that back. We can't take things from here."

"I'm just looking at it. You put yours down, too. I can't believe all those are sitting there going to waste."

"We need to get home," she said.

"Text Mom and let her know we're on our way."

She looked at her phone. "I don't have a signal."

"I saw a tower before we came in here, so you should have one," he said.

"How long are you going to keep looking at those? Come on, leave it in there and let's go."

"It's sticking out from the rest," he said, reaching for it.

"Whatever," she said, stepping toward the window.

"Okay," he said, "meet me over by that barn in a minute, probably get a signal there."

She turned and gazed out the window. "Okay. It looks different from in here," she said.

She turned back to him and he was already gone.

CHAPTER ONE
The Victorian and the Farmhouse

KAYLA RAMSEY BOUGHT A HOUSE. Two houses, rather, an ornate 1890 Victorian at the edge of the Flint Hills town of Sycamore Falls, Kansas, and a dilapidated 1870 farmhouse on the hill behind the Victorian.

She didn't need the second house or what the seller left in there.

* * *

During her first evening in the Victorian, she gazed out from the back porch at the hill. The old farmhouse up there was a dark silhouette against the night.

She felt a strong urge to get up there. After staring at it for a while, she headed back inside the Victorian to the empty parlor, to the boxes stacked along its walls, and strolled around.

Unpacking can wait a couple of days, she thought.

Nightfall settled in.

She spent the rest of the evening writing the opening of her upcoming blog series, "The Influence of Art on a Flint Hills Town and Vice Versa."

Kevin was part of the art community here and her old friend was a major reason she moved out here.

* * *

The next day, she spent the morning pulling items from a dozen boxes in the parlor.

A knock at the door interrupted her.

Kevin!

She invited him in.

"Welcome to Sycamore Falls," he said. "I've seen this house from the outside, but have never been inside."

"You like it?"

He looked around. "I do."

"What're you going to do with those forty acres out back and that old house? How'd you ever afford all this?"

"I had no idea Mom was that well off or that she'd leave that much to me."

"Did you two ever make up?"

"We didn't. And I'll regret it forever."

"I'm sorry to hear that."

"I've thought ahead though. I set up a trust with my cousin as beneficiary. The property deeds to the trust should anything happen to me."

They caught up on things until he had to leave.

* * *

By mid-afternoon, she grabbed her binoculars, went out the kitchen door, and up the gravel lane, through the field to the old farmhouse.

As she hiked, a gust on a neighboring hill pushed a wave through the grass that rolled over to her, the tallgrass singing as the breeze flowed past.

A red-tailed hawk soared down over Sycamore Falls' roofs that dominated the valley. She pulled out her binoculars so she could glide with the bird.

She turned back to the farmhouse. It looked shabby. It was a popular style in the 1800s, with wraparound porch. Overgrown brush obscured its stone foundation. A newer style barn stood nearby. She went up to the old house, climbed the rickety porch steps, and peeked through the etched door window. Brenda had abandoned more than just the house when she sold it to Kayla. Old broken down furniture still sat on frayed area rugs. She could see through to a room in the back, a library lined with shelves full of old books.

How odd, she thought. A snapshot in time. Too bad this place is a dump. Wonder if it's salvageable. Have to get someone up here for an estimate.

* * *

She stepped off the porch and walked the perimeter of the house, following a gravel driveway around the side. Trees that hadn't been trimmed in ages shaded the backyard. A gnarly tree had wound its way around a deteriorating shed. Two rusting metal T ends of an old clothesline still stood minus the lines that held drying laundry of times past. She trudged along a woods edge and stopped short of stumbling over a rock outcrop hidden by overgrown grass mostly covered with fallen twigs and leaves.

She veered away from the trees and stared up at the back of the old farmhouse, at the old screened-in back porch, up at the second floor balcony then gazed over at the barn. All was quiet, except for the singing of the breeze through the prairie and the occasional clank of a loose downspout.

She went around to the front porch and headed up through the door into the foyer. She hadn't been in since inspection and the house smelled stale like before. The wooden staircase along the wall was a look she liked. She went to the living room and opened some windows. At least the windows weren't stuck.

As she walked through the living room with its peeling shell pattern wallpaper, which must have been from the 1940s, she felt impressions of past generations. She would have to check with the Historical Society for information about the former residents, perhaps back to the house's nineteenth century beginnings.

She went into the library and settled onto one of the old chairs against a wall opposite the bookcase and stared at the bookshelves across from her. An eclectic collection of old books stared back: frayed old books that looked like they'd been there for decades. So many to explore. She looked forward to digging into them. Many of their authors were long gone. The authors' minds could still communicate with readers' minds, one-way communications from authors dead for decades.

She scanned across the old books.

* * *

Next Door Neighbors by Josephine Lawrence had a couple of bookmarks. She went to the bookcase and pulled the book from the shelf then flipped to the first bookmark at page 32. Toward the middle of the page were words underlined in pencil: not one to make a stranger feel at home. Another bookmark on page 37 had underlined in pencil: Why don't you go out and see around a little?"

After a shrug and another scan at the old books, she noticed that *The House of the Seven Gables* by Nathaniel Hawthorne had a bookmark. She pulled the book from the shelf and opened to the bookmark at page 274. Near the top, underlined in pencil was: attempt to connect a by-gone time with the very present. Another old book, *Daddy-Long-Legs* by Jean Webster, had two bookmarks. She grabbed the book. On page 54, underlined in pencil was: I find that I am the only girl in college who wasn't brought up on "Little Women." On page 95, underlined in pencil was: The scenery around here is perfectly beautiful.

Kayla started taking pictures of the pages with underlined passages then she spotted *Little Women* by Louisa May Alcott. It had a bookmark. She pulled the book from the shelf and opened to bookmarked page 397. Underlined in pencil were the words: something about the election.

A couple more books had bookmarks.

The Best Short Stories of 1915, edited by Edward J. O'Brien had a bookmark.

On page 193, underlined in pencil was: <u>After all, who knows anything about a work of art but the artist?</u>

She puzzled over the underlines, but she had work to do.

* * *

Out the door, down to the Victorian where those unpacked boxes waited. As soon as she got there, she started digging into them. Lamps, kitchenware, small framed prints, bath items, and books.

Books. What about those books with underlines? What was that about? She pulled up the pictures she took of them. Just random words and phrases.

Still more unpacking to do, but she needed groceries. The books with underlines and any others up there, she would investigate after she got back.

* * *

Kayla knew of a supermarket at the other end of town, but instead headed on foot to a mom-and-pop grocery downtown.

From the south end of Main Street, she stopped and gazed up the wide street, at the old buildings that lined it and imagined a past with 1960s cars cruising the street and occupying diagonal parking spaces; pedestrians along the sidewalks entered stores here and there. She then conjured a Main Street from a couple of decades before that with behemoth automobiles of the 1940s crowding the street and men and women on the sidewalks dressed to go out.

"Can I help you?" said someone, knocking her from her reverie.

"Oh!" she said to the woman, feeling a bit embarrassed. "No, thank you. I'm new here and was just looking around."

"Well, welcome to our fair town!" the woman said.

Kayla headed on up the sidewalk.

The building that housed Weber's had the ornate old architecture common to Midwestern towns.

The relic wooden screen door banged shut behind her with a ring of its little bell. An older man behind the wooden counter nodded and she stepped up to introduce herself.

"Sure, I know who you are. You bought the Barlow place," he said.

Kayla glanced around the store. Had it not been stocked with current products, it could have been from decades before.

"This has been preserved well," she said, "the tin ceiling and all."

"It's all original," he said. "Oh, and my name is Hank Weber."

"Nice to meet you," she said. "All original?"

"It hasn't needed much. We've kept it maintained, including that old screen door. This store has been in my family for two or three generations. My grandfather started the business back in the 1880s."

"Impressive."

Weber smiled and attended to something behind the wooden counter.

"I'm glad to see it's doing well."

"We've had better times."

"So the store's been in continuous operation ever since its founding?"

"Well, things got a little tough at times, but we managed to keep it going. He turned to do a little moving of products from one shelf to another. "Are you enjoying the property?" he said.

"I love it. The big old Victorian is beautiful. The old farmhouse is interesting, too."

Weber stopped what he was doing for a moment. "In what way?"

"I can imagine its history. It looks like Brenda abandoned it with little effort to clean everything out, except to throw sheets over some things. And there's a bookcase full of old books that look like they haven't been touched in years."

"You could try selling those old books to The Niche over on Second."

"The Niche? A used bookstore? How did I miss that! Now I'll never get anything done."

Weber snickered and resumed his work, grabbing a box of crackers, shoving them next to similar boxes.

"Well," he said, "Brenda just decided it was time to move and I don't think she cared what happened to that old house. Her cousin talked her into moving. She was happier in the bigger house, the one where you live now, than that decaying old farmhouse. I've known her since she was a kid. She was never the same after her mother died years ago. Mr. Barlow deeded the house to her and moved out later and it just wasn't right Brenda being out there by herself all those years, but she stayed at the property most of her adult life.

"Never socialized or had a job. She lived on her inheritance and finally had to sell the place."

"Had to sell? That wasn't my impression. I thought she just wanted to live in town."

"Uh huh." Weber started to head back to the store room. "Just tap the bell if you need anything. Excuse me."

Kayla grabbed a basket, gathered up some items, and placed them on the counter. Weber returned by the time she was ready to leave.

"Well," she said, "I'm really happy to have the property."

Weber placed the items into Kayla's reusable bag and rang up the bill. "Oh, that's nice," he said. "Brenda's been kind of withdrawn, more than usual, since she sold it." He smiled. "Take good care of it."

"I plan to and I might even fix up the old farmhouse."

"That old farmhouse probably isn't worth keeping."

"I want to get an estimate for fixing it up. Can you recommend anyone?"

"Well, my niece has a remodeling business over in Mound Grove. Let's see, I think I have her info here." Weber pulled a card from his wallet, handed it to Kayla.

"Thanks," she said, then turned to leave.

He smiled at her and nodded. "Thank you, and come back."

Kayla resisted the urge to find The Niche and took her groceries home to the Victorian. She was planning to go back downtown to meet Kevin after a while in the Artists Loft above the Historical Society.

She mulled over the underlined passages in those books up in the farmhouse and pulled up the pictures she'd taken of them.

She would have grabbed the books if she'd had room in her bag.

CHAPTER TWO
Rock Hound

MILDRED HELD ONTO HER FLOPPY HAT and kept an eye out for cattle as she bent down to pick some loose stones off a rock slab that was imbedded in the hilltop.

Another fossil for her collection. She placed it in her bag and looked around while pulling her hat down against the gusty breezes, and adjusting her sunglasses.

She was glad Mr. Moore let her scavenge around his property. Would the new owner of the neighboring land allow her to? The previous owner certainly didn't want her around.

She trudged on through the tallgrass. There was an old house a ways ahead. She continued toward it along the grassy ridge and came to a barbed wire fence that must have been at least a mile long. It ran left and right, over the contours down the hill toward another house down there, and the other direction, down the west side of the hill to the woods along the creek. Mr. Moore's land was large, indeed. She carefully pulled wires apart, squeezed through the fence, and headed toward the old house. A plate-sized stone on another rock slab along the way tempted her. With her rock hammer, she carefully lifted the stone off the slab. No snake under it, but an arrowhead the size of her fist sat there. She had found different sized arrowheads before, but this was a really nice one.

"I need permission," she muttered.

She held it up with both hands to inspect it, twirling it over. A gust nearly knocked her down and sent her hat sailing. She turned and lunged for the hat, pulling it back on, and dropped the arrowhead in the grass next to the slab, then nudged it back to its spot, replacing the stone cover. The wind calmed and she continued to the old house.

A few minutes later, she reached it and started walking down the gravel lane to the big house at the bottom of the hill.

A younger woman answered the door.

"Hello," said Mildred, "I wonder if I could traipse around your hill and do a little prospecting. I'm a rock hound. I found a big arrowhead up by the old house and I'd like to look some more. I'll leave that one for you, but if I find some smaller ones, I'd like to keep one, with your permission."

"That's fine. I'm Kayla, by the way, new in town."

"Glad to know you, Kayla," Mildred said, smiling. "I'm Mildred. Well, thank you and welcome to our community."

Kayla thanked her and Mildred turned to leave, stepping off the porch. Kayla watched her head back to prospecting up on the hill.

But now, Kevin waited at the Artists Loft downtown.

CHAPTER THREE
From Time to Time

KAYLA STEPPED INTO THE HISTORICAL SOCIETY, into what might once have been an early twentieth century dentist office. She could only imagine the horrors.

Several old pictures on the wall caught her attention. She stepped over to a portrait and gazed into the eyes of a woman from the 1880s. The woman gazed back. She was somewhat young, distinguished looking with hair pinned up. Could she and Kayla have been friends if not separated by an accident of time? Kayla regretted this being only a one-way meeting.

She sighed, wishing she knew more about her, and caught a glimpse of another portrait, this one of a man, perhaps a similar age, also looking distinguished, hair neatly trimmed and parted on the side. He was a teacher according to the placard. She wondered if he, too, could have been a friend if they were of the same time.

The woman projected an air of success. A shame they didn't mention or know her profession, domestic or otherwise.

A woman sitting behind a table interrupted Kayla's thoughts. "My name is Caitlin. May I help you?"

Kayla smiled, realizing she had been ignoring Caitlin.

She looked over at Caitlin. "When I look at old portraits, I imagine what it would have been like to know the person."

Caitlin smiled. "To be contemporaries with someone from long ago, yes. Wouldn't that be an interesting thought experiment?"

"It would." Kayla stepped around and took in more old pictures.

"The man's portrait was found at a school from the 1800s that had been demolished," Caitlin said. "The woman's portrait was donated by someone here in town."

"Too bad we don't know more about these people," Kayla said. "Why was that old school demolished? Some of those old school buildings lasted a long time."

"It was a wooden one-room schoolhouse destroyed by fire," Caitlin said.

"I'm glad his portrait was salvaged."

"There's also a damaged class picture from the school in storage awaiting restoration."

"I'm sorry, my name is Kayla Ramsey. I just moved here."

"Then welcome to Sycamore Falls."

Kayla gestured to a stairway. "Is that where Kevin O'Brien's studio is?"

"The Artists Loft. I think he's there now. He mentioned you. Why don't you go on up?"

A group of artists working at easels and the smell of paints and thinners greeted Kayla in the cavernous brick-walled loft as Kevin welcomed her and took her across uneven wood floors. Large canvases with landscape scenes leaned against a brick wall.

"Welcome to the Artists Loft."

"So, the Historical Society is just a front?" she said to Kevin.

"They like us here. We attract some tourists."

"You bribe tourists?"

"We do. With historic decaying buildings and art shows."

"Is that enough?"

"I have other ideas."

"Show me those landscapes along the wall."

Kevin led her to them. Five paintings of what looked like the same hill in order of progression from a grassy hill, to the same hill with a group of people in tribal dress gathered on top, to the same hill with a road up it, to the same hill with a farmhouse on top.

Kevin pointed at the canvases. "These paintings were done by five artists, a tag team effort."

"Like a relay," said Kayla.

"Right." A woman with dark, graying hair down to her back, wearing a long flowing dress stepped over to them.

"Hello," she said, "I am Mara Shaw."

Kayla turned to Mara and introduced herself, then said, "I am admiring these works."

"That's your hill throughout time," Mara said.

"Fascinating."

"Kevin shouted to the artists at the back of the room. "Hey, Kayla's going to have us up to her property to set up this weekend!"

Kayla laughed. "Say what? Set what up?"

"We would love to set up our canvases on the hill behind your house," Mara said. "There's a wonderful view up there."

"Of course, Mara," Kayla said. "I'd love to have you all up. I've only been there a little. That grass is pretty tall."

"Welcome to the Flint Hills." Mara said, nodding. She thanked Kayla and went back to her canvas.

"So, what's it like here?" Kayla asked Kevin.

"Wonderful. I never thought I'd settle in a place like this, but there's a lot of good going on here. And the town setting is awesome. I've only been here for a year, but other artists have been here longer. And now we have a writer in town."

"I'm sure I'm not the only writer here."

"No, but you're the only one I know with a following."

"So this is a far cry from teaching Linguistics, right, Professor? Being a Flint Hills artist?"

"I still explore that subject. Subtle differences in dialects across Kansas. Like some places, there's an unusual usage of one word swapped with a variant of it."

"What word?"

"I'll tell you later. And it'll be in my article in the Winter issue of *Geographical Semantics.*

"Will it be available online?"

"Probably with a trial subscription. But the public library here subscribes to it."

Some of the artists looked up from their easels.

Kevin turned to lead Kayla out.

Mara came back over. "We look forward to setting up on your hill."

"Great to meet you, Mara," said Kayla, "and I'll look forward to this weekend."

Kevin led Kayla to the stairs.

Mara smiled as they left. "I'm glad we have a friend there. Brenda never allowed us onto her property."

Kevin took Kayla downstairs and out into the noon sun. "Lunch?" he said. "There's a diner around the corner."

"Sure. Why didn't Brenda allow you guys onto the property?"

"Who knows?" he said. "She didn't like visitors near the old farmhouse."

"Strange."

"Yeah, I was glad to see her sell the whole property. It got to be too much for her anyway."

When they reached Third Street, he gestured down it. "She bought a small house over there and no one hears from her much."

"Muriel, my realtor, told me Brenda thought about tearing down the farmhouse and Mr. Weber also suggested I not bother with restoring it."

"Brenda abandoned it to move to the Victorian but maintained it for a while," he said. "Then let it go for a few years, which is a shame, because it could have been a really nice house with good potential instead of becoming another dying rural house in the country ready to fall into ruins. Are you going to let that happen?"

"I haven't decided," she said. "It needs a lot of work. Hey, I saw some interesting old portraits on the wall in the Historical Society lobby. I kind of lost myself in them. Wishing I could have known the people."

"That's so you."

She looked around Main Street. "Is the town healthy?"

"It's been better. I'm told the town worked well a while back. Especially in its heyday: Nineteen Fifties and Sixties and a few years beyond. It could be better. We can contribute. The town welcomes new businesses. We're a new industry here that can feed into other existing ones. In obvious ways, tourists will patronize local businesses. But I've got another an idea that will utilize more local companies in other ways.

"What's your big idea?"

"Not so fast," he said. "I want to get things sorted out in my mind first. Figuring it out is the challenge. The tornado was a setback a couple of years ago."

"I remember. Made national news. If your efforts help, what can I do?"

"Like I said, we have a writer in town. One with a following. He gestured about. "People are looking for ideas. We need to pay attention to what works and what doesn't."

"And what used to work," she said.

"People are open to anything new," he said, stopping and glancing at his phone. "Okay. Um, sorry I have to skip lunch after all; I have to get back to the Artists Loft."

"No problem, I've got unpacking. See you soon?"

"Then." They hugged and split.

* * *

Kayla got back to the Victorian and relaxed for a while. Those bookmarked books at the farmhouse waited for her.

She grabbed a quick shower, drove up to the farmhouse, and went into its library. Mid-afternoon sunlight flooded the spacious room of books.

"What have you seen during your times, old house?" she said, sending eerie soft echoes bouncing throughout the empty main floor rooms.

From the middle of the library, she looked around at the walls, bookcases, hardwood floor, and wood trim.

"If only these walls could talk." Echoes again.

She stared at the old books.

The bookmarked ones waited to be explored.

Next Door Neighbors had a bookmark she'd missed. She pulled the book out and opened it to that page. Page 150 had a sentence underlined: <u>She was glad to have the library table placed at her disposal.</u>

Kayla felt silly when she looked for the table. No table in here.

She put a couple of the books with underlines into her bag and sat in a chair across from the bookcase. She felt the quiet permeate her, a rare moment. Not a sound intruded as she took in the look of the room with the sunbeams casting spots all around.

The spine of *Destination Unknown* by Agatha Christie glowed in a stray sunbeam. Kayla checked her bag for room then went to the bookcase and pulled the book out.

A breeze swirled around her. The sunbeams vanished, the room was cooler, freshly dusted, and neater. A small table sat in the library's corner nook. It was cloudy outside. She glanced out the tall window. An early 1950s car sat just outside on the gravel driveway.

A male voice in another room startled her.

She jumped back to the chair, out of sight from the other rooms. He kept talking.

That's not Kevin, she could tell, frozen at the thought that somebody sneaked in without her noticing. She had no way out without being noticed. Should she confront the intruder or make a run for it?

She was still holding *Destination Unknown,* so she went to the bookcase, and reshelved it. The male voice faded. The sunbeams slanted in like before. She listened for the intruder to leave. After a minute, all was quiet. She went over to the window. No old car outside. The room looked shabby again and the little table was gone. After a while, she decided the intruder was gone, so she tiptoed through the living room. No one around. She took a deep breath and walked straight through the foyer in a way to assert her ownership and dashed out to the porch. No sign or sound of anyone out front. She was alone.

"What was that!"

She decided not to worry about having an overtired hallucination, nothing that sleep wouldn't fix. She would put it out of her mind and look forward to Kevin's group coming up on Saturday. After heading down to the Victorian, she crashed for a couple of hours.

What a day.

* * *

Saturday afternoon, Kayla stood by Mara and easel halfway up the hill behind the Victorian.

"Look out at that vista," said Mara, "at the hills, the dark blanket of buffalo covering the prairies, the tree-lined river in the valley."

"Beautiful," said Kayla. "I can imagine the buffalo." Kayla looked everywhere, then realized Mara was talking about how it was throughout the ages.

Kevin and the other artists set up on a level spot just below them.

"There's Old West Hill Road down there," Kevin said, pointing down to where an abandoned gravel road curved around the base of the hill, then out of view. "That's where Mrs. Barlow crashed years ago."

"Doesn't surprise me somebody would crash there," Kayla said. "You can barely see that road. Visibility must be poor."

"It wasn't grown up in brush back then," said Kevin. "The county maintained it then."

But gravel is gravel, easy to skid on around a curve," said Mara. "I'm not surprised Brenda sold the place with those bad memories. She was only a teenager when her mother died down there."

"And there are those missing kids who were last seen hiking along there a couple of weeks ago."

"Missing kids?" Kayla said. "That would have been just before I took possession of the property. Brenda was probably up here packing around that time. We were working toward closing then. What kids?"

"A boy and a girl," Mara said. "Their mother thinks they might have come up here, but Brenda said she would have known if anything happened here. Anyway, no sign of them ever found."

"You mean. . . nothing?"

"No," Mara said, "A lot of people are still searching."

"Did an investigation turn up anything? Are there any hidden wells or anything that I'm not aware of yet? Could the kids have gotten lost or fallen somewhere?"

Kayla cringed at the thought. Trapped in an abandoned nook somewhere or down an abandoned well.

"They searched the whole property including your Victorian house and the house up here. Brenda did help with that. She stuck by the investigators at every turn when they went through the houses and around them."

"I think kids would be more interested in poking around a barn than old houses," Kevin said.

"Don't underestimate the range of kids' interests," said Mara. "That barn never had much in it. I don't think Mr. Barlow used it. Mrs. Barlow's crash wasn't long after he built it and he moved out soon after and deeded the property to Brenda when she was twenty-one."

A woman with short gray hair stepped over to Kayla from her easel.

"Kayla," said Kevin, "this is Mrs. Weber, of Weber's Grocery."

Kayla was about to offer her hand. "I met Hank the other day."

"I know. It's nice to know you." She glanced up at the farmhouse. "I hear a few people think you should demolish that old house."

"That seems to be a growing consensus," Kayla said. "Mr. Weber said it."

Mrs. Weber leaned close to Kayla. "Don't you let anybody pressure you into anything."

Mara took an interest in the conversation.

"Thank you, Mrs. Weber," Kayla said. "I'm thinking it over and am going to get an estimate for restoring it. There are some nice things about it that you just don't find in many houses."

Mara stepped over to them. "Of course, if you decide to remove the house," she said, "there'll be a nice clear area up there."

Kayla shrugged.

"I'm sorry, I didn't mean to intrude, but if you find a compelling reason either way, search within your heart for the right answer."

"Thank you, Mara. So, when was Mrs. Barlow's crash?"

"1961," Kevin said.

"So long ago."

Kevin started an outline of rolling hills on his canvas and the beginnings of a house on a hill.

Kayla went over to him. "Are you going to do those puffy clouds?" she said, pointing toward the sky.

"Haven't decided yet.   Sometimes I move things around."

"Oh, right. Hey, I didn't mean. . ."

"It's all good. I get questions like that all the time. We have to take criticism sometimes."

"But I wasn't criticizing—"

"It's okaaay, Kayla."

As the creative work continued, the sun continued its path toward the west.

Kevin pointed down to Kayla's Victorian, its upper floor and roof bathed in the late afternoon sun in contrast to the darker trees behind it. "That looks creepy," he said.

"Thanks," Kayla said. "I'll remember that next time I'm heading home just before dark. Why don't you paint it like that for a Halloween display?"

"I'll remember that."

Mara looked away from them.

Kayla and Kevin both laughed.

"Hey," Kayla said to Mara, "you should have seen us when we were dating."

"Never boring," Kevin said.

"Ever thought about getting back together?" Mara said.

Kayla and Kevin both cringed.

"No."

"No."

"I'm sorry. That wasn't cool," Mara said. "I just thought with you moving out here after Kevin did, Kayla."

"We're still best friends," Kayla said.

"We are," agreed Kevin. "But no, we'd never make it together."

"So did anyone ever come up with an idea of what happened to the kids?" Kayla said.

Mara shook her head.

Kayla walked a few feet around the hill and peered up at the farmhouse. It looked different now. Not just the house, but the area around it that was partially hidden by the contour of the hill. A place of two tragedies. What else of its history?

"Would any of you like to come up and walk around the property with me tomorrow? I'd just like to have someone with me in case anything turns up."

"They searched everywhere thoroughly," said Mara. "There's nothing. I'm sure the kids got lost somewhere else. They could have run away for all we know."

"I will," Kevin said. "I'll come by tomorrow."

Kayla nodded and smiled.

She started admiring Mara's work.

"Green hills rippling to the horizon with buffalo just like you described it," said Kayla.

Mara pointed the brush at the scene. "The hills are sacred and the Tribes came together on this hilltop. From up here, we watched the buffalo herds so we knew where

[28]

to go for essential hunting. Does the scene make an impression?"

"It does."

"I hope you always remember it."

"I will."

I don't care—there is something strange about the house—I can feel it.
—Charlotte Perkins Gilman
from "The Yellow Wallpaper"

CHAPTER FOUR
The Farmhouse and the Barn

"DON'T YOU WONDER SOMETIMES?" said Kayla as she sat on one of the square boulders that lined the hill up by the farmhouse. She pointed out at the grassy hills vista and continued, "Do you wonder what it was like up here before western settlement?"

"I've thought about stuff like that, including in Kansas City," Kevin said. "Mara talks about the once pristine nature of the area and it's the subject of many of her paintings. Her Tribe's land from long ago."

"She's welcome to come up here anytime."

"She's planning a whole series similar to that multi-artist mural you saw."

"Too bad Brenda didn't let her up here to paint this view," she said.

"Mara has painted this view from memory."

"Is it on display anywhere?"

"Nonstandard Artifacts Gallery downtown."

They headed up the porch steps and paced around. Kevin peeked through the front door.

"Have you been inside?" he said.

"I went in the other day and during inspection and when I first came to look at the property. This time, I want to take someone with me. There's something creepy about this house."

"Creepy house. Sounds fascinating. Have you spent the night in there yet?"

"It's in bad shape and no power yet and I wouldn't feel comfortable in there because of that." She pointed down the hill. "No, I bought the whole property mainly for the Victorian and a little land. That house is my home now."

Kevin shrugged. "But this old farmhouse is creepy even during the day? How? Have you seen any mice or rats or evidence of them?"

"Brenda hired an exterminator just a week or so ago right before we closed the deal. Although it won't take long before they take up residence again."

"Then what's creepy about it?"

"I have to show you sometime."

"At some point you'll want to start straightening things up in there if you plan to keep it."

"I need to clear Brenda's junk out or get her to, to keep the rodents out."

"I saw those bookcases in that back room. If you want, give me the key and I can come up here with boxes and toss all those books in, the ones you don't want to keep."

She didn't answer.

"Are we going in?" he said, leaning toward the door.

Kayla unlocked the door and hesitated as she took the doorknob.

"Well?" he said. "There's probably nothing Brenda hasn't already told you about the house."

"I had very little interaction with her. She hasn't told me much of anything. All I know has come from you guys and Muriel."

Kevin started to step inside.

"No, wait," Kayla said. "In fact, let's go see the barn and hike around a little."

He shrugged. "Okay, whatever, let's go."

The quiet barn waited. A breeze flowed toward it as if pointing the way.

[31]

They headed over.

"How did negotiations go after you made the offer?" Kevin said.

"I think she was ready to sell. I got a bargain."

"From what I've heard."

"Hank Weber mentioned something about her having been alone out here."

When they reached the west side of the barn, Kayla said, "I went in the barn briefly when I looked at this place."

They grabbed the handle and shoved the overhead door up. The breeze swirled into the empty barn. No typical barn smells, hay, animal, or machine.

"Nothing," Kayla said.

Kevin stepped in and looked around. "At least Brenda didn't leave you a mess in here. I wonder if she or her parents ever used it."

"Brenda's had a lot of hardship," Kayla said.

"She has," he said. "A lot of people think she's weird, but it's not her fault."

They wandered around the inside of the barn looking for anything that indicated it'd ever been used.

"Maybe as a garage?" she said.

"I don't know. There aren't any oil stains or anything else that smells like a car ever lived in here or that Brenda used it for anything except to keep a lawn tractor."

"Imagine all that work, Barlow building this thing for nothing."

"He must have had a reason."

The wind started to whistle through the cracks in the structure.

"I like that sound," she said.

Kevin frowned and looked up at the rafters and around the barn, to the cracks around the doors and windows.

[32]

"It stopped," Kayla said. She pushed her hair behind her ear. "Did you hear it?"

"Uh huh."

A few minutes later, Kayla led Kevin out of the barn to the farmhouse backyard.

"Good thing we're wearing long pants," Kayla said as they trudged along the woods edge. "Watch for snakes, right?"

"Right. Mostly black rat snakes and other nonpoisonous ones around here, although you have to be careful around rocks and streams. Rattlers in the fields, copperheads in the woods."

"Eeek."

"The rat snakes eat the poisonous ones. And other predators get them, too. Hawks and owls."

"There weren't any snakes in the barn," she said.

"They're in there. You just didn't see them."

"You're really getting to know the area, aren't you?"

"You learn a lot about a place spending a year there in all four seasons. How'd you survive in KC without seeing me all that time?"

"It was easy," she said.

"Say what?"

"Don't worry," she said. "I got used to being apart after the split. You know, we could have made it if we tried." She then regretted bringing that up.

He shook his head. "Yeah, okay, let's not get into that."

"You're right. Hey, thanks for coming up here with me," she said.

"For sure. I'm enjoying it. It's a plus having a place to set up an easel." He tapped her shoulder with the back of his hand.

"Yeah, just using me?" she said. "But really," she continued, "it's nice getting acquainted with people in a new place."

As they approached the edge of the woods, Kayla ducked. "Watch out for those old clothes line wires," she said.

"What wires?" he asked.

"The ones that used to be there."

"Huh?"

"Gotcha," she said, chuckling.

He followed her to the woods edge.

They rounded the edge of the woods toward some trees that protruded into the field.

"Something in there," Kayla said, pointing to a large bluish object.

Kevin glanced into the woods and saw it, then stopped and stared.

"What?" Kayla said.

"You noticed it first," he said, "an old abandoned car in the woods being devoured by trees."

Kayla stopped and looked toward it. "Right."

"Those are fascinating," he said. "Let's go look at it."

Kayla shrugged and they headed toward it.

The hood was partially open, revealing a rusty engine.

Kevin ran his hand over the side. "An early 1950s Bel Air."

"Hm," Kayla said.

"I'm overwhelmed by your enthusiasm," he said.

"What? I think they're fascinating, too. A part of history."

That old car in the gravel driveway.

"Gives me another idea," he said.

"What I always wonder is why an expensive thing like that ends up abandoned in the woods."

"Or how does a house end up like that, too, right? When a car doesn't run anymore out here, what do you do with it?

"I'm sure the woods grew around it," she said.

Kevin gestured to the side of the car. "This is probably where the trees ended, where the trees grew around the car. The woods behind your farmhouse will devour the house someday, too. That's why a lot of landowners out here do yearly spring burns. Keeps the tallgrass healthy and prevents woods from taking over the grassland."

Kayla wondered whether she should do anything of the sort. Did Brenda ever do spring burns? Would other landowners assist with that? Did her land require it?

She joined Kevin looking into the car's front seat area where some of the upholstery had survived. The dash had wires sticking out of the cavity that had held the radio; most of the interior had deteriorated with ground visible through some rusted out holes in the floor.

Something moved under the car. Kayla jumped.

"Okay, let's go," she said.

They exited the woods into the field.

Up on the small ridge, they took in the view and waded through the grass back to their cars.

Kayla sighed and looked at the farmhouse. "There's so much to do in there."

"Those bookcases in that back room," Kevin said. "Really, I can come up here and start packing them."

"It's good. I can do it," she said quickly.

"I'm happy to help."

"Thanks. I'll let you know."

* * *

That night, Kayla sat in the quiet study in the Victorian updating her journal and blog, and the first article of her Art Influence series, and caught up on social media and comments from her multitude of readers, but she couldn't get that

Eric T. Reynolds

farmhouse out of her mind. What to do with it? No matter how strange it was, it belonged to her and *she* would decide what to do with it.

"I didn't buy this Victorian so I could get that broken down old place, but I don't need to be nervous going in there."

She needed to go through the rest of the books in there, too, the one last thing to do up there, then get an estimate.

It'd been a long day. She hauled herself up to bed and was asleep in no time.

I tell you, books are the depositories of the human spirit,
which is the only thing in this world that endures.
—Christopher Morley from *The Haunted Bookshop*

CHAPTER FIVE
Replay

SHE WOKE THE NEXT MORNING TO A RECTANGLE OF SUNSHINE draped across the floor, onto the wall. She rolled onto her back and dozed a little while staring at the ceiling. Along with the rest of this house, there were tiny flaws, microscopic cracks she'd never noticed before. The house wasn't perfect, but no amount of money could buy the history of this grand old house. The same could be said for the farmhouse, but its condition outweighed its historical value. Or did it? Another visit was in order.

After a shower and breakfast, she poked around the boxes stacked along walls and corners. Once again, she thought of the old books that waited for her. By late morning, she abandoned unpacking and drove up there.

At the front door, she felt the urge to go in, an obsession with the house building daily.

Inside the front door, she noticed the antique woodwork with nicks and scratches, and on the nineteenth century hardwood floors beneath the old rugs. What about renovating this place? Was it worth the expense and effort? It could be a money pit. She'd think about it for a while. If this had been the first house she toured on the property, she would have walked.

And yet, now you can't fight the urge to explore it.

She headed into the library. Those dusty old books sat there. A shame this house wasn't in better shape for this room must have been nice.

She knew the weird sensation before wasn't real, but decided to grab *Destination Unknown* again. She pulled out the book. A breeze swirled around her and the sunny day outside turned cloudy like the last time.

The same male voice came from another room.

She stepped away from the bookcase and looked out the window. The old car sat outside on the gravel drive like before.

That antique wreck in the woods.

She reshelved the book. The voice faded. Sunlight returned and all was still. It was an exact replay of last time, so this time she was sure nobody was in the house with her. She went from the library through the living room to the foyer. No one there. Out on the porch again, she saw no one in the yard. She was well rested this time, so that was no hallucination. She'd always got a good sense of impressions from an old house. That had to be it.

She went back inside to the living room.

"But I didn't imagine it. The library *did* change around me."

Kayla stood in the middle of the old living room and gazed at the walls, at the flaws, and started to think what it would take to repair those. Mostly cosmetic, she could do that herself: the crown moulding, wood trim, and wood floor, but the ancient wallpaper from the 1940s with its pattern of shells had to go. She liked the vintage look, but it was in bad shape—and what about the rest of the house? Again, would it be worth the expense? Next, she went back to the bookshelf.

"Now, what?" she said, brushing dust from some of the spines.

She started pulling other books out. None caused the library to change like that one book.

She gave up the search for more weirdness and headed out the door, down to the Victorian.

"Well," said Roger, "when literature goes bankrupt I'm willing to go with it. Not till then."
—Christopher Morley
from THE HAUNTED BOOKSHOP

CHAPTER SIX
A Special Old Book

THE NEXT MORNING, AFTER GETTING LITTLE SLEEP, Kayla figured the best thing to do was to purge the anomaly experiences from her mind and go downtown. There was that bookstore Weber mentioned, The Niche. She'd go there then go see Kevin.

* * *

She found The Niche on Second and Main. Kayla wandered in and browsed through the aisles of tall bookcases and reading niches with lamps and cushy chairs. It was mostly empty except for a tiger-striped cat holding down one of the bookcases. A paw protruded from an upper shelf. After a while, Kayla came across an old, old copy of *The Portrait of a Lady* by Henry James and reached to pull it off the shelf.

"Okay," she mumbled, "you aren't going to change anything, are you?"

"That book might," said someone on the other side of the shelf.

"Oh!" Kayla said. "I didn't realize you were there."

A woman peered at her through the books. "The shelves have ears," she said.

"Apparently," Kayla said, a bit embarrassed.

[40]

The woman made her way around to Kayla's aisle. She wore a long, flowing brown and beige dress with a Southwest pattern.

"Hello," she said, "I am Ronnie. I co-own The Niche with Marsha who comes in this afternoon."

"How long have you been open?" asked Kayla.

"Since eight this morning."

"I mean—"

Ronnie chuckled. "I know what you mean. We opened The Niche four months ago."

"How is business?"

"Going well. We're the only used bookstore in the county."

"Congratulations on knocking off the competition."

"Hopefully, new competition won't knock us off. No, really, I'd welcome another."

Kayla nodded. "So would I. You can't have too many bookstores in my book."

"And you can't have too many books in my bookstore."

"Ah, you got me. And I'm sorry, my name is Kayla Ramsey."

"The arts blogger! I've been following you for a couple of years. So nice to meet you."

Kayla nodded. "Always a pleasure to meet a reader."

"Yes, I'm certainly a reader."

"Kayla glanced around at the multitude of books. "Of course you are—you got me again."

"You got yourself."

"Careful or you'll end up in my blog."

Ronnie chuckled. "Not very original, Kayla. But I'll be glad to misbehave if that'll get us a mention. How fabulous."

Kayla sighed. "What is it? About 9:30? I haven't had my full dose of caffeine yet."

"I have a fresh pot of coffee on or there's tea," Ronnie said. "Why don't you take that book to one of the comfy alcove chairs and relax for a while? I'll bring you a cup."

"Thank you. Tea would be nice."

As Kayla took the book and settled into a niche along the wall near the front of the store, the tiger-striped cat scurried to her and hopped up onto the arm of the chair. Ronnie came by with a mug of tea and set it on the table by Kayla.

"Thank you, again," Kayla said. She started sipping her tea and opened *The Portrait of a Lady*. She was careful, because the book was old. And then she came across something. Inside the front cover was an inscription written in an older style of cursive:

> *Dearest Mary—*
> *Enjoy this for Book Club,*
> *and have a most blessed birthday—*
> *Love,*
> *Cousin Margarete*
> *May the 4th, 1885*

I *have* to have this! Kayla thought.

She looked through the book.

After a while, Ronnie came by with her camera. "May I take your picture? I'm starting a new tradition of collecting pictures of famous patrons."

"I'm okay with a picture, and I'm flattered, but I'm not famous."

"You must be with all your followers."

Kayla started to open the book. "I was hesitant to show you this in case it's not for sale now, because I want the book."

"The inscription?"

"Yeah, somebody gave it as a gift in 1885."

"I'm aware of it. We get a lot of books with inscriptions. We don't want the bother of keeping track of them and we don't want to start keeping books aside that we had otherwise planned to sell. A little surprise bonus for our patrons. You'll probably come back now."

"I would have anyway—"

"That book was in a batch of old books somebody brought in. You probably have some interesting old books among those that Brenda left in that old house."

That's an understatement, thought Kayla.

"You know about all those books?" she said.

"Hank Weber mentioned it."

Word gets around, Kayla thought. "He told me about your store."

"Excuse me," Ronnie said. Someone entered the store and Ronnie turned toward a woman with reddish gray hair pulled into a long ponytail. Ronnie scooped up the cat and went to greet the woman.

"Hello, Brenda," she said.

Brenda sighed and lifted her ponytail. "Getting warm out," she said.

"Summer's not for a while," said Ronnie.

Brenda shrugged and headed into an aisle.

Kayla held the book and stood to leave. When she reached the checkout counter, Ronnie glanced to the aisle where Brenda went.

"Okay," Kayla said. "She's all yours."

"Thanks. Before you leave," said Ronnie, "have you been to the library on Main?"

"I want to get over there. It's on my list to do right away."

"It's a brand new one that replaced the old Carnegie Library. The old one was in bad shape and not ADA compliant. The new one is fantastic."

"Sounds wonderful."

As Kayla left, Ronnie said, "And, Kayla, those books Brenda left, bring them by and I might be able to take some off your hands."

Kayla thanked her and headed out onto Second Street. Should I worry about Brenda? she thought. Is she all right? Poor woman.

* * *

Kevin waited at the Historical Society.

They had decided they would go on a short walk around town. A good distraction to help take her mind off things. Try not to think about it for now, she thought, then go up later and go through the books.

She reached the Historical Society building and met Kevin in the little front room. He noticed her worried expression.

" You okay?" he said.

"I'm okay."

"Something's bothering you."

"No. Fine."

"So everything's okay and nothing bad's happened?" he said.

"I'm good."

"You're not regretting the move and thinking of moving back to KC?"

"I love my new place. And the town. I definitely made the right decision. I'm anxious to get to more writing on my article. Getting to know people here, and then. . .there's the farmhouse."

"What about it?"

She wasn't about to tell him about the anomaly yet.

[44]

"It's a dump, but I want to consider renovating it. I'll get your thoughts on that sometime. I went in yesterday and I can imagine the generations of families who've lived there. I want to find out if there's any info on previous owners of both houses."

"We can look into that. I'll make a historian out of you yet," he said.

"I've got lots to write about."

He shrugged and gestured to the exit. "Let's go."

They walked a ways up Main and Kayla stopped and stared at the brick side of a building with a "Red Rock Cola" ad painted on the wall.

"That looks surprisingly fresh," she said.

"Volunteers restored it a couple of years ago."

"That's fantastic."

"There's something else I'll want to show you there, so we'll come back by."

They headed on to the corner of Third and Main. As they crossed at the intersection, Kevin pointed to a hotel.

"Nice old hotel," said Kayla.

"Built in the 1880s."

"I like the architecture."

"Spanish Mission Revival. Not the original building style, the original was similar in looks to some of the other buildings here downtown. The hotel was renovated in the 1920s to this style and reopened. And it's on the National Register of Historic Places."

"Can we go in sometime?"

"We can."

They walked another block.

"Are you hungry yet?" Kayla said.

"I could eat."

"Let's grab lunch and take it to the park."

They got sandwiches from Danny's, headed back south to the city park, and found a shaded area under a tree.

After Kayla finished her lunch, she sighed and lay back in the grass, clasping her hands behind her head, and stared up at where the sun filtered through the tree foliage.

"So peaceful here," she said. "What do you want to show me near that Red Rock Cola ad?"

"You'll find out."

"Whatever." She closed her eyes for a moment then heard a female voice over her.

"Are you enjoying the property?"

Brenda was standing over her, staring down at her.

"Oh," Kayla said, sitting up. She stood and extended her hand to Brenda.

Brenda shook it.

Brenda looked down at Kevin. "And how are you enjoying our town, Kevin?"

"I like it here," he said. "I'd been looking for a picturesque place like this far from a city with an active arts community."

Brenda glanced up Main and managed a small smile. "There's more going on now, and The Niche is a nice little bookshop."

"It is," said Kayla.

Brenda shielded her eyes and looked into the distance beyond the west trees. "You can see that old farmhouse up there from here," she said. "You should tear that ugly old thing down."

"I just moved into the Victorian and am still unpacking. I haven't decided yet."

Brenda frowned and looked away.

"Want to join us a while?" Kayla offered.

Brenda looked across the park. "For a minute." She pointed toward the playground. "I played on that merry-go-round over there when I was a kid. It hit me in the head once. I was stupid and jumped in the middle of it. There's something to be said about jumping into something without knowing what you're getting into, you know?"

The anomaly. She knows.

"I'm thinking of getting an estimate on fixing up the farmhouse."

"I know." Brenda put her hands on her hips. "I think it's best if you raze it. I was going to, but never got to it. Then I figured you would after seeing it."

"Maybe," said Kayla.

Brenda turned and left.

"Why does Brenda care about that house?" asked Kevin.

Kayla decided she needed to demo the anomaly to him. She wouldn't tell him ahead of time.

"Are you going to tear it down?" he said.

"I don't know yet about tearing it down," she said. "So, you want to go see the old place with me?"

"Are we going in this time? I've already seen the barn and we've already hiked. I want to see the house."

"We'll go in. I want to get some more unpacking done first, so how about in a day or two?"

"Okay," he said, standing up, "And then I'll show you what I was talking about near the Red Rock Cola ad, but I need to head back to the Loft now."

"No problem. Thanks for showing me around."

"For sure."

He hugged her and they split.

As he went on his way, Kayla decided to stay in the park for a while. She wandered past the playground to the middle of the open area and basked in the sun for a moment. Gazing back at the merry-go-round, she drifted into a daydream of the park in the 1960s where a little girl ran and played. The girl skipped to the kid-occupied merry-go-round and reached for

[47]

one of the extended hands of riding kids who faced out. The girl stopped and held her hand out still so the riders could slap it as they swung by bringing out laughter among the girl and others. One kid grabbed her hand as he rounded by her, pulling her over. She fell inward: one of the seat corners hit her head. She jumped up, screamed, and ran to her mother over at the ballfield. Kayla's daydream dissolved when present day kids converged onto the playground.

Later, when Kayla got home, she sat on the sofa with her prized purchase, the old copy of *The Portrait of a Lady*. It seemed durable enough that she could safely open it again. She eased the front cover open and ran her fingers over the birthday script written by a hand over a hundred years in the past. She summoned her imagination and thought of the woman who wrote it in 1885. Margarete was her name, addressed to her cousin Mary. What was their story? Kayla wondered. Maybe she could find out about them. Mary was obviously a reader. Kayla thought about her conversing with her book club friends about this book. She wanted to put a face with the name. The woman in the portrait at the Historical Society popped into her mind.

She sighed and found a special place for the book on the mantle, placing a bookstand there to display it opened to show the inscription inside cover. She likened it to releasing the essence of the book's first owner. This would just be a part of filling her house with the wonders of the past along with the placement of Mom's antique wood furniture pieces. She could handle living in the past along with the present.

* * *

The next morning, a storm woke Kayla early. After dozing a while, she rolled out of bed and decided to stay put at the Victorian and finish more unpacking. The forecast didn't call for anything severe. Wind and sheets of rain swept against the house during the storm's beginning, then calmed most of the rest of the morning to a steady shower.

By early afternoon, the rain ended. The urge to get up to the farmhouse gnawed at her. The more she thought about the anomaly, the more she had to experiment. The sun came out and as she got ready to go, a car pulled up out front. A fortyish woman stepped out of the car and skipped over puddles as she made her way onto the front porch.

Kayla opened the door to greet her.

"Hello," the woman said. "I'm Jennifer Dodd. May I come in?"

"Yes, of course," Kayla said, inviting Jennifer into the parlor. "Do you have time for tea?"

Jennifer nodded. "Yes, thanks. I have a few minutes." She glanced around for a moment and fixed her eyes on unpacked boxes stacked along the walls. "I'm sorry," she said. "I should welcome you to Sycamore Falls."

"Thank you, said Kayla. She took Jennifer's raincoat and gestured to the sofa.

"I hope you like it here," said Jennifer, sitting on the sofa.

"I do like it here," Kayla said. "I've only been here a short while and downtown a couple of times."

Jennifer sighed. "The town isn't what it used to be."

"That's common in a lot of towns all across the Midwest," said Kayla. "But you had a tornado. I hear things are improving here."

"Some. Well, anyway, I don't know if you've heard, but my son and daughter are missing. I mean, they just. . ."

"I'm so sorry. I heard about it. I understand they were seen on Old West Hill Road."

Jennifer nodded. "Near your property."

"What are their names?"

Jennifer pulled out a tissue. "Megan and Caleb. They're my twins."

Kayla reached out to offer a hug.

"Thank you. I'm okay. It's hard. I'm a single mom. A couple of people want to help, but no leads yet. I'm a teacher and it's hard to focus. School's out, but I have summer activities coming up."

"Where do you teach?" Kayla asked.

Jennifer stashed her tissue. "I teach History at Sycamore Falls High."

"History's an interest of mine," Kayla said.

Jennifer managed a smile.

"Tell me about Megan and Caleb," Kayla said.

"They turn fourteen in two months. Megan's a math whiz and was also a finalist in the county geography bee. Caleb's a landscape artist and won Reserve Grand Champion at the county fair for his painting of the Flint Hills last August. His painting is on display at a gallery downtown."

"Such accomplishments. You must be proud."

"I am," Jennifer said, suppressing a sob. "Some of my students, although a little older, know both of them."

Kayla took a step back and lowered her gaze. "What about the investigation?"

"I haven't been satisfied with it. I don't think they're being thorough enough."

"Where could they have gone?" asked Kayla.

"We don't know and there aren't any leads. They're curious and love exploring the rocky hills, streams, and wooded valleys. A lot of tempting places to go."

"What can I do for you?" Kayla said.

Jennifer forced a small smile. "I would like permission to look around your property."

"Of course. You're welcome to. There's quite a bit of ground."

"I appreciate that. And I would like to look around the old farmhouse up on the hill a bit."

"Around the outside?" Kayla said. "The shed, the barn? You could come up anytime for those."

"I just want to look around for any abandoned wells or maybe check that basement."

"Wouldn't the investigation have done that?"

"They did, but I don't think Brenda was very cooperative about letting anyone access to the property even though she was getting ready to sell it."

"Yeah, she insisted on being there when my realtor showed me the property. A bit unusual. Whatever I can do to help."

Tears welled up in Jennifer's eyes and she uttered a soft "Thank you," and turned to leave.

* * *

After Jennifer left, Kayla headed up to the farmhouse. When she got up to the old porch, she gazed out at the sunlit hills to the east which glowed in contrast against the backdrop of dark clouds of the receding storm. She went into the house and headed to its library. She stood in front of the bookcase, staring at *Destination Unknown*, then she pulled the book out.

A breeze swirled around: cloudy outside and male voice from another room, a replay of the previous times. She spotted the same 1950s car outside, then crept into the living room. The shell wallpaper looked fresh and in good shape. A natural Christmas tree adorned with bulbs and popcorn strings, and dripping with tinsel icicles sat in the corner with presents. She stood against the wall and peered around the corner.

There he was. Mr. Barlow as a younger man! In the foyer talking to someone in another room. Kayla remained still, trying to listen. He gestured about something, turning this way and that. He spoke about the barn and some other things.

[51]

She slipped back to the library and reshelved the book.

The voice stopped and all was quiet after the library returned to normal.

She caught her breath, looked around the room, and out the window. The old car was gone. She looked toward the foyer to make sure no one was still around. Everything happened just like the other times, the other library and the return to the normal one. She felt chills even though it was quite warm. She paced around the living room trying to figure out what to do. She had to get Kevin up here, but wanted another look at the books for now.

She scanned the bookcase and put the bookmarked books that were still there into her bag.

* * *

That evening, back at the Victorian, she contacted Kevin, asking him to come to over the next day. He said he could for a while in the afternoon, which was fine because she had more unpacking and writing to do in the morning. The Victorian was finally starting to shape up, but she still had pictures leaning against walls and lamps not plugged in. The kitchen was in pretty good shape, but in the rest of the house, still a lot to do. That anomaly at the farmhouse claimed a lot of her attention and sapped her energy. It interfered with settling in she wanted to do.

* * *

The next day, about the time she expected Kevin, the doorbell rang. She hopped up from the sofa and glimpsed Jennifer on the porch. She decided not to answer just yet and waited through another doorbell ring, then watched her turn and head for her car.

A couple of minutes after she drove away, Kevin showed up on foot.

"I didn't want to come here when she was at your door," he said, closing the door behind him. "Figured you didn't want to see her right now."

"Not right now. There's something about the farmhouse up there."

"I want to see what you're talking about," Kevin said, smiling.

CHAPTER SEVEN
Something To Show You

KAYLA AND KEVIN HEADED UP.

"I mean really weird," she said as they stood in the farmhouse's foyer. "Something I have to show you."

"How long will it take? I want to see what you're talking about, but I need to get back to the Loft."

"It won't take long."

Kevin looked around at the foyer's cracked walls and ceiling and raised an eyebrow.

"I can't describe it," she said.

Kevin held out his palms. "Okay."

As they stood in the living room, he glanced around.

"I see what you mean," he said. "Some weird vibes here."

"No," she said, grabbing his hand. "In here." She led him to the middle of the library. "Now, stand here and don't touch anything."

"I promise not to upset the delicate cosmic balance."

"Shut up and watch." She stepped up to the bookcase and pulled out *Destination Unknown*. The day turned cloudy, the male voice came from the other room, the old car sat outside, and no Kevin. Everything replayed like the other times. She reshelved the book, the room returned to normal, and she turned to look at Kevin.

"Well?" she said.

"Well, what?" he said, rolling his eyes.

"What do you mean, 'what'?"

"I mean, what do you want me to see?"

"Did I disappear when I pulled that book out?"

"Um, no."

"You didn't notice anything about me when I pulled out the book?"

"You didn't pull the book off the shelf. All you did was take hold of the book and let go."

"You mean, you didn't see me disappear or anything?"

"See you what? Like I said, you just grabbed and let go of that book."

"Then the book stays in current library and a copy goes with me," she said.

"Kayla, explain to me what I'm supposed to be seeing."

"Come over here. Stand here." She pointed to the floor in front of the bookcase.

"Okay."

"Pay close attention to me and this book."

She pulled the book out and went to the cloudy day with male voice in the other room and kept the book off the shelf for a few seconds this time before reshelving it.

Back in the normal library, Kevin stood there rubbing his eyes and put his hand on the bookcase.

"So?" she said.

"Uh, yeah, you faded away. It was weird. Sorry, I'm a little freaked out right now."

"No, you're okay." She grabbed his shoulder. "How long did I fade?"

"Maybe a couple of seconds. Totally invisible. Holy crap, what am I saying?"

"This is why I needed to show you. I should have prepared you better. Now it's your turn."

"Say what?"

"Come on. Just grab this book and pull it out. Then put it back right away. That's very important."

"What's supposed to happen?"

"When you pull the book out, the room changes."

He stepped back and shook his head.

"No, really!" she said. "I want you to experience it."

She stepped aside and gestured to Kevin to go to the book.

"Take hold of the book and pull it out. The room will change. After a second or two, put the book back."

He pulled book out and after a moment, turned to look at Kayla.

"Well?" she said.

"What was that?" he said in a whisper, looking around the library, then he peered into the living room.

"There's somebody in this house."

Kayla snickered.

"Shh," he whispered.

"Did you hear a man's voice coming from the foyer?"

"I did."

"It worked for you, then!"

"It didn't last long. As soon as I pushed the book back in, I couldn't hear him."

"You mean, you returned to the normal library. Dare I suggest: you returned to *the present*."

"Holy crap. What are you saying?"

"You saw it, you felt it. It suddenly got cloudy and cooler. Look at that shabby wallpaper in the living room. When you go to that other library and peek into the living room, the wallpaper looks newer."

He shrugged. "I'm thinking it's more likely that pulling on the book triggered a rigged mechanism that cooled the air and just then some guy came into the house, and he's probably still in here."

"No. We're in our own time now. We went into the past. I'm sure of it. Quite a ways back, I'm guessing. I saw Mr. Barlow as a younger man during a previous shift."

[56]

"Shift?" he said

"Whatever we call it. How about timeshift?"

"Fine."

"Okay, we're trying something else."

"I don't know," he said. "Is this safe? I don't want us getting electrocuted or something. If there's wiring there, it's probably really old."

"There's no wiring," she said. "Let's go."

"I don't know."

"I'll go first," she said. "After I fade, the book should still be here. Pull it out."

"Okay."

She pulled the book out and shifted to the cloudy day and male voice. After a few seconds, Kevin didn't appear with her. She reshelved the book.

Kevin was there in the normal library, waiting. "You left for a few seconds."

"Did you pull the book out?"

"I chickened out."

"Okay, you go first. I'll join you."

He reluctantly grabbed the book and pulled it out, faded.

Kayla did the same and faded to the cloudy day and male voice.

Kevin stood against the opposite wall.

"It works," said Kayla.

He went to her. "What do you mean?"

"One person can join someone who's already timeshifted here."

She pointed to the bookcase. "Okay, I'll reshelve my book, then you do the same. See you in the present."

She put her book back and faded to the normal library, waited for Kevin. After a minute, he didn't appear.

"Crap!"

[57]

She pulled the book out again and faded to the cloudy day.

Kevin was over by the window.

"You're still here," she said. "Let's go. She pointed to the bookcase. "Reshelve your book."

They reshelved their books and returned to normal time.

Back in the present, she said, "You scared me!"

He shrugged. "Just taking a look around."

"Convinced now?"

"Getting there," he said. "The old car from the woods was outside and that voice was Mr. Barlow's."

"Yep," she said.

He shook his head. "I think I'm done."

"Don't you know what this means? One person can go to a past timeline already in progress. Before, I thought this only worked one person at a time."

Kevin started pacing. "What if you went into the past and didn't know you could get back here by reshelving the book that timeshifted you?" he said.

"You'd be stranded."

"Right."

"The kids!" they both shouted.

* * *

Later that afternoon, back at the Victorian, Kayla and Kevin were in the parlor munching on crackers.

"Do we need another witness to this?" Kevin said.

"We?" Kayla shook her head. "I don't want to show it to anybody yet. Just you."

"I was in Weber's the other day," Kevin said, "and heard Hank talking about Brenda and your property and he mentioned you seemed like you'd take care of it, but thought you ought to remove the farmhouse."

"You think anyone else knows about that anomaly?" she said.

"Probably depends on how long it's been there."

She reached for a cracker and frowned at the crumbs that had dropped. She went to the hall closet and grabbed the vac from the wall, handed it to him, and he swept the crumbs around his feet.

"Still thinking about how Brenda has insisted I tear the farmhouse down," she said. "It's a dump, but fixed up, it'd be really cool with that view from the front porch. I'm going to get an estimate to renovate it. I'm not tearing it down soon. Especially with the anomaly."

"And then you can go on your own private little adventures." He winked at her. "And me, too. If you ever do want to get rid of that house, sell it to me."

"What would you want with it? Besides the anomaly?"

"Research," he said. "Second thought, it's kind of scary there. You need to be careful who you show it to."

Kayla shook her head. "As I said, I don't plan to show it to anyone just yet."

"Best to keep it between us for now. The question is, can we go back in time and explore out and around in that time, or are we stuck in the library?"

"Wait. I remember something."

"Something you saw?"

She pulled out her phone and scrolled through pictures she took of underlined passages. "Actually, yes. Here, one of the underlined passages in *Next Door Neighbors* says: 'Why don't you go out and see around a little?'"

"That's pretty direct," he said.

"The only way to know is to go try it," she said. "Those passages are messages."

"You think the house is talking to you?"

"Maybe, but I think mainly the town is. Although I can't help but sense something else is, too."

"Something else?"

"Um, yeah, like it's asking me to keep an open mind about something, of which I don't know."

"You need an open mind to deal with all this."

"I need to catalog the books."

"Didn't you want to be a librarian a while back? Now you can. Anyway, I've got to get back down to the Loft, okay? We can talk about this more later."

Kevin put his hands on his knees to prepare to stand.

"So tomorrow," she said, "I want to go down to Nonstandard Artifacts and see Jennifer's son's painting."

"It's impressive." He got up and headed out.

Kayla spent the rest of the evening decorating in a style from years past with antique tables, desk, and chairs she'd inherited from her mother that had been in the family for generations: her connection with the past. There was still more to do, but she decided to head up to bed and crash.

* * *

The next day, she went to Nonstandard Artifacts Gallery. Some of Mara's artwork was on display. A lot of her paintings were landscapes of the Flint Hills among landscapes by other artists.

As Kayla browsed, Mara entered and noticed Kayla studying one of her grassy hill paintings.

"Hello, Kayla," Mara said upon entering, extending her hand.

"Is that my hill again?" Kayla said, taking Mara's hand.

"It is. A pre-study for a large painting." She started to whisper. "I'll be unveiling it soon."

"It's gorgeous."

"Thank you. There is young Caleb's masterpiece," she said, pointing to the opposite wall." I'm afraid I'm in for some competition."

A tall painting of a green grassy hill hung on that wall, the scene showing a slanted orientation of a hilltop with a house on its upper slope. The house curved upward at an angle.

"Remarkable," said Kayla. "Any idea who influenced him?"

"A surrealist artist in British Columbia, Laura Zerebeski. Caleb's a genius like his sister. Those two like to experiment with their talents. I think the stretched out house was his idea although he said Megan put him up to it, like a dare. Oh, I hope they find those poor kids." Mara pulled a flyer from her bag. "I'm having a party and an auction Friday evening at my home to raise money to aid their recovery, would love to have you over." She leaned close to Kayla. I'm going to reveal the large painting of the hill to auction off," she whispered. "Those two are very special to all of us and I am optimistic they'll find their way out of their troubles." Mara wiped a tear away.

CHAPTER EIGHT
Auction

MARA LIVED A BLOCK OFF MAIN, the first house from downtown on her street. Kayla arrived late and a good crowd was there.

She hoped to see a familiar face or two and was happy when she spotted Kevin, Ronnie, Mildred, and others in the dining room. The living and dining rooms connected through a wide cased opening, the woodwork in Mara's house ever as beautiful as in Kayla's Victorian. There were over two dozen people scattered about, most of whom she hadn't yet met. Ronnie was next to the dining room table talking to someone. That must be Marsha, Kayla thought. She would have to introduce herself and compliment her on The Niche.

Kevin, who was talking to an older man near the fireplace, waved her over to introduce them. Kayla waved back to indicate she would be there shortly. After making her way through the crowd of people, she reached Ronnie and Marsha.

"I love The Niche," Kayla said to Marsha.

"Thank you. It's our dream come true," Marsha said.

A slight commotion in the living room interrupted them. People made way while Mara brought out several easels, including one with a veiled canvas. After she lined the easels up next to a wall, Kayla followed a stream of people into the living room with Ronnie and Marsha. Kevin and the man he'd been talking to caught up with her.

"If you'll all indulge me," Mara announced, "I'd like to present my latest work." She pulled the cloth away from the veiled one and revealed a scene showing a gathering of people on a grassy hilltop. The people wore indigenous clothes; one stood gazing out, holding a hand over his brow in bright sun.

"My people, long ago," Mara continued. "Scouting the buffalo grazing in the valley, perhaps not far from this very spot." She pointed at the floor and smiled.

"Silent bidding cards for these works are on the table," she said, pointing to a console along a wall.

Mara left the paintings and mingled to utterances of "congratulations" and other praise with a "well done" from Kevin when she made her way past.

After people gathered around the paintings, a line formed at the silent bidding console.

Kevin turned to Kayla and the older man he'd been talking to.

"Brett Moore owns property west of town, near yours," he said.

Moore's gray eyes sparkled. "Yep, I've been keeping watch on your property for years," he said to Kayla.

Kayla raised her eyebrows. "Keeping watch?"

"He's just kidding," Kevin said, then reached toward a bowl of chips that sat on an antique mirror-backed side table. "He has a ranch with a few head of cattle."

"Do you live out there?" Kayla said.

"No, I live in town now, but I'm out there most every day. When Brenda Barlow lived on your property I stopped by once in a while to help out with things and make sure she was okay. I helped keep that farmhouse maintained until she moved to the bigger house. She told me to stop coming by after that. She let the farmhouse go, I guess. Pretty sure she didn't hire anyone else for the upkeep. And I don't think she went up there much recently."

"What sort of work did you do at the house?"

"Ohhh, occasional things like minor plumbing. A bunch of us reshingled the roof a while back and I fixed wood rot around some windows. Did she ever do anything with that back room? She had that den blocked off from the living room. Seemed a waste."

"She made it into a library," Kayla said.

"Good," at least she put it back like it was. I think it always had bookshelves in it even before the Barlows owned it."

"What did the Barlows use that newer barn for?" asked Kayla.

"Nothing," Moore said.

A petite older woman came over.

"Well, hello, Mildred," Kevin said.

"What'cha doing there, young fella?" she replied, then gestured to Kayla. "Is she your friend? She was so kind to let me do some prospecting up on her hill the other day. I got some right nice specimens for my collection. Say, that wind sure whips around up there. I'm taking somebody with me next time. It blew me over a couple of times and I must have bumped my head, because I had a hard time seeing the town in the valley when I got up."

"I'm glad you're all right," Kayla said.

"Oh, it was nothing more than me tripping over my own two feet," Mildred said. She excused herself and went to the other side of the room.

Moore smiled and stepped away. Kevin leaned closer to Kayla. "I've been trying to get whatever I can out of him about the place," he whispered. "He tells me what he knows and doesn't seem to be bolding anything back, but he doesn't seem to know much."

"He's been in the farmhouse," Kayla said.

"Apparently not often or recently," Kevin said. "He wouldn't know about the anomaly. I guess no one in town besides us and probably Brenda, know about it. Notice how we always go back to the same time with that book."

"I noticed that the second time I went," Kayla said.

"Have you tried pulling out any other books?"

"A couple," said Kayla.

"So, what if there's another book that also takes you back in time?" Kevin said. "To a different time."

"That's worth exploring," she said. "And if there are other books, then that means the kids could be in one of any number of past times. I did find a book or two, a couple more timeshifters and cataloged the bookmarked books," she said.

"Any new bookmarks?" he asked.

"I'll show you," she said, "There's Brenda talking to Brett Moore."

"Catching up, I'm sure."

"Probably discussing how I need to tear the farmhouse down?"

"No doubt."

"Have you felt the thrill of a windy day?"
—Serena Truman Robinson

CHAPTER NINE
The Story of Art, and Graffiti Murals

A DAY OR TWO LATER, just when Kayla was finished unpacking so she could start concentrating more on the Victorian, she found herself standing up on the hillside in front of the farmhouse beneath a big gray sky. A cool breeze blew through her hair. As the gusts waved through the grassy hillside, a pleasant chill sent goosebumps down her bare arms. She imagined soaring on the breeze out over the rolling landscape.

Distant sheets of rain draped over the hills, from one to the next. A lightning bolt split a lone cottonwood on a far hill.

"One thousand one."

"One thousand two."

"One thousand three."

A few seconds later. . .

"One thousand ten."

And the distant rumble. . .two miles away—time to get inside.

She decided she wouldn't touch any books this time, but just crept around the house, to the kitchen to check for timeshifting artifacts there. The old kitchen was mostly barren and dated compared to the expansive one at her Victorian house. The neglected gas stove was a relic and would have been frightening with its corroded burners and rusted scratches across the top had there been any fuel in the tank outside.

She stood on tiptoes and noticed a few ceramic plates in an open cabinet. The cabinetry had been painted light green at one time and aside from the plates and debris on the aged linoleum floor, the kitchen was empty. A faded rectangle on the wall next to the stove revealed where the fridge had been. She reached into the cabinet and grabbed one of the plates. Nothing happened. Not part of the anomaly. She spotted an old 2014 calendar hanging on a nail and flipped through it. It wasn't a timeshifting artifact so she abandoned the effort in here. Apparently, timeshifting didn't happen in the kitchen. Only the books in the library so far.

Wind gusted against the house followed by the patter of raindrops on the roof and metal gutters. She ran to the front door and pushed it open. One of her favorite smells: the scent of rain at first drops. She breathed it in, then headed into the living room.

Did *any* items outside the library timeshift? She wasn't finding any. The wind and claps of thunder picked up as the sky grew darker and rain battered against the windows. The house grew gloomier as the storm grew noisier. No severe weather in the forecast so she wasn't going to worry. What would happen with the timeshifting books in a tornado?

The house and its timeshifting anomaly so fascinated her that it didn't feel weird being alone in a deteriorating old house with dark clouds looming outside during a thunderstorm. She glanced into the library. Wind whistled through one of the windows from its upper seal. She stepped in and scanned across the book spines. Did each book lead to a different time?

She already tried some books at one end of the bookcase with no result, but she could try more later.

After a couple of minutes, the wind let up and the storm faded to a steady rain so Kayla went out onto the porch and sat on the swing to watch the rain flow across the rolling prairie. There was nothing like watching the rain out there for losing oneself in thought.

Those underlined messages! She pulled up the pics on her phone and scrolled through them.

How did they get underlined? Who did that? Some random thing from way back? Another layer of weirdness in this house.

She headed in to the library and sat in one of the chairs where she could stare at the books. Was there a way to tell which books had timeshifting ability or were there other indications. A book caught her attention. She got up and went to the bookcase.

Looking at the titles, she remembered a couple of phrases from the underlined passages. Glancing at the pics she took, she noticed: <u>After all, who knows anything about a work of art but the artist?</u> and <u>She was not one to make a stranger feel at home</u>

If the underlined passages were messages, these pointed to two books, neither of which had bookmarks: *The Story of Art* by Ernst Gombrich and *Stranger in a Strange Land* by Robert A. Heinlein.

Even though she wasn't going to touch any books this time, she went ahead and pulled *The Story of Art* from the shelf. A breeze whisked around her. It was nighttime with ambient light coming from another room, all quiet except for baritone clunks of a grandfather clock around a corner. In the low light, she opened *The Story of Art* and was able to make out the copyright year of 1950.

She peered into the living room. In the low light, she noticed that the wallpaper with the shells was in much better condition during this time.

Muffled talking outside broke the silence. She went to the window. A bulky sedan had just pulled along the drive. The driver cut the lights. Three people got out of the car and headed around the house toward the front. Time for her to go back to normal time. She shoved the book back in.

Back in normal time, she pulled *Stranger in a Strange Land* from the shelf.

She timeshifted to a sunny day with early fall colors outside. Two women in another room were arguing. Kayla tried to eavesdrop.

"I'm going out now." one said.

"We're not finished, young lady. I'm not having you gallivanting off to some college with all those crazy beatniks and who knows what," said another.

Beatniks?

"Mother!" said the first.

Stomping followed, then the opening and slamming of the front door.

"Brenda!" the mother called out the door. "Come back here now!"

Kayla could hear Brenda's voice from outside.

She reshelved the book and shifted back to normal.

A young-sounding Brenda? The book certainly did take Kayla back to an earlier time as did the others.

Mulling over the anomaly, she decided she needed to see Kevin and more of Sycamore Falls. She was becoming so obsessed, she was missing meals and her work.

She contacted Kevin who said he would meet her downtown the next day at Fourth and Main and take her around town again.

* * *

They strolled down Main under a blue sky and puffy clouds floating over while a breeze gusted along the street and around corner buildings.

They went past the restored "Red Rock Cola" ad.

Kayla pointed at it. "Let's go see it up close," she said.

"Definitely."

They went to the brick wall.

She leaned close to see if she could see any of the original.

"This is cool," she said, lightly brushing her fingers over it, then she turned to head back to Main. "Okay, thanks for showing me this."

"Wait, there's something else." He led her toward an alley behind the building and they turned down it.

"Oh!" she said, trotting along.

"Graffiti Alley," he said, catching up.

Kayla stopped and regarded an old brick wall on the back of a store building covered with graffiti murals.

"Sycamore Falls kids, mostly, including one by Rift Raft Carafe from Emporia," he said.

"I've heard of her," said Kayla. "She's all over Kansas and the Midwest. That's a lot of talent from here. Crossroads district in KC has murals on old brick like this."

"So does Sycamore Falls."

"Well, yeah."

They continued up Main a few more blocks and walked over the scar in the street where old train tracks had once crossed Main. The historic old train depot sat to their right about a block away with the original "Sycamore Falls" sign still on the building. The old depot had a new roof and the original reddish-brown bricks on the lower façade with freshly painted curved timber roof support beams under the eaves.

Kevin gestured up and down where the tracks had been. "Passenger trains came through regularly," he said. "This one handled east-west trains. There's another depot few blocks from here that handled north-south trains. The depots house some business offices now."

They walked along the railway's ghost track.

Kayla stepped to one side, stopped for a moment, and closed her eyes. Thousands of passengers rode by here

[70]

decades before. She imagined the train easing to a stop along the depot platform with women, men, and children stepping off the train while others boarded, people dressed up in traveling clothes, looking their best as they went to visit places near and far or arrived in Sycamore Falls.

Kayla had never been on a train. Amtrak had good direct routes from KC to Chicago, LA, and St. Louis, but she never got around to it. Flying and driving were too convenient. She figured in the old days when many people traveled by train, cities and towns across the Midwest were more important since they were stops on the train lines long before anyone ever heard the words "flyover country." One day she would consider a train trip.

"Pshhhhhh!"

She snapped out of her imaginary world to Kevin making a seesaw sweep with his hand.

"Ding ding ding ding," he said.

She jumped back.

"I didn't want you to wander onto the track," he said.

"So I have an imagination," she announced.

"So you do."

She put her hand on his back and shoved him onto the ghost track and jumped away before he could grab her arm.

"Cute, but I've got to go," he said.

"Let's go around the town more, later," she said. "But now, I need to go try more timeshifting."

"You're obsessed."

"I can't stay away. I've got to get back to it."

"Maybe the house *is* communicating with you."

"*Something's* trying to?"

* * *

Kayla sat in a wingback chair in the parlor of her Victorian the next morning, her feet propped up on the small coffee table. She had windows open for now. Curtains sailed inward from an occasional breeze that brought in the scent of lilacs. She made progress on her article and caught her blog up, the old hotel, Graffiti Alley, trains past, and old grocery stores. She tried to focus and not to let her mind wander to the farmhouse and the anomaly. She glanced over at the book on the mantle with its inscription and smiled.

Tires crackled on the drive outside. She peered out the window and saw Kevin exit his car. As he stepped toward the house, she went out to the porch to meet him.

"You okay?" she said.

He nodded. "That house. How can you cope with that?"

"I'm having trouble staying away."

"As much as it's drawing you in, I'm worried about you getting lost or hurt in the past."

"But we know how it works. I'm not in danger if I'm careful. And I want to try something else." She walked to the edge of the porch where she could lean out and see around to the farmhouse and pointed up to it.

"I want to try an experiment."

"No. I don't like it there."

"Come on," she said, "let's go."

He stayed on the porch while she headed to her car and he followed after she started the engine.

They drove up.

"What's your experiment?" he said.

"You'll find out."

They pulled up and went in.

"Let me get those windows open," she said as they stood in the living room.

"At least there's a good breeze up here," he said.

He followed her to the library.

She stood in front of the bookcase. "We need to try something."

Kevin cringed.

Kayla curled her index in a 'come here' gesture.

"Oh, Kevvv," she said.

"What now?"

"Okay, we do this: I pull the book, timeshift, then you grab the same book and timeshift. My copy will go with me so it'll still be here to pull out. We both set our books down. There's a little table in the corner niche in the past timeline."

"Is that the experiment?" he said. "Sounds easy enough. Didn't we try that before?"

"I want to make sure" she said.

Kayla pulled out *Destination Unknown* and timeshifted. The scene replayed and she set the book on the little corner table.

Stepping to the middle of the room, she glimpsed Mr. Barlow in the foyer. He talked and gestured, then glanced toward Kayla. She ducked behind the wall and heard him say the same thing as before.

Someone went into the living room. Kayla grabbed the book and held on to it, ready to reshelve if she needed to quickly.

A young girl stepped into the library.

"Who are you?" the girl said.

She shrugged and returned to the living room.

Kevin finally faded into view holding his book and placed it onto the corner table.

"Welcome to this past timeline," Kayla said in a whisper. "I just saw young Brenda. I'm about to head back to the present."

Kevin leaned an ear toward the living room to listen to the male voice.

The young girl stepped back into the library and looked at both Kevin and Kayla.

"Who are you all?"

Kayla reshelved her book. "Let's go," she said to Kevin. He started to reach for his book.

Kayla faded back into the present, stepped aside and waited for Kevin.

He didn't appear after a bit.

"Oh, crap!" she said.

She went to the past timeline again and he was there looking out the window. Young Brenda was gone.

"You stayed here. Did you talk to Brenda?"

"She stayed in here for a sec, then left."

"Come on!" She took his hand and dragged him to his book on the little table, gesturing toward it and to the shelf. She reshelved her book and timeshifted to the present. A few seconds later, Kevin faded to the present.

"You scared me, again!" she said.

He shrugged. "Did you see the old Bel Air again? It looked new. They had a 'vintage car' and didn't know it. Ha!"

She nodded. "Duh. Don't do that again."

"Not sure I want to go back again anyway," he said. "When do you think that was?"

"I'm saying, 1954."

"You sure?"

Kayla ran her finger along the spine of *Destination Unknown*. "No, but the book was published that year."

"True, that Bel Air looked like it was only a couple of years old."

"Never mind that. We've verified one person can join another in a past timeline already in progress. We need to find the timeline the kids are in and join them."

"I still don't feel comfortable doing that," Kevin said.

"But it works. We have to."

He didn't answer.

"Okay," she said, "those kids *must* be stuck somewhere back there and I'm going to find them. I'll go myself if I have to."

"I think you should contact the sheriff."

"I've already thought about that and I will as soon as I rescue the kids. Who knows how the sheriff will react to something like this? Need to work through that carefully."

Kevin went into the living room and flopped onto a corner chair. "I want the kids found, too. We don't know enough about this weirdness."

"We know enough to convince me," Kayla said. "We've tested my hypothesis and it's repeatable. Anyone can go back and join someone who's already there."

"I've got to think this over," he said.

She went over to him and put her hand on his shoulder. "Then let's try it one more time. This time, don't get distracted."

"Yeah, okay."

They went back to the bookcase. Kayla grabbed the book first and timeshifted. Kevin followed her and they returned to the present together.

"So it works," he said.

"Practice," she said.

He shook his head. "I still think we should go to the sheriff."

"The sheriff'll think we're crazy," Kayla said.

"Not after we demonstrate it," he said.

"All the time it'll take to demo this and train him to use it, the kids are stuck. No, I'm going back to look for them first."

Kevin grabbed Kayla's hand. "You're familiar with time paradoxes, right?"

"That doesn't apply here. It replays the same each time like it's an independent timeline that doesn't lead to us.

"Well, perhaps we've already changed something and we're not aware of it."

"There's no evidence of that. These are just time fragments that don't lead to us. They must jut out into a different dimension and don't affect our time. It's like a time 'stub'. You've noticed when we put the book back, we return to our present and all is as it was. The entrance to the little time fragment we create just goes away as far as we're concerned. We can find the kids and bring them back from one of those fragments. The fragments remain as long as someone from the present is active in them. Bring the kids back and that fragment's deleted from our access."

"I don't know, Kayla," he said, shaking his head.

"Okay, watch. I'll prove it." She took a nail file out of her bag. "Watch."

She went to the bookcase, pulled *Destination Unknown* out and timeshifted to the cloudy day and male voice. She took her nail file and scratched a tiny nick on the left end of the bookcase in an obscure spot and snapped a picture of it.

She reshelved the book and timeshifted back to the present.

"Well?" Kevin said.

She stepped over to the left end of the bookcase. "I scratched a tiny nick here," she said, showing the picture to him.

"Okay, nothing there," he said. He slouched back on the couch. "I don't think you should."

"We just need to rescue those kids! I'm going and I want you here as a precaution."

She won that one. They agreed to take a break and meet back here later.

* * *

Next afternoon, Kayla sat in her parlor with a mug of tea catching up on writing. She had been mulling over the future of the farmhouse. That was an interesting contrast, she thought, when much of her experience up there was in its past. But its past could help her decide. What shape was the house in during the past? The inspection report didn't note any structural problems. What if she could compare the house's past with the present and get an idea of its condition over time, could that help her decide on its fate? She needed to avoid emotion in her decision. Emotion that the view from the porch up there gave her, emotion from the house's historical timeframe, and other aspects that were irrelevant when concerning the condition of a house. An estimate would help her decide.

She looked around the Victorian, walked through the parlor, living room, study, dining room, and considered the historical aspects of this house.

"Why can't I be satisfied with this one, the house, I bought the property for?"

She sighed, eased onto the sofa, opened her laptop, and dove into her article.

A minute later, Kevin tapped on the storm door.

She kept typing and shouted, "Come on in!"

He stepped in and sat across from her. "I've never seen anyone type that fast."

"I'm keeping up with all this."

"So I assume you're not publishing that."

"Just documenting it for personal record. A lot going on. I want it all down. I'm also finishing up an article installment, update that I promised my readers, and I labeled the bookmarked books."

"Hey, if you're busy, I'll come back."

"No, stay. I want to talk about this," she said, setting her laptop on the cushion next to her.

"Did you see any evidence the kids were in the farmhouse?" asked Kevin as he sat across from her. "Or that anyone besides us has been in there?"

"Hard to tell," Kayla said.

"I'm just thinking about the kids. Do you think the farmhouse library is the only place? Do we need to explore other possibilities before looking for them trapped in the past? We haven't even tried touching any other potential artifacts in the house."

"I have," she said. "In the kitchen. Nothing happened. Just books so far."

"So, you sure it's just books? It's only been the couple you've tried so far, right?"

"I've tried several, but not a lot. I've shifted back to a couple of times."

"Maybe we go up and try more books," he said.

"Getting brave now, are we? Or just curious?"

"I want *you* to try them!" he said. "And anything else in that room, or house? It seems to be confined to the bookcase. Is it books, or location that matters?"

Kayla shrugged.

"Have you been in the basement yet?"

"Briefly during inspection. With no power, it's too dark down there to see much."

"Okay, how about we go there tomorrow," Kevin said.

"I like this new you. Curious. Might I say adventurous? How about tomorrow after lunch?"

* * *

The wooden steps to the farmhouse's basement creaked but seemed sturdy enough. Two flashlights barely penetrated the gloom aimed toward the stone foundation walls; the basement was mostly empty.

"Pretty dank down here with the dirt floor," she said. "Is a dirt floor unusual?"

"Not in old houses in the country Watch for snakes."

"Eeek."

"They show up in dirt basements sometimes, but not often. This basement may have been used for food storage way back for items that didn't require an ice house."

Kayla stumbled and fell flat over a rock outcrop. Kevin helped her up.

"Treacherous," she said, brushing herself off.

"Those rocks don't look like they were there naturally; natural outcrops are common up on a hill like this, but these might have been placed here for one of the original footings. Found or quarried nearby. They placed them where they located support beams.

Kayla aimed her flashlight up at the sub-flooring and over to the stairs.

"Those inside basement stairs would have been added sometime in the twentieth century," he said. He directed his light to an opening in the foundation wall where steps led to outside. "That's where the original cellar door was. The only access to the basement was through there, from outside. They made a lot of improvements and additions over the years.

Kayla shined her light next to it on the stone foundation and panned along the wall of stones to a blackened recessed area in the upper part of the wall.

"That was the coal shoot. Sometimes they had a little iron door there. There's probably a covered window well outside where coal was once delivered through."

Kayla went over and ran her finger along the stones of the shoot then went over to Kevin and brushed the soot onto his arm. "There," she said, "a souvenir from the past."

"Thanks, I'll never wash that arm."

"Then you won't change your habits."

[79]

"Of course not. And I think we're below the library," he said, "and the bookcase is right about there." He shined his light up at the subflooring.

"Okay, there's nothing here under the bookcase," she said, shining her light on the dirt floor, at the rock that had tripped her. "Let's head on up. If we're to find those kids, then we need to go try."

Back in the library, Kevin said, "We should check the books around the one we've been using to see if location of the book is important."

"Ready?" she said.

Kevin watched as she grabbed a random book not far from the original and pulled it out.

"Nothing," she said.

She reshelved the book.

"Okay, how about one we know about?" she said. "This one—the second one I discovered."

She grabbed *The Story of Art*, pulled it out.

Nighttime. Light filtered in from another room. Quiet except the clunks of the grandfather clock around a corner. *Out of the Silent Planet* protruded out from the books around it. She pulled it out, felt a breeze swirl, and timeshifted. It was about to rain and it looked like the residents were moving out. Several movers had just taken boxes from the living room. A man approached the library. Kayla ducked to a corner.

Two other men entered the living room. "We'll have an estimate by tomorrow, Mr. Nolan."

"Thank you," Nolan answered quietly. "We might sell the bedroom suite. Please give me two estimates, one not including moving the bedroom suite."

"It's nice, Mr. Nolan."

Kayla reshelved the book, jumped back through the nodes to the present, and looked at Kevin.

"Anything?" he said.

[80]

"Nighttime, same as before with this book. Not sure when it was, but some light came from another room. I heard a little talking."

Then I pulled out another book, and went back farther. The residents in that timeline were moving out. The Barlows didn't live here yet."

"Okay, so we have a couple of books that take us back to different times," said Kevin.

"A few. Maybe it is based on location in the bookcase."

"It's a good start."

Kayla rubbed her chin. "Or is it?"

"What?"

"*Stranger in a strange Land* was published in 1961, the year it takes you to. *Destination Unknown* takes you to 1954, late in the year, November or December. I don't know when *Out of the Silent Planet* takes you yet, but it was published in 1938, so I figure. . ."

"Oh, hey," he said, smiling.

"Anyway, regardless of that, when we search for the kids, we have to figure out how to get around without being discovered. After all, we're in someone's house just appearing there suddenly."

"No more of this today," he said. "This is wearing me out."

"Then let's discuss this again tomorrow and start a real plan. You're not getting out of this."

Kevin groaned. "Okay. See you tomorrow."

* * *

The parlor was shaping up well at the Victorian and Kevin helped Kayla hang some large pictures. The portrait *of* her late mother went on the wall opposite the fireplace. Kayla originally thought about displaying it in the study.

She stood back from it. "That works. Mom would have liked it there."

Kevin grabbed the antique wall table and placed it under the portrait. "There," he said. "Does that look okay?"

"I think." She unpacked a small lamp and placed it on the table. "Glad there's an outlet here."

"The wiring was updated, right?" he said.

"It was, otherwise I would have negotiated for it during inspection period."

She stood in the middle of the parlor. "You know, in this room is where the owners would have entertained their guests on a Sunday afternoon in this house's early days. They closed off the rest of the house to visitors."

"That was tradition."

"If they had a piano, they would sing together or they played cards. There were so many events here over the generations who lived here. I can imagine over a hundred years of celebrations, of triumphs, tragedies. That's what's in an old house."

"You don't need the farmhouse anomaly, you have that ability engrained in you," said Kevin.

" Not exactly. I've always imagined the history of things. The anomaly doesn't prop that up. The anomaly's a new thing. Don't you imagine stuff like that when you go into an old place?"

"Sometimes. Maybe."

A knock at the door interrupted them.

Kayla went and opened the door for the sheriff and Jennifer who stood down by the sheriff's car.

"Ms. Ramsey?" the sheriff said, "Ms. Dodd would like to take a look around your property, around the farmhouse."

"I told Jennifer she could go up and look anytime," Kayla said, smiling.

"She wants to go in the farmhouse."

Kayla and Kevin stepped toward him. "Do you have a search warrant?" Kayla said.

[82]

"No," the sheriff said, "you don't have to let us if you don't want to."

"It's okay, Sheriff, um. . . ?"

"Rick Hernandez," he said, extending his hand.

She shook his hand and glanced at Kevin.

"We've met," Kevin said.

"No problem. I'll go up with you," Kayla said.

"Thank you."

Kayla and Kevin drove up ahead and met them in the farmhouse's front yard. They followed Rick and Jennifer around the outside and stopped at the shed in the back.

"Okay if we look in here?" Rick said, taking hold of the shed door handle.

"Sure. I've only peeked in a little," Kayla said.

Rick pulled the door open to reveal shelves stacked with paint cans, used brushes, and tools, and an old sickle and hand saw, both rusted with rotted wooden handles, hanging in the back.

"I've been so busy, I haven't cleaned this out yet."

"Those belong in a museum. Watch for snakes if you go in there."

She turned to Kevin. "What about the old tools? Can the Society use them?"

"Maybe. I'll talk to the society president. She's been talking about a county museum."

"Okay," Rick said, "let's go."

Kayla and Kevin followed Rick and Jennifer around to the front of the farmhouse and they all convened on the front porch.

Rick took Jennifer to the front door. "Okay if we go in?" he said to Kayla.

"We can, but please don't touch anything. I want to preserve things how they are. It's a snapshot in time. I might fix this place up someday but for now I want to keep it as is even in its condition."

[83]

"I imagine this place needs a lot of work."

As Rick and Jennifer headed toward the library, Kayla caught up with them and stood in front of the bookcase when they wandered through the living room.

"Looks like those books haven't been touched in years," Jennifer said, her eyes focused on the middle shelf. "Except for any you've gone through, right? Hard to resist looking through some of these old books, I imagine."

"It is," Kayla said. She leaned against the bookcase and placed her hand in front of the timeshifting books.

Jennifer and Rick decided to go to the foyer, up the stairs, and Kayla remained in the library.

After they came back downstairs a few minutes later, Kayla met them in the foyer.

"Nothing upstairs," Rick said. "I pulled the attic trap door ladder down. Completely empty up there."

"I guess there's nothing to see here," Jennifer said. "I hoped we could find some clues."

"Thank you, Ms. Ramsey," Rick said, and they headed out the front door.

"Phew, no problem," Kayla mumbled.

After they left, Kevin frowned and glanced around. "Of course, you could have shown them the timeshifting."

"I'm not ready to yet."

"I figured."

"Let's head back to the Victorian," Kayla said. "You need to finish helping me."

Late that afternoon at the Victorian, Kayla sat in one of the wingbacks in the parlor with her laptop, catching up on writing while Kevin slouched back on the sofa and napped.

It took her a while to notice, because it was gradual. As she continued deep in her writing, she sensed a change about the room. A shaft of sunlight came from a west window. The sunlight streamed from there into this room, casting a spot on the floor in front of the snoozing Kevin before edging past his feet, then slid over to drift up the east wall.

Kevin stretched after a bit and sat forward. Then he stood and bright sunlight struck his face.

He groaned and shielded his eyes.

"Gotcha," said Kayla.

He stepped over and kicked her foot. "You planned that?"

She chuckled. "Hardly, but it'll change as the year progresses from one season to another."

"If I know you, you'll be considering stuff like that in your decorating."

"Lighting affects mood and the personality of a room and, this way, the room has a different look for each season."

"It might cause you to stumble into something."

"Not if I'm careful." She stretched and put her hands behind her head. "So I want to get ready to check those past timelines for the kids."

"We should just do the timeshifting books we've found," he said. The kids should be nearby, right? Because if they just go back there and drop the books then they might be afraid of what happened and stick around nearby."

"I've seen no evidence of them in any past timelines, have you?" she said. "They might try to head to their home, such as it was back in time."

"They might have hid, been confused about where they were. They could have been in any of the past timelines you've visited. So are you going to let the sheriff in on this, or are you trying to be a hero?"

She frowned. "It has nothing to do with being a hero. Like I said, I'll call the sheriff in after we master this thing and we find the kids, but for now I don't want word of this thing getting out. I don't want to risk anyone getting lost. We know how to navigate this thing. Training others takes time. Look how you didn't take to it."

"I was nervous and I also got curious."

"My points exactly," she said. "After the kids are found, then just think what we can do with this. We can observe history, history of the house's past families."

"More than that. We can go anywhere."

"And take Jennifer back. But first, we rescue her kids. I'm sure we can do it. They must be in a past timeline."

"Yeah."

"No more stalling. We go up to the farmhouse tomorrow morning," she said. "Period."

"We will."

CHAPTER TEN
Together

THE NEXT MORNING, Kayla pointed to *The Story of Art*. "This one," she said.

"Good luck," Kevin said, stepping back.

"I'll get back here soon as possible. It's not like people are going to remember me then since it resets every time we go back."

"So you've said."

Kayla pulled out *The Story of Art* and timeshifted to the nighttime library with ambient light coming from another room and the clunks of the grandfather clock. She crept toward the living room and peered around. The scene replayed with the car pulling around the house. She thought about sneaking outside, but wasn't sure the kids would have gone out in the dark after being thrown into a strange situation like this. How unfortunate the kids picked a nighttime timeline if this was the one. They had to have hidden somewhere. The basement? A dark corner? Or maybe they did sneak out and go to their own house of the past. Or the barn. Kayla decided she'd wait quietly in the library while the Barlows came in and until they went to bed, then she'd try to sneak out. She stashed her copy of *The Story of Art* into her bag and found another copy on a chair which she put in her bag with the other one.

After a while, the last of the lights around the house went out and the muffled upstairs footsteps and talking faded. A few minutes later, Kayla tiptoed through the darkened house, cringing every time she stepped on a squeak in the floor. She got to the front door. It was unlocked and she could slip out without waking anyone upstairs.

Out onto the porch, she could see out over the moonlit hills, a ghostly impression of a sunny day with the landscape clearly visible beneath a not quite full Moon. Occasional trees cast sharp shadows. Frogs and crickets echoed throughout the valleys, accompanied by the occasional thumping of an oil well. She crept down the porch steps to the front walk that led to the barn and made her way over around to its moonlit south side that faced away from the house. She looked for a way in. The south window was up a little. She went to peer in. Too dark inside to see anything except where the moonlight shone through the window and cast a white rectangle on the floor with Kayla's shadow in it.

She gasped when something moved by the moonspot and she almost screamed when a moonlit face behind the window rose up to meet hers.

A girl's voice. "Who are you?" she whispered through the opening.

"I'm Kayla. Are you Megan?"

"I am!"

Kayla made a shh! gesture.

Megan lifted the window. "How did you know my name?"

"I'm here to take you home."

"Oh!" Megan tried to contain her excitement. She lifted the window higher, climbed through the opening, hopped onto the ground next to Kayla, and hugged her. Kayla patted her back.

Footsteps on gravel broke the silence.

A man came around the corner and emerged into the moonlight. "Who's there! Who are you and what are you doing here?"

Kayla took Megan's hand and led her toward him. "Just go with what I say," she whispered to Megan. They stood next to Barlow.

"I'm so sorry. My daughter slipped away and I just found her up here."

"Then you best be heading home," he said. "It's late and I have to get up in the morning."

"Yes," Kayla said, "are you satisfied, young lady?" She turned to Barlow. "Believe me, she'll be punished."

"What are you doing with my book?" he said, pointing to one of *The Story of Art* copies poking from Kayla's bag.

"She's in big trouble. I found the book on her. She must have gotten into your house and taken it." She turned to Megan again. "How does reform school sound, young lady?"

"You mean juvie?" Megan said.

"Shhh!"

"All right," Barlow said, "no real harm done. Just give me my book back."

"If you'll permit us," said Kayla, "I want her to take the book and put it back from where she took it."

"My family's trying to sleep," he said. "I don't want any commotion."

"I'll go with her and make sure she's quiet."

"I don't know."

Kayla ignored Barlow's reply, grabbed Megan's arm, and faked a forceful yanking of her toward the house. "Come on." She pulled her to the porch amid Barlow shaking his head.

"Just keep it down," he said quietly.

He followed as they tiptoed onto the porch and waited for him. Kayla led Megan in to the library. Barlow watched.

"Put it back exactly where you got it," Kayla said as they stood in front of the bookcase.

Megan reshelved her copy of the book and faded.

Barlow stood in the living room and approached Kayla. "Where is she?" he said. "I want my book back."

Kayla reshelved her copy and shifted her way to the present.

Kevin was there, slack jawed with Megan who stood in the middle of the room.

Kayla pulled a granola bar from her bag and gave it to Megan.

"Where'd you find her?" Kevin said.

"Wait, give her a chance to calm down before we start talking. She gestured to a chair for Megan to sit. Megan started pacing instead. After a few minutes, she regained her composure.

"We'll explain it to you, honey, you're home safe," Kayla said to her. "Can you tell us where Caleb went?"

"I don't know. We were going to meet at the barn and he went somewhere else.

He wanted to look at that story of art book and he pulled it out. Then I pulled it out, too, and the house turned kind of dark. We didn't know why it had gotten dark earlier than normal. I told him to leave the books alone but he started to grab *Out of the Silent Planet* sticking out of the shelf. When I turned away, he said to meet him at the barn, then he was just gone." She wiped her eyes. "We have to find him."

"I know where he is," said Kayla. "I'm going back to get him."

"Kayla," objected Kevin.

"Quiet. I know where he is. She reached for *The Story of Art,* pulled it out and timeshifted to the nighttime library. *Out of the Silent Planet* sat in the bookcase sticking out a little.

"Of course." She pulled it out and timeshifted earlier.

It was daytime, raining outside, some activity over in the foyer. She held the book. On a corner chair, a boy about

[90]

thirteen or fourteen sat cowering. *Out of the Silent Planet* and *The Story of Art* sat on the chair with him.

"Are you Caleb?" Kayla whispered.

The boy nodded.

"Come with me, I'm taking you home."

Kayla faced him. "We can't keep those." She told him to reshelve *Out of the Silent Planet* and hold onto *The Story of Art*.

He complied and faded. Kayla reshelved hers and followed, escorting him back to the present. Kevin and Megan were waiting.

Megan threw her arms open. "Caleb!"

Caleb lunged at her and returned the hug.

They had a tearful reunion and after the kids relaxed, Kayla pulled another granola bar from her bag and offered it to Caleb.

Kevin gestured to the chairs.

Neither sat.

Kevin and Kayla filled them in on the situation.

"I wish I knew the date during the nighttime library," Kayla said.

"I saw a calendar hanging in the barn during the day," Megan said. "It was on November 1950."

"So, 1950," said Kayla. "A few years before my first timeshift with *Destination Unknown*."

"What about Mom?" Caleb said.

"I just saw her a couple of days ago," said Kayla. "She misses you and we'll have you with her right away."

"Can you both keep this a secret?" Kevin said. "This is a dangerous place. We don't want anyone else getting lost like you did."

"I'm not touching those books again," Megan said.

"Nether am I," said Caleb.

"You can stay at my house until your mom comes over," Kayla said.

"I don't want to stay here," Caleb said.

"No," said Megan.

"Not here," Kayla said. "I don't live in this house. The one down the hill."

Both kids sighed.

Caleb looked around and peered into the living room toward the foyer.

"They're not here," Kayla said.

* * *

Kayla and Kevin took Megan and Caleb down to the Victorian.

They got them settled onto the sofa in the parlor.

"Two timeshifting levels," Kevin said to Kayla.

"The possibilities. And something's been bothering me," Kayla said. "If that house had been bulldozed, the kids could have been lost in a past timeline."

"Then what?" Caleb said.

"I don't know," Kayla said. "But don't worry. I was never going to tear the house down before you were found. Not yet."

Kayla sat on a chair with a package that had been left on the porch.

"What'd you get?" Kevin said.

She opened the package and showed him.

"Silver certificates. One-dollar bills," she said. "A hundred of them. Got them online." She pulled a bundle out and fanned them. "They're in decent enough shape. If either of us needs money in a mid-twentieth century timeline, these'll be good to have. Better than trying to pass off current bills. Got an assortment of some minted in the nineteen forties and fifties."

"I'm sure those weren't cheap."

"Not bad. There's no demand for them now. I had some already. My mother used to collect them."

[92]

"I'll go get some take out," Kevin said. "Megan and Caleb must be hungry. Right, kids?"

Both mumbled "Uh-huh." He started for the door.

Soon after, he returned with takeout from Danny's and everyone convened in the dining room.

After they finished eating, both kids, exhausted from the day, returned to the sofa and collapsed.

Kayla went into the kitchen out of earshot and called Jennifer.

"I have a lead on Megan and Caleb," Kayla told her. "Can you come over right away?"

She ended the call and Kevin joined her in the kitchen.

"I just checked on them," he said. "They're worn out, both asleep on the sofa. Is Jennifer coming over?"

"On her way," Kayla said.

"I'll stick around."

"Good. I'm planning a demo."

"You're what?"

We've got to explain it to her. I want to let her in on the secret, try to get her buy-in so she and the kids don't tell anyone," she said. "We don't want people flocking here, like I've said."

"Right. You've got a challenge on your hands."

Jennifer pulled into the drive. Kayla peeked out the window to make sure she was alone.

Kayla answered the door just as Jennifer stepped up to it to avoid a doorbell ring and invited her in.

"Would you like something to drink?" Kayla said.

"No, thank you. I'm anxious as you can imagine."

"Yes, of course. In a bit, I want to take you up to the farmhouse."

"So there's something there?"

"There is. It's not a bad thing. Something I need to show you."

[93]

"I wondered."

She led Jennifer into the parlor. The kids were leaning against each other, dozing.

"Oh," Jennifer said in a hushed tone, not looking directly at them, "Am I interrupting anything? I didn't know you had kids."

"I don't—"

Jennifer stared at them, then: "My babies!"

Megan and Caleb snapped awake, jumped up, and rushed to their mother with arms out, nearly knocking her over.

Jennifer embraced them.

Kayla stood back, giving them room.

After the excitement subsided, Kayla said, "We still need to go up to the farmhouse right away."

"We do," Jennifer said, sobbing. "I want to see where you found them."

"Let's head up."

"Do we need to call Sheriff Rick?" Jennifer asked.

"I plan to ask him to meet us up there soon," Kayla said.

"Right," Jennifer said, "show me first."

"I will."

* * *

At the farmhouse, Kayla and Kevin led Jennifer and the kids into the foyer. "Follow me to the library, Jennifer, that's where it happened," Kayla said.

Megan and Caleb remained in the foyer.

Jennifer laughed. "Whatever happened, it figures it was in a room full of books!" She tried to suppress her laugh and turned look back to them in the foyer.

Caleb smiled and kept quiet.

"A big reader, he is, as is Megan," Jennifer said.

They stepped into the library and Kayla pointed to *Destination Unknown.*

"The best way is to show you," she said. She showed Jennifer how to timeshift and prepared her so she had the right expectations. Jennifer timeshifted and the 1954 timeline replayed for her as it had for Kayla and Kevin, cloudy day and male voice.

She returned seconds later and stared at Kayla and Kevin wide-eyed. "What happened! I heard a man's voice in there with my kids."

Kayla stepped over to her, took her wrist, and led her a step away from the bookshelf.

"You timeshifted," she said. "That's what we're calling it anyway."

Jennifer sat in one of the chairs, elbows on her knees, head in her hands trying to comprehend the experience.

Kayla stood next to her and put a hand on her shoulder.

"Thank you," Jennifer said. "At least they're safe. If this thing timeshifts as you say, then they could have been lost forever."

"Yes," said Kevin. "We don't understand it, but it does take you back."

"It could be a tool to study history," said Kayla. Then, "I'm sorry, it's a bit early to discuss that."

"I guess so. Once I get over the shock of this, I might jump into that."

"I'm sorry," Kayla said.

"No, it's fine. You're right."

Jennifer gestured toward the parlor. "It was suddenly cloudy and I heard a man talking in there."

"You heard Mr. Barlow back in the 1954."

She gasped.

"That's what happened to Megan and Caleb, only with a different book. That story of art book, we think, took them back to 1950."

"It figures. An art book," Jennifer said.

"In fact, Caleb went farther back in time from there. Megan managed to sneak out of the house and spend the nights in the barn in 1950."

"I sneaked inside to get food sometimes," said Megan from the foyer.

"Those two. Always pushing the limits," Jennifer said, smiling. "So, what now? Can you go back farther than 1950?"

"We think so. We don't know how far back Caleb went. I think 1938."

"I'm planning to try that one," Kevin said.

"Well, I know you wanted to call Sheriff Rick up here," said Kayla.

Jennifer held her hand over her mouth. "Should we yet?"

"I've been reluctant to," Kayla said. "But I need to and we need to explain finding the kids and cancel the Amber Alert. I'd hate for them to get in trouble, accused of running away."

"No, they're such good kids."

"Let's wait a day or so," Jennifer said. "I want to spend time with my twins. And we'll need to return the donations from Mara's fundraiser after Rick announces the kids are safe."

"Of course. Then you'll need to keep the kids home until we talk to Rick," said Kayla.

"We really should contact Rick right away," Kevin said.

"I am," Kayla said, "We need to get this anomaly figured out and present it all to him. It's pulling me back, like trying to communicate with me, with something to say. This isn't for personal adventure. It's *speaking* to me."

Kevin shrugged. "We can call Rick when you're ready to demonstrate this to him, but hurry up. People are waiting to hear the kids are all right."

"Kids!" Jennifer called to the foyer. Megan and Caleb skipped into the living room and stopped a ways before reaching the library.

"Yes?"

"We have to keep quiet about this until we talk to Sheriff Rick and we have to stay home until then. It won't be long. Since I'm not teaching summer classes, I'll have time to spend with you. We have some catching up to do."

"Okay," Megan said.

Caleb nodded. "Are my paints and canvases still in my room, and the easel?"

"They are," Jennifer said, "I *knew* I would see you again soon!"

Still in the library, she opened her arms and beckoned them for a hug, but both kids held back from the library.

"Oh, of course," she said, "I'm sorry." Jennifer went to them in the living room for a hug.

She turned to Kevin and Kayla. "My head is spinning. I'm thinking of all the things this could be used for now. Witness the past in person."

"True," Kayla said, "eventually, but we're limited to the past timelines the books are set to take us."

"A pity. Well, it's something to consider. I wonder what the sheriff's department will do with this place."

"It's your property," Kevin said, "you don't have to let them do anything."

"Unless the house is condemned because of what happened to Caleb and Megan. That's why I want to timeshift more. I need to know what it's trying to *tell me*."

"For your ears, maybe," said Kevin.

"Well, Jennifer said, "I need to get my family home and rest up after all this. I need a couch and some mindless activity to recoup from all this."

Kayla smiled. "Be careful about the kids being seen!"

Jennifer nodded.

"We're not going out or talking to anyone." Megan said.

Jennifer held her hands out. "Your phones."

They handed them to her, then they all headed to the front door and left.

Kayla and Kevin went out to the front porch and watched them drive away down the gravel lane, leaving a trail of dust.

When Jennifer's car was out of sight, Kayla and Kevin sat on the porch swing. A cooling breeze floated in from the north.

"You think they'll be good?" Kayla said, extending her feet and legs.

"I do," Kevin said, "although they'll be tempted to talk and it'll be hard for Jennifer to contain her joy when she's out."

"All the more reason to get to exploring the past timelines and contact Rick," she said.

"Right," he said. "We need to find out all we can quickly before we call him up here."

"Glad you agree. We might not have another chance to really investigate this timeshifting thing," she said. "I've *got* to do it. I want to check for books or objects that go farther back like *Out of the Silent Planet* that took Caleb back."

"So, what's next?" Kevin said, dropping his feet to the floor of the porch.

"I've been thinking," she said. "First time I walked along downtown after moving in, I noticed some of the things this poor town is suffering. Across Main from Weber's and the Historical Society, there are a lot of empty stores. There are a couple of open stores another block down and a place or two on Second and on Fourth like The Niche and Danny's Café. Good location with the courthouse there. I don't know what the town was like in its heyday. If I did, I'd have an idea what the good times were like. I know you talked about it a little."

"Part of your article? I thought you were more focused on art's influence."

"I am. It fits together. This is an evolving process as I notice new things here. My readers are interested in my experiences here and I said I'm going to document over time how the town works to renew itself and the art thing figures within that. There's a lot of interest in that from my readers, some as far away as the UK, but most of the interest is from across the Midwest and South. A lot of towns around are similar."

"You may not have lived here during its heyday, but you have a way," he said.

"I knooow," she said.

"So I have an idea," he said. "We're at the mercy of where each book happens to take us, but *The Story of Art* goes to 1950.

"Right," she said. "1950. Megan verified."

"Okay," Kevin said, "but we should both go back to 1961."

"We will. First, I'm going to 1954 again. We haven't explored there yet, because I need to find a good way out of the house. It's busy when you first jump into that timeline."

"You just need to duck in a corner and wait."

"I will. After that, I'm calling Rick and we figure out a way to keep him at bay and we go together to 1961."

"I suppose."

CHAPTER ELEVEN
Holiday

KAYLA PULLED *DESTINATION UNKNOWN* off the shelf and felt the swirl of wind. The timeline replayed, cloudy day, male voice in another room. This time, she looked out the window past the old car to the hills and sky beyond. It looked like snow was on its way. She needed heavier clothes for this timeline, so she reshelved the book. Back in the present, she hurried down to the Victorian, grabbed a heavy coat and scarf, and changed out of the skirt into jeans, sweater, and winter boots.

Back in the farmhouse, she quickly timeshifted back to 1954 again with *Destination Unknown.*

The timeline replayed. After a while, Barlow was in the living room conversing with a couple of men, one holding a clipboard.

Kayla waited in a chair tucked in the library's corner.

She leaned toward the living room to eavesdrop on Barlow and the men.

"I'm going to replace it," Barlow said.

"Well, we can help you tear the old one down," the clipboard man said.

"I'll want a clear spot next to it for the new barn."

"You want us to bid that, too?"

"You can give me an estimate, but I'll probably build it myself. And I want that gravel lane down to West Hill Road straightened and oriented due east down the hill."

"We'll bid that, too. Let's go take a look at the barn before it snows," the clipboard man said.

They headed for the foyer.

A moment later, they went out the front door. Kayla glanced out the window. Barlow was next to the barn with the contractors.

A minute later, a woman went out to the porch and shouted. "Marlin! Take me to town before it snows!"

Barlow answered, barely audible.

"I'll get Brenda ready," the woman shouted.

Kayla would bide her time until they left.

About twenty minutes later, the house was quiet. If snow wouldn't have been on the way, she might have poked around the house a little. Instead, she headed outside, leaving the front door unlocked. A few flakes started to fall. She went around to the back of the house, went a ways into the woods, and trudged through the leaves beneath the bare tree limbs. There was beauty in walking through woods in winter. The underbrush was mostly gone and navigating all the twists and turns was easy. The snow picked up. A ways into the woods now, she stopped and listened to the hypnotizing crackle of snow on the scattered dead leaves as the flakes landed. She stood still, squinted, and stared, could feel the illusion that the ground was moving upward against the falling snow.

The trail led down the hill, deeper into the woods. She hiked down it, for how often does one get a chance to hike in Flint Hills woods in 1954? After she went a ways, she came along the edge of a small ravine where someone had dumped old bottles. The clutter of junk included a batch of old blue Milk of Magnesia bottles, other non-descript broken bottles, and additional assorted vintage junk. She snapped a photo, then turned and saw the rusted body of a Model T Ford, lonely and decrepit, surrounded by saplings and banks of leaves that had collected around the bottom of the car. The car had remnants of an engine and the interior was practically nonexistent, only the steering wheel and what was left of the steering column. She snapped pictures. "This is for you,

Kevin." She gazed past the car into the deep woods and felt in tune with nature.

After indulging in the meditative moments, she spotted open prairie where the trees thinned out uphill and she hiked a ways up toward the grassland. She needed to get to town, so she quickly made her way up.

Out onto the grass, she hiked to the hilltop where she had a view of the hills blanketed in a patchy layer of white beneath the fog of the light snowfall. It wasn't that cold with the snow falling. She spotted West Hill Road, went to it, and hiked her usual route to Main Street.

The snow hadn't accumulated yet and cars headed up and down Main without hazard. She would say Main Street was "decorated to a T." The cross wires at the intersections were lined with greenery and multicolored lights, which were on even during the day. The lampposts along the street had candle-like attachments. People swarmed the sidewalks, stepping in and out of stores.

Her previous imagining of Main Street of the past didn't match the reality around her. With the winter weather and decorations, the town was different and had a vibe to it that she felt part of as if this was *her* town and she belonged here, which happened a lot during some of her jaunts to the past, so that was nothing new. She was predisposed to it like when you go on vacation and imagine what it'd be like to live in the place you're visiting. This wasn't something she could explain to Kevin. This Sycamore Falls seemed so *normal*.

A Five and Ten, Ben Franklin's, Sherry-Wilson's, and Denny-Paul's were in business and busy. A middle-aged man carried a frozen turkey out of Weber's and loaded it into the trunk of a massive rounded black car while a woman held the trunk lid. The door to Weber's opened and a young Hank, leaned out and waved. The woman went back into Weber's. Kayla managed to make it across the street through some accumulation of snow and approached the man who had just loaded the turkey.

"Hello, sir," Kayla said. "Are you ready for Christmas?"

"Yes, ma'am, I am. It's going to be a good one for us. I just got a job at the high school here. I'll be the custodian."

"Congratulations. That's wonderful. Where are you from?"

"Wichita, born and raised."

"Welcome to Sycamore Falls."

Now it really felt to Kayla like this was her town, not just this one in the past, but Sycamore Falls in general to which she welcomed him.

He smiled, thanked her, and resumed his task.

Kayla took in the general upbeat mood of people going about their downtown holiday shopping.

She needed to head back to the farmhouse, so she went down Main and slogged her way through two inches of snow. On West Hill Road, she encountered a car sitting on the side of the road. Mr. Barlow was putting chains on the wheels. Mrs. Barlow waited inside the car. Kayla hiked past through the woods next to the road, avoiding detection, then emerged a ways past the curve and trudged up the snowy hill to the farmhouse. The front door was still unlocked so she went in to the library and reshelved the book, returned to the present, and went home to rest up before calling Sheriff Rick.

CHAPTER TWELVE
Demo

THE NEXT DAY, SHERIFF RICK WASTED NO TIME getting to the farmhouse. He stood in the middle of the library with Kayla and Kevin. A little later, Jennifer arrived with Megan and Caleb. The three of them remained quiet in the foyer, waiting for Kayla's signal before Jennifer brought the kids back toward the library.

"Where's Jennifer?" Rick said while Jennifer and kids were still out of view. "She should be here."

"She'll be here in a while," Kayla replied. She pointed to a spot on the floor next to the bookcase. "I need to show you something, if you'll stand here, please."

Rick tipped his hat back and dragged a sleeve across his forehead. "Something there?" he said.

She pointed at *Destination Unknown*. "Take hold of this book, pull it out and don't let go, whatever happens. It's very important to keep hold of it no matter what you see."

He reached for it and Kayla stepped back.

Sheriff Rick timeshifted to the cloudy day and male voice.

He started to let go of the book. Kayla and Kevin weren't there. The room was different.

"Kayla?" he said.

A male voice came from another room. "Who's there?" Barlow said from the foyer.

Rick set the book on the corner table and stepped to the middle of the library. Barlow peered around the corner from the foyer.

[104]

"Who are you?" he said.

"I'm meeting with Kayla on business, who are *you*?" Rick said.

Kayla faded into the room.

"Rick," she whispered, extending her hand to him. "Get the book off the table and come with me." They timeshifted to the present, Rick took his hat off, and took a deep breath.

"What the hell was that?" he said.

Kevin gestured to one of the chairs. "Have a seat, Sheriff, and we'll discuss what just happened."

Rick sat. "Is that the weirdness Brenda has mentioned about this house?" he said, placing his hat on his knees.

Kayla nodded and sat in the other chair. "I'm sure she never went into any details."

"Clouds just went over and some guy was in the house," he said. "Does whatever this is have something to do with Jennifer's kids?"

"It does. It, um, changes the setting you're in," she said. "Listen, Sheriff, it's true."

"What kind of setting?"

"To a different time."

"So. . .did the kids get lost somewhere through whatever this is?"

"Yes, they did," Kayla said.

"We need to rescue them," he said.

"We already have," Kayla said, smiling. She called to the foyer. "Jennifer!"

Jennifer and the kids entered the living room and Rick jumped up, and ran over to greet them amid cries of joy.

"Well," he said patting Jennifer on the shoulder. He shifted his attention to Megan and Caleb.

"So fine to see you both!"

Megan and Caleb both threw hugs around him.

"Looks like we can cancel the Amber Alert!" he said.

"How are you going to write this up, Rick?" Kevin asked.

"Have to think about it, but until then, what with this weird transporting to another time, did you say? I'll have to make this off limits until I figure out how to explain ending the Amber Alert."

Kayla frowned.

"What would you do?" said Kayla. "This is my house. There's been no crime committed."

"To ensure the safety of everyone, until we figure this out."

"What are you going to do," Kevin said, "restrict access because there's dangerous time transferring here? How're you going to explain that?"

"Tell me more about this thing," Rick said.

"By removing the book from the shelf, it takes you to the past where you can observe and experience it," Kayla said. "I don't know how it works."

"There's no precedent for this," Kevin said.

Rick shook his head. "Okay, we don't know what it is, but as a precaution, I'm thinking about restricting access."

"I have work to do here and this is my house," Kayla said. "How about we make a deal? I need access to my house. I'm just as afraid of that thing as you and frankly I'd rather work on my house than play around with some freaky thing like that. So, let me have access to the rest of my house, eh?"

"Depends. How widespread is this?" the sheriff asked.

"Just the books. I've tried objects all over the house."

Kevin nodded. "She has. There's nothing else here."

"I want to inspect the rest of the house," Rick said.

"That's okay," said Kayla.

Rick left the library.

"What if he finds something and timeshifts?" she said, whispering.

"Go," Kevin insisted, "catch up with him."

Kayla joined Rick and after they poked around the living room, upstairs and the kitchen, they returned to the library.

"Like when I was here before," Rick said, "everything checks out, but I'm going to think about this and I'm not going to do anything yet. Part of our deal is that you don't talk about this.

"Agreed," said Kayla.

Kayla nodded and handed him the front door key."

"How are we wrapping this up?" Kayla said.

"What we can do now," Rick said, "is announce the kids are found safe and cancel the Amber Alert. Say they went to their aunt's in Mound Grove who took them camping in Colorado for a couple of weeks. She and Jennifer had a miscommunication and the aunt thought Jennifer knew. They were deep in the mountains without service and couldn't contact Jennifer. I'll let you know before I decide to restrict access to this thing. Be careful and keep it quiet."

Kayla and Jennifer were satisfied with that. After Rick and the others left, Kevin and Kayla stood in the middle of the library.

"So we have a some time left," Kevin said. "Let's get ready to go to 1961."

"Tomorrow."

CHAPTER THIRTEEN
Interviews and Research

THE NEXT MORNING, KAYLA AND KEVIN STOOD IN FRONT OF THE BOOKCASE.

"Let's go," she said.

They timeshifted with *Stranger in a strange Land* to the sunny autumn afternoon. They remained quiet while the women in the other room argued.

"Listen," Kayla whispered.

After Brenda stomped out, it sounded like Mrs. Barlow headed outside as well. A car drove away and the house was quiet now. Kayla and Kevin crept into the living room and approached the foyer. No noises from anywhere such as the kitchen, dining room, or anywhere else.

In the foyer, Kevin started out the front door and said, "Ready?"

They stepped onto the porch. The Ford receded into the distance down the lane past the Victorian.

"Wow," said Kayla, "look down at my Victorian as it was in 1961. Still looks the same except less trees in the backyard among the mature ones that were already there."

A clank of a tool in the barn interrupted them and they got back against the wall of the house. She took Kevin's hand and led him off the porch and around a hidden side of the house.

"The place looks nicer in this time," she whispered, looking up at the white, well-maintained clapboard siding.

"Yeah," he said, "that lead-based paint isn't peeling or anything."

They sneaked around to the backyard, past the clothesline draped with sheets and went to the shed.

"Let's duck in here until Barlow goes somewhere else," Kevin said.

"The woods are farther back from the house and yard now: you were right about that," she said.

They stepped into the shed. A neat arrangement of shelves lined one wall. The sickle hung on the wall, already old and rusted.

"Barlow's keeping that old thing," Kayla said.

"Looks about the same in our time," he said.

"Fascinating to see something in the past that's already old."

They looked over at the house.

"I haven't been on the back porch," she said. "It's not safe in normal time."

"Shh!" They ducked low in the shed and watched Barlow trudge across the backyard and disappear back into the barn. He emerged for a moment and grabbed some lumber from a stack of boards outside the overhead door and dragged the boards in, the sounds of sawing and hammering following.

"Let's take a peek on the back porch," Kayla said. "Then we need to get into town."

They crouched low as they made their way across the backyard to the porch steps.

"We might have to make a run for it," Kevin said. "And he's downwind from us. You're not wearing perfume, are you?"

"No I'm not. Are you? You should know with your dog sense of smell."

"Just covering all the bases."

Barlow finished up in the barn and started toward the house. They ducked behind the porch as he went up the steps opposite their side. After he went inside, they sneaked over to the barn. Both overhead doors were open now and they headed inside from the west.

Their shadows stretched in the afternoon sun toward the east opening.

"He's almost done with it," Kevin said.

"Not a lot different than in our time. He really didn't use it, but maintained it well."

"Hey, look," said Kevin, walking over to a 1961 calendar hanging on a nail. "He has September 21st circled. First day of fall."

"Can I help you folks?" They nearly leapt to the rafters.

Kayla turned around first and saw Barlow's figure silhouetted against the sunny backlight. "He saw us sneak over here," Kevin whispered.

"Oh, hello, sir," she said, "we didn't mean to trespass. We're out for a long walk and wanted to admire your new barn."

"Yes," said Kevin, "nice workmanship."

"You best be moving on then," Barlow said.

They nodded at Barlow and turned to head out the east door to the grass along newly laid concrete and started to walk down toward the gravel road.

"Weird," Kayla said. "I wonder if he used this new driveway."

"Maybe he used it later."

Kayla stopped. "Hey, look," she said. Movement on the road caught her attention.

"I see her," Kevin said, stopping to look as well.

A young woman emerged into a shaft of sunlight, her form glowing against the trees behind her.

They reached the gravel road. The woman was gone when they got there.

"Let's get into town," Kevin said. "You brought money, right?"

"I did."

"Let's get a room and check out the town," she said. "I hope I pass okay in this skirt."

She fanned it.

"Mid-length," he said. "Pretty sure that's within early sixties length."

"Should be."

They walked around a bend in the road.

"Somewhere along here," he said, "Mrs. Barlow crashed."

"Not surprised," Kayla said. "Gravelly road on a curve. What time did it happen?"

"Not sure."

"Feels weird to walk right over where she's going to die."

They dropped the subject and continued on to Sycamore Falls, passing her Victorian house along the way to Main Street.

The motel room was cheap though acceptable.

Kevin sat on the edge of a twin bed. "It makes me nervous to be back here this long, overnight."

"Not me," Kayla said. "I feel a sense of well-being, like I'm supposed to visit here."

She slid into her twin bed. "Stay in your own bed tonight."

"Yeah, fine. I got over you long ago. The check-in guy thinks we're married."

"Shhh."

Both rolled over and fell asleep.

* * *

[111]

1961 Sycamore Falls was vibrant and alive as they walked up Main Street next morning. All the familiar buildings were there with stores open for business, the men's shop Denny-Paul's and women's shop Sherry-Wilson's.

Cars occupied most of the diagonal spaces, a lot of 1950s models and a few rounded black 1940s behemoths interspersed here and there. Traffic was heavy compared to normal time. A flashy new 1960 or '61 cruised by getting admiring glances from pedestrians.

Kayla pointed to the manikins in the Sherry-Wilson's display windows. "Look at the skirts. I'm right in style. You, on the other hand with your hair. You beatnik."

Kevin shrugged. "I'm in style for a hipster. The word existed in 1961. Anyway, look at this place. I hardly recognize it."

"Any place is going to change from 1961," she said. Different stores, different cars, people wearing different styles."

"People in our time want to see the storefronts again and cars downtown like this."

They walked another block.

Kevin stopped. "Look, across the street at that five-and-ten. Recognize that building it's in?"

"Nonstandard Artifacts Gallery," she said. "Let's go in."

"But we need to cross at the crosswalk. We don't need any legal trouble no matter how minor."

They went over to the store and stepped in past the checkout counter with its old style cash register.

About halfway back along the model kits, Kevin pointed to the wall above. "That's where a couple of Mara's paintings are in normal time."

"Look," whispered Kayla, gesturing up toward the checkout counter. A young girl bought a drawing pad, box of charcoal drawing sticks, gum eraser, and left.

[112]

"Is that Mara?" Kayla asked.

"Not sure."

Out on the sidewalk, Kayla said, "But think of it. If that's Mara, then she just bought art supplies in the room where her paintings will one day be displayed."

Kayla stopped and glanced back at the establishment next to the five-and-ten.

"We passed it, you know," said Kayla.

"Hm?"

"Rexall Drugs. With its soda fountain. They made real sodas. That's why most people here call soft drinks 'pop' not 'soda.' I still hear 'pop' in our time."

"Hey, I know. I'm the linguist."

"Just an observation. I started saying 'soda' quite a while back and also I think a lot of Midwestern Millennials call it soda."

They came upon the entrance to JC Penney's. A teenage boy worked out front, sweeping the sidewalk. He smiled and stepped out of the way as Kayla and Kevin continued walking.

Ahead, a twenty-something man arranged fruit in display boxes outside a grocery store.

Kevin grabbed Kayla's hand and stopped. "That's Hank Weber as a young man," he whispered.

"Shall we say hi?" she said.

"Okay," Kevin said.

"I just want to say 'hi' and see what he was like."

They reached him and stopped.

"Good afternoon," Weber said.

"Nice weather, isn't it?" Kevin said.

"How original," Kayla whispered, discretely jabbing Kevin in the back. "Nice store, you have," she said to Weber.

"You really topped me with that," Kevin whispered back.

"You folks from out of town?" Weber said.

"Visiting from Kansas City," she said. "Say, I'm a writer for a new newspaper called *Spaces*. May I ask you a couple of questions?"

Kevin gave an apologizing glance. "If you'll all excuse me, I'll take a little walk," he said.

"Thank you," Kayla said. Then to Weber: "I'd like to browse in your store for a moment, but I don't want to interrupt your work so I'll be back out in a moment."

"That's all right, I'm finished out here. Any excuse I can have to be out in the nice weather."

He accompanied Kayla in and she picked up some picnic items. They went to the end of the canned food aisle.

"I'll start," she said, "by asking, how is business?"

"Oh, it's good. Steady, just like I like it."

"Who are your customers?"

"I have regular customers from around town, and occasional out-of-town visitors. Most local customers are loyal. Some are friends. I also deliver milk, so I'm the milkman around town."

"Are your customers typically young or old? Men or women?"

"Younger ladies, usually, shopping with their young-uns. Occasionally, men stop in for something on their way home from work. That's more common in summer just before the weekends when a lot of families have cookouts. I prepare by having plenty of steaks, ground beef, and hot dogs available. If I order too much, I mark them on sale on Monday."

"Do you have competition?"

"In a sense, but there's enough business for me and for Fishman's Grocery down the street. People seem to prefer our meats and they go to Fishman's for produce. They get the best apples. I hate to admit it, but they're better than I get."

"Who are your suppliers, not just for produce?"

[114]

"There are a couple of suppliers in Wichita and Salina whose routes we're on. Dairy mostly from a Wichita distributor. I sometimes get fresh eggs from a couple of farms near town, but most of the dairy farms are farther away."

"How long have you lived in Sycamore Falls?"

"Born and raised."

"Do you manage this store by yourself?"

"No, my dad still works with me."

Kayla put her pad and pencil away. Do you mind if I take your picture here in the store?"

"Not at all." He posed holding a can of peas while Kayla snapped a pic with her small black digital camera.

"One of them newfangled ones, I see," he said.

"Yes it is." Must be similar-looking enough, she thought. Not so different.

"Thank you, Mr. Weber," she said, then turned to leave.

"You're quite welcome."

* * *

Kayla stopped Kevin in the middle of the crosswalk. "Oh my God, that was so fascinating, and he realized my camera is indeed a camera. I used flash so it'd pass for the times."

She clutched a brown paper bag.

"What's that?" he asked.

"A bag, you know, one of those flexible paper things you carry groceries in."

"Good thinking," he said. "That reminds me. Another word thing."

"Oh boy, I live for that."

He chuckled. "Here it's called a sack. In the East, it's a bag and it also is in St. Louis."

"I call it both. Why's it called a bag in Midwestern St. Louis?"

[115]

"St. Louis is a displaced Eastern city. Layout, architecture, you name it."

"Whatever." She shrugged then pointed up Main. "Speaking of architecture, that downtown church has nice architecture."

"The Methodist church. The sanctuary's pretty impressive. And. . ."

"And, what?"

"That tree in front of it. It's not there in our time."

"What kind of tree is it?"

"Not sure."

They reached the other side of the street.

Pointing to the sweeping boy, Kayla said, "I want to talk to him."

"Don't interrupt his work."

"He can keep sweeping while I talk. Let's go."

The boy stepped out of the way like when they approached a few minutes earlier.

"Hello, there," Kayla said. "I am a journalist with *Kansas City Spaces* newspaper. May I ask you a couple of questions?"

He stopped sweeping and leaned on the broom. "I have to finish soon."

"Oh, I'm sorry."

"That's okay, I can work fast. You might want to stay clear of the sweeps."

"Thank you. Are you in high school?"

He nodded. "I'm a junior at Sycamore Falls High."

"If it's not too personal, are you working to save up for anything?"

"I'd like a car, but I'm actually saving up for college."

"Do you know where you want to attend?"

"Somewhere not far away. I have a girlfriend here." He looked down for a moment.

"That's nice," Kayla said. "What's her name?"

"Brenda," he replied. "I'm set to go up to Boys State on Friday and I was going to see her Thursday night, but she's busy."

Kayla smiled and nodded. "I'm sorry."

"It's all right," he said, "Hey, will I be mentioned in your article?"

"I neglected to ask you your name."

"Mickey MacGregor. Please don't mention the part about my girlfriend breaking our date."

"I won't and thank you, Mickey. Good luck with everything."

He smiled 'thank you' and returned to his work.

Kayla and Kevin turned and headed north.

Out of earshot, she said, "Wow, Brenda?"

"She must have been strong as a girl," he said. Too bad about Thursday."

"But yeah," she said. "He's going to miss her when he's gone. I think it lasts for a week. Not exactly forever. Interesting insight into her past during this time. And that argument she had with her mother about college."

Kevin gestured to the north. You up for a walk?"

"Sure, then I want to eat. It's about lunchtime our time."

"Come on," he said.

They headed up Main a ways, past the courthouse and turned east through a residential area.

"The bungalows and craftsmans look nice in 1961," she said after they went a block or two. To see these houses decades before our time, what an amazing thing."

"Looks like the kids are home from school," he said, referring to a group of kids in a front yard.

A block down, a kid set a can onto a sidewalk. Other kids scattered and ran to hide.

"Look, they're playing kick the can," Kevin said.

"I've heard of it, but never played it."

Some kids played it in our neighborhood. My parents said kids all over played it when they were kids."

"Are some of these houses still around in our time?"

"Still there. Most of them still in pretty good shape, those that were spared by the tornado and a few that fell into disrepair over time."

They walked along and Kayla noticed a rock-lined creek to her right running parallel to the street spanned by driveway and sidewalk bridges to homes.

"What's that creek?" she said, pointing down to the flowing water.

"Storm drainage."

"Looks natural, a tributary to Elm River?" she asked.

"It is. Keeps the town from flooding the right way."

"Suburban KC with all its concrete drainage channels and culverts could learn a thing or two from here. It's still here in normal time, right?"

"Still here, the same, doing its job," he said.

She took a deep breath and looked around. "So where are we headed?"

"Sycamore Falls used to have a college," he said.

"No way! How cool."

"It was active in 1961 and into the sixties a few years," he said. "I never dreamed I'd see that."

They picked up the pace and after passing another train depot and a water tower, they went by Sycamore Falls High and reached the college a block later.

Kevin pointed to a three-story brick building toward the middle of a city block-sized campus. Near that stood a large white house with tall pillars.

"College students in 1961," she said, gesturing toward the buildings.

"The founder of the college was from New England. It's affiliated with Barb-Henry College in New Hampshire."

"Come on," she said. "Let's eat. We can picnic on campus."

They crossed the intersection and wandered onto the large open area between the two buildings and sat in the grass.

"You fit right in," Kayla said.

"I'm sure there are plenty of subtle differences. I'm not going to fool anyone here."

They pulled out the makings for sandwiches and started consuming.

Two students, male and female approached, the young woman carrying a guitar.

"Uh-oh," he said. "Real beatniks."

"No," said Kayla, "this is an opportunity."

The young woman crouched next to them and smiled. "Hey bean! You wanna bash ears?"

Kayla got a puzzled look.

"Oh," the woman said to Kevin, "is she a cube, a square?"

"No, she's a gas."

"Your hair is cookin'," the guy said to him.

"I need to refuel," said the young woman.

Kayla offered her some bread and cheese.

She accepted the offer gratefully.

The woman sat crossed-legged and positioned the guitar to play.

"I'd like to sing a song," she said. "It's a new song called 'Five hundred Miles'."

"Oh," said Kevin, "that's the 'you can hear the whistle blow a hundred miles' song."

The woman uttered "ah" in agreement. She sang the song and rocked back and forth as she sang. . .

"If you missed the train I'm on

[119]

You'll know I am gone
You can hear the whistle blow a hundred miles. . . "

"I know that song," Kayla said.

"Your friend's a gas to know this song," the guy said to Kevin.

"I'm going to take a train ride someday," said Kayla.

"Take a friend with you," said Kevin.

The guy looked toward a small group of people headed by. "Some cats in our galaxy."

They exchanged several 'Hey beans!' and the two joined the group and headed on.

The guy had a bouncing gait and snapped his fingers on the beat of each step.

Kayla wanted to interview some students, beatnik or otherwise. She had blown her chance with the beatniks.

Kevin gestured to a group of students dressed in jackets and ties, skirts, and blazers.

"How about them?"

Kayla stood up, stretched, and faced a group of three headed toward them.

They arrived, a young man and two women.

Kayla retrieved her pad and pencil and decided to start right in. "Hello there," she said. "My name is Kayla and I am a columnist with a new paper in called *Kansas City Spaces*. May I ask you some questions?"

"Oh, yes," they answered simultaneously.

She directed the first question to one of the women. "May I ask your name, major, and where you're from?"

"Name, rank, and serial number," said the guy."

"It does seem to be standard," the young woman said. "We should wear nametags. Well, yes, I am Susan, business major, and I'm from Massachusetts."

The other woman volunteered. "My name is Judy, my major, economics, and I'm from Connecticut."

The guy said, "I am Moondoggy—haha—I'm just kidding. I'm Jeff Goldsmith, majoring in Political Science, and I'm from New York."

"Very good," Kayla said. "I see you're all from the Northeast. How is it here for you? That is, how welcome do you feel here in Sycamore Falls?"

All three echoed a chorus of: "Very."

"People talk to us a lot and they're easy to get to know," said Susan. "People are friendly here."

"The locals call us 'Barbies'," said Jeff. "I heard a group of boys passing by us yelling in cadence: 'What do our sisters play with? Barbies! Barbies!'"

"Barbies. Okay."

"We don't mind," Jeff said.

"Do any of you have part-time jobs here?"

"I'm here on scholarship," said Judy.

"Me, too," said Susan.

"And me," said Jeff.

"In what way do you interact with people here?"

"Some of the older kids like to hang around us," said Jeff. "High school and junior high kids."

"Do their parents mind?"

"Not that we've noticed."

"Differences between here and where you're from?"

"Slower pace here," said Jeff.

"Yeah," said Susan.

"I like it," said Judy.

"Our hills are bigger and we have more forests," said Susan.

"I see," Kayla said. "Of course the places you're from are hillier and more forested than most places."

"I guess you're right," said Susan. "The scenery around here is perfectly beautiful."

Kayla suppressed a gasp.

[121]

The students left; Kayla and Kevin gathered their things to leave.

"I didn't know you spoke Beatnik," Kayla said.

"I minored in Beatnik and know enough to get by. If those anomalies had been available then, I could have come here for field study."

"Yeah, right," she said.

"Don't be a cube."

"Okay, let's go." Kayla pulled up a picture on her phone. "Look. It's right here. One of the underlined passages. Susan said it verbatim. 'The scenery around here is. . .'"

"Freaky cool."

* * *

There was enough time to walk down Main Street again, this time on the other side of the street from most of their earlier walk. A peaceful sunny September afternoon for a walk.

They walked by Sherry-Wilson's where two women stood regarding the manikin displays.

One of the women turned toward Kayla and said, "Hello, my name is Hazel. Are you the reporter with *Kansas City Spaces?*"

Kayla and Kevin stopped.

"Yes, I am," Kayla said, smiling.

"My husband owns Bruce-the-Plumber. Would you like to interview him?"

"I may. I'll have to check the schedule."

The woman nodded. "Thank you."

Several men and women crossed Main at the intersection ahead and started to head toward them.

Hazel looked at her friend then at Kayla. "Word gets around."

Before the group reached them, Mickey came up from behind wearing nice pants with an "SF" letter sweater, holding hands with a girl in a plaid skirt and red sweater with penny loafers and bobby socks. They were a perfect picture of a classic early sixties high school couple.

Brenda!

Kayla glanced at Kevin.

Kevin started turning to walk away. "Well, I believe I'll go—"

Kayla grabbed his arm and pulled him in back.

After his phony stumble, she whispered, "No way!"

Mickey and Brenda stepped up.

"Hi," Mickey said. "Remember me?"

"Of course," Kayla replied.

"This is Brenda."

"Pleased to meet you, Brenda."

Brenda clasped her hands behind her back. "Likewise," she said, her voice younger, but recognizable.

Mickey put his arm around Brenda and said, "It was swell seeing you again." He steered Brenda away from a group of girls headed past them.

"I guess they made up," Kevin said.

One of the women still standing there heard Kevin's comment. "Excuse me for butting in. That poor girl."

"She has problems," the other woman said.

"Mickey is such a nice boy," said the first.

"He's good to her," said the second.

"Why, the girls swoon when he enters the room."

A minute later, Kayla and Kevin bid goodbye and excused themselves.

"Well, interesting stuff about Brenda," Kayla said. "What about the town?"

"I get good vibes," Kevin said. "The stores are in business and people seem happy."

"Except Brenda. I feel sorry for her," said Kayla.

"You should reach out to her after we're back in our time," he said.

"Have you?" she asked.

"I haven't," he said.

"Easy for you to dish out social advice when you don't follow it!"

"Touché."

"Okay," she said. "I'll give her a chance. I don't know how she'll take to advances of friendship."

"Won't know until reaching out to her," he said. "Look at that poor girl. She could have been happy, had a happy life."

"And yet," he said, "I'm seeing the beginnings of one of Sycamore Falls' upcoming problems."

"What?"

"Some kids are planning to leave after high school and not come back."

"You can't tell that for sure. Some will go off to college and return."

"Some will return, a lot, maybe, but some will move away, too."

"Even if true, what to do about that?"

"That's part of my big idea," he said.

"What—go back in time and not let young people leave?"

"You've said it yourself—the timelines don't lead to us and dead end after we return to the present, remember?"

"You keep talking about your big idea. What if you die, damn it?"

"I'll write it down. In fact, it's on my computer at my place."

"Password protected, no doubt," she said.

"My idea is sitting on my printer. Geez, here we are in 1961 arguing about a computer. Got any punched cards on you?"

"I can punch you," she said. She took a deep breath and stopped to look around. The makings of another small mob appeared in the next block. "Walk in front of me," she said.

"Why? They know about me, too. That's your public."

"Based on a lie. There's no *Spaces* paper."

The "mob" was another group of teens headed their way aiming past them.

"Don't let fame get to your head."

Kayla growled. "It's not fame."

"Okay," he said. "We should head back, don't you think?"

"Good idea, but I'm still hungry. There's that diner. I want a piece of 1961 pie."

"You talked me into it. Pie's a good antidote to being nervous about being here."

"I love being here," she said. It's like I'm *supposed* to do this. The town wants me to."

"You've said that. Pie awaits. "

A large, black sedan with rounded hood, trunk, and fenders pulled into a diagonal spot just ahead of them and a sixtyish woman stepped out. She was wearing a flowery dress and hat. She headed up the sidewalk ahead of them.

Kevin leaned over to Kayla and said, "Think she's still around?"

Kayla pulled away and slapped his arm. "Say what! Crap, why don't you go ask her name so you can go look for her grave later?"

"Stuff like that just pops into my head."

"How perceptive. You don't know. She could be very, very old in our time."

"Pushing her 120s maybe."

They reached Lenny's Café.

Through the "Lenny's" stenciled plate glass window, they saw several tables with shiny metal napkin holders and glass sugar dispensers. Several patrons sat at the counter devouring their meals accompanied by drinks in glass glasses. Behind the cashier, a wall-mounted display case had slices of pie on little plates. Two young women with bouffant hairstyles sat at a table next to the window with ice cream sundaes in pedestal glasses. One smiled when she noticed Kayla glancing in.

"Did you see the display case?" Kayla said.

"Cherry pie's waiting for us."

They went in and got a table by another window.

A waitress came and took their pie order.

Kevin took a discrete video around the diner.

"You've been taking videos all day. What're you going to do with them?"

"Battery's almost dead."

"No doubt."

They'll be handy."

"Historical Society? How're you going to explain that?"

"Not for public consumption. Just recording what things were like back now."

"I can see the value of having them."

"Not like I do."

Kayla smirked. "Oh, well, now."

"I want a good overview of life here in 1961."

"You're really into it. Part of your big idea?"

"I'm not saying."

Kayla chuckled and leaned over the table toward him "When she took our order, she was staring at your hair," she whispered.

"Yeah, maybe I'm a beatnik for real. All I need is a goatee like one of the guys in those beatniks' galaxy."

"My hair's not all that stylish, either," she said.

They finished, Kayla paid, and after one last look around 1961 Lenny's Café, they left and continued on Main. "Let's head across the street," she said.

"Okay," we go down to the crosswalk. We don't need to be cited for jaywalking, and that reminds me of something else to be nervous about. Getting in trouble with the law."

"Relax!"

"We need to be careful and not get ticketed, or worse. I'm so uncomfortable being back here."

"Is the pie wearing off?" she said.

"There's no lasting effect, just the anticipation."

"I feel at peace," she said, "as I said, like I belong in one of these past timelines."

"You worry me. Don't get used to it," he said. "I want you around in normal time."

"Aw."

They walked around for a while longer and Kevin stopped to look at the bank clock. "It's 4:45. Ready to get back?" he said.

"I am. I'm tired and would like to get back home and crash."

"Me, too."

"Let's go."

They made their way back down Main to the street that led to West Hill Road, then up to the farmhouse's porch.

Brenda stood by the barn conversing with her father while they opened the overhead door together. When the door was up, Brenda and Mr. Barlow glowed in the bright sunlight that streamed through the barn.

Kayla and Kevin stepped up onto the porch.

Brenda noticed and started toward them. "Can I help you!" she shouted.

"Let's go!" Kayla said.

They ran in, to the library.

Mrs. Barlow called from the kitchen. "Is that you, Marlin? Brenda?"

At the bookcase, Kayla and Kevin reshelved their books.

[127]

Back in present time. "Phew, that was easy getting back," Kayla said.

"Getting back was, but I feel much better being in normal time," Kevin said. "We risk getting complacent, thinking it'll always be easy to return."

They headed into the foyer.

Kevin pointed toward the kitchen. "To think Mrs. Barlow was right there just seconds ago."

"Seconds plus well over half a century ago while Brenda and her dad were out in the barn," Kayla said.

"What do you suppose they were doing?"

"Scheming. So now that we're back in normal time, you going to tell me your bright idea?"

"Let me gather my thoughts."

"You've had plenty of time. Come on."

"Tomorrow."

CHAPTER FOURTEEN
Reconnaissance

KAYLA SPENT THE EVENING online researching Mrs. Barlow's crash.

She waited until the next morning to contact Kevin: "Meet me at Danny's for lunch. 12:30."

"See you there," he replied.

* * *

He had a table at Danny's when she arrived.

"Ordered you a veggie sub," he said as she sat across from him.

"Thanks, that works."

"So, what's up?" he said.

"Those underlines in the books," she said. "I mean, how? Why?"

"It's obvious," he said.

"Yeah, they do seem to point to things," she said. "Other books, timeshifters. What mysterious person put them in there?"

Kevin shrugged. "Brenda."

"I don't know. They're creepy."

"Well?"

"Maybe it wasn't a person and they got there another way," she said. "The town, the house, or that other thing that's pulling me to timeshift."

"Anyway, how you doing?" he said. "You find something? Besides underlines?"

"No. Your big idea first."

[129]

Kevin sighed. "At first, I thought about offering tours of the past through the library."

"Um, no," said Kayla.

"Go back and enjoy 1961 homemade pie, see the old school, the town, whatever. Authentic atmosphere."

She finished chewing. "Look who's talking. So you think exploiting this would be good?"

"I do."

"It would require a tour guide. You up for that?"

"No," he said.

"I'd do it," she said. "We aren't going to be able to open it up to people to go alone."

"Hang on," Kevin whispered. "If we can't take people to the past, we can bring the past to people. We have the perfect research tool. And we create tours around Sycamore Falls with vintage props based on its past. Not in a cliché-ish way, but authentic."

"What vintage props?"

"Old cars for tours of the town, houses decorated in period furnishings, old style restaurants. I figure somebody like Myrtle could provide antique furnishings on loan from her antique shop, a marketing opportunity for her with the tours."

"Just avoid cliché-ish stuff like I said like fake fifties restaurants, whatever."

"Maybe Danny would do one," said Kayla.

"No, Danny's is already doing great as it is now."

"So I'm still putting my thoughts together. Obviously, it'll take an investment."

"A sizable one."

"See? I didn't think you'd take me seriously."

"I am, I want to hear more when you've got a plan," she said.

"Okay," he said, "you got that out of me, what's your 'discovery'?"

[130]

"I found Mrs. Barlow's obit in the *Sycamore Falls Prospect* archive site." She pulled it up on her tablet.

* * *

Mrs. Velma Barlow died Friday, September 21, 1961, in a one car accident at approximately 7:20pm on West Hill Road. Survivors include her husband, Marlin, and daughter Brenda of the home, . . .

"That was the evening Brenda had a date with Mickey that she broke."

"They seemed to be getting along when we ran into them in front of Sherry-Wilson's."

"Of course. To be expected."

"So then, what?" he said.

"And so, what were Brenda and Barlow doing at the barn around then on the day we were there?"

Kevin shrugged. "Barlow had the 21st marked on the calendar hanging in the barn."

"We know when it happened and I think he did something," she said.

"Can't know for sure."

"We can. Go back and stay until that evening, hike there, and watch."

Kevin groaned.

* * *

So they did.

In the library, Kevin said, "Let's go with the timeline replay to when we encountered Barlow in the barn."

"Why?"

"I want a better look at that calendar."

They timeshifted to 1961, went through the initial replay, and Kevin snapped a pic of the calendar just before Barlow told them to be heading on.

They went out the barn's east door like before and saw the woman down on the road again.

"Is that Brenda for sure?" Kevin asked.

Kayla pulled out her binoculars and verified. "It is. She's looking at some rocks along the side of the road."

Once in town, they got the same motel room and stayed until September 21st. That day, Kayla managed to interview more students at the college. No beatniks there this time. After their excursion, they headed down Main Street and Kayla spotted Mickey across the street out in front of JC Penney talking to several classmates.

"Let's head over," she said.

"This one won't remember you from the other timeline."

"I'm sure all else is the same and Brenda has broken their date for tonight."

They reached a crosswalk and headed over.

"Mickey looks down in the dumps," he said.

Kayla and Kevin tried to eavesdrop as they walked past.

"You hear anything?" Kevin said.

"I didn't."

"Me, either."

They kept walking, left them behind, then headed over to Lenny's Café for supper where Kevin talked more about his idea and the inspiration gained from this trip back.

"So, you're glad we took this journey?" she said as they finished paying and walked out to the sidewalk.

"Yeah, but let's head on."

They left just in time to get to the winding gravel road below the barn before sunset. A convertible driven by a high school student passed them along the way.

"That was Mickey," Kayla said. "Looks like he's headed to Brenda's house."

"Just couldn't stay away from her tonight," Kevin said.

"Aww."

Kayla and Kevin continued along the gravel road and at about sunset, they rounded a bend where they saw two people ahead piling rocks onto one side of the road. A convertible sat nearby.

"That's Mickey and Brenda," Kayla said in a hushed tone as she and Kevin stayed low along the edge of the road.

Mickey and Brenda finished their task, embraced, and kissed.

A muffled "Bye" or two, then Mickey jumped into his car, pulled around, and sped toward Sycamore Falls, the sound of his car soon fading. Brenda headed up toward the barn. Kayla and Kevin crouched behind a bush in the waning daylight. The sound of distant wheels on gravel echoed around the still of the evening, drawing closer.

"That's not Mickey," Kevin said. "Look."

A Ford sedan headed toward them.

"The barn," said Kayla. "Look at the barn!"

Brenda darted in front it. The car reached the bend. It rounded the curve. Brenda heaved the overhead door up. The sunbeams poured through the barn. Blinding light struck the car's windshield. A wheel hit the rock pile. Wheels locked. The car skidded, overturned, and ejected the driver.

Barlow rushed from the house to the barn.

An argument ensued.

Shouts of "No!" from Barlow followed as he started to run down the hill.

Kevin and Kayla got to the side of the road and started to head up to the farmhouse.

"It was Brenda! Mickey was in on it!" Kayla said.

"Maybe Barlow was going to do it but Brenda did, ruining his plan after he spent all that time building the barn at that orientation."

"No way to know, but there's no question Brenda murdered her mother and Mickey was an accomplice."

"Barlow harbored a criminal for a long time and he built the murder weapon."

[133]

Kayla and Kevin reached the porch and ran in to the library.

Back in the present, Kayla scanned along the books again.

"Here's another old book with a bookmark, *The Witness Stand* by Hugo Münsterberg," she said. She opened bookmarked page 78. Underlined in pencil was: <u>Man has the power to hide his knowledge and his memories by silence</u>.

"Okay," Kayla said, then she read it to Kevin.

"Any questions about Brenda underlining these?" she said.

"She didn't," he agreed.

"No wonder she wants this place torn down."

CHAPTER FIFTEEN
Cattlemen's Day

A DAY LATER, Kevin saw Kayla headed to Weber's. He joined her on the sidewalk.

"How are you holding up?" she said.

"I'm coping."

She patted his shoulder. "Are you done with timeshifting?" she asked.

"No. I want to see 1938 before Rick thinks about restricting access to the library."

"Okay, I've got more I need to do before he does, too. Something's drawing me back. I need to keep going."

"No more for me until tomorrow," Kevin said.

"I'm going back to 1950 now," Kayla said. "I'll check for more ways to jump back farther, but we haven't seen Sycamore Falls in 1950.

"Dress the part."

She stood back and gestured to the jeans and blouse she wore. "This look okay?"

"I think women wore that in 1950."

They went up to the farmhouse.

Kayla pulled out *The Story of Art,* and timeshifted to the nighttime library and the clunks of the grandfather clock. She let the timeline replay and duplicated her sneaking out like when she rescued Megan. The waxing gibbous moon awaited her outside like last time, so she'd be able to walk into town with plenty of light. The frogs and crickets accompanied her moonlit walk. The stroll was without event, if plenty creepy. She'd get into town and watch it start the day. Her internal clock was still on normal time, so she would be wide awake for quite a while even though it'd be early morning here in a few hours.

She made it to downtown before sunrise and started up Main Street, which had a little traffic: mostly late 1940s black sedans and pickups with rounded hoods, fenders, tops, and oversized shiny chrome bumpers. She walked by a service station built into a brick-front building with its overhead door up and a sign above that said "Chuck's Auto Service." A 1940s car that sat in the shadowy back of the service bay faced her as she peered in. It idled roughly, the whole car vibrating as it stared at her, as if pleading to be set free. She took a short video and continued on to Second Street, turned and walked along Second a ways around several blocks, timing her walk so she'd get back to Main Street by around mid-to-late-morning. There was a little residential traffic, a late milk delivery truck, and a man delivering groceries from his station wagon. She got a quick pic of the car and the man.

1950 Hank Weber.

Morning wore on. She went back to Main Street. Lenny's Café was open. An early lunch, late breakfast waited for Kayla there.

But before that, she found the original Red Rock Cola ad on the side of the building. She walked up to it, drawing a stare or two when she ran her hand over the painted bricks and snapped a picture. It was only slightly faded.

Lenny's had mid-century appliances like a red metal Coca Cola fountain dispenser with the familiar logo. She seated herself in a booth along the wall and a young woman came to take her order, wearing a restaurant uniform and what Kayla thought was a cutesy little hat. "Nice to see you here," the waitress said. "Didn't you make it to the pancake breakfast early this morning?"

"I missed it," Kayla replied with a smile.

[136]

Somebody played a selection from the vertical discs behind curved glass on the Seeburg Select-o-matic jukebox, filling the diner with "The Hucklebuck."

Kayla knew this song from an old *Honeymooners* episode where Ralph Cramdon, dressed in a "hip" letter sweater and loud striped jacket, was learning to dance.

Kayla hummed along. "Herrre's a dance, you should know! Whennn the lights go down low! . . .Do the Hucklebuck Do the Hucklebuck, If you don't know how to do it, boy you're out of luck. . ."

A teen couple rushed onto the open area and started dancing, holding hands, twirling, skirt flying out. The boy lifted her up, flipping her upside down. Kayla wanted to cheer at their skill. Another couple joined them in the same dance moves with simultaneous flipping of girls, heels up. Some of the older patrons gasped.

"Kevin ought to see this," Kayla muttered.

The song ended, followed by another swing tune and "Long Gone Lonesome Blues" by Hank Williams. Music of different genres followed as more patrons kept arriving and feeding the jukebox until the place was full. Something going on in town today? she wondered.

Kayla finished her breakfast, paid at the register, and headed out onto the sidewalk.

Outside, she wondered about the strange look the cashier gave her when she paid.

The beginnings of a parade were starting a ways up Main Street.

She went back into Lenny's to the cashier.

"They're gathering for the parade," Kayla said to her.

"It starts at 1:30 this year," the cashier said. "Are you visiting from out of town?"

"Yes, I am. I came out from Kansas City."

[137]

Kayla smiled and headed out to the sidewalk. She looked a few blocks up at a float or two crawling along, following a marching band from which the drum cadence echoed.

A teenage boy in boots and hat led a calf up the street toward the parade.

Kayla crossed the street and continued along that side of the street. She stopped so she could get a picture of Lenny's when she saw the cashier out front with a police officer. The cashier pointed straight at Kayla. The officer waved at Kayla with a gesture telling her to wait while he trotted across the street toward her.

Kayla gasped.

The officer stepped sideways between the parked cars and came up to Kayla.

"Miss, Violette at Lenny's says you gave her a counterfeit bill."

"Oh my!" Kayla said. "But how?"

He pulled it out and regarded it.

"We expect some of these floating around during Cattlemen's Day celebrations, but this one is so unusual that I need to talk to you about it. Can you come with me to the station for a moment?"

Kayla gasped again.

He pointed to the police station a block south.

"Yes, sir," she said. "Of course."

They walked briskly to the station. He led her to a desk.

As he settled into his chair, he spread a five dollar bill out.

"Can you tell me where you got this?"

"I don't remember," she said, "in change somewhere."

"Not at a store here in Sycamore Falls?"

"I don't know. Maybe, or possibly in Kansas City where I'm from."

"The odd thing is the bill doesn't have all the usual traits of a counterfeit bill," he said. "The paper is authentic, the printing is good, and no smearing or anything else not right except it says 'Series 1953-A' so unless you're from three years from now, this bill is all wrong and I don't want to find these getting around town. Do you have anything else to say about it?"

"No, sir, except that the mint does make mistakes sometimes."

"Then this is a rare one," he said. "I saw a double-strike nickel once, but I've never heard of a misprint like this. If this came from the mint, it could be worth a lot."

"I see."

"I'll let you keep this, but don't spend it anywhere."

"Thank you, I won't," she said, suppressing a sigh. She took the bill and tucked it away, thanked him, and left. She was about to kick herself for that lapse, not checking the money before spending it.

She resumed her walk. The high school band marched by. A band of younger kids followed, Kayla assumed a junior high band. After the bands, a convertible rolled by pulling a float flanked by people on horses, men, women, boys, girls, and the boy with the calf went by. Watching the marching bands brought nostalgic feelings from Kayla's high school band days.

She went along the sidewalk a ways more and came to a Rexall drug store.

Not being able to resist, she stepped in to the soda shop. One stool not occupied by any of the teenagers at the counter was free so she took it. While she waited for the busy soda jerk to finish making a couple of drinks for waiting customers, Kayla marveled at the young woman practicing a now lost art of working at the soda fountain. When it was Kayla's turn, she decided splurging with a chocolate soda was the right thing to do. After all, when would she get the chance. . . ?

The young woman placed a tall pedestal glass under a curved spigot and pulled the lever to add a squirt of chocolate, opened the shiny metal flap of an ice cream vat and drew a couple of scoops into the glass. She added another squirt of chocolate, then filled the glass with phosphate soda water, added whipped cream and a cherry. Kayla savored every sip and spoonful as she devoured every ounce. After finishing it off, she glanced outside. The parade was still going, although it seemed to be getting close to the end. She listened to the teens around her talk about school, boys, girls, football, teachers, and who had the best float, horse, or car. A couple of them were talking about a new over-six-foot-tall basketball player, Clyde Lovellette, who would start at KU in the fall. She reached into her bag and started an audio recording on her phone.

After a moment, the manager came over and leaned toward the window area. "Looks like rain later."

Uh oh. Kayla didn't want to get caught in that. Maybe it'd hold off long enough to explore a little more.

She retrieved some silver coins from her bag and paid for her soda.

The girl accepted the coins including a tip. "Thank you. How was it?" she asked.

"It was delicious," Kayla said.

"It's my first day today."

"You did very well."

The girl smiled and attended to another customer. Kayla went out to the sidewalk. She wandered a ways and watched the remnants of the parade. A black 1940s convertible rolled by with a man in a suit sitting up on the back of the rear seat waving at the crowds. A banner on the side said, "Vote for Frank Carlson, Kansas' Favorite Son for U.S. Senate."

Kayla overheard several people talking.

"I liked him as governor," said one.

"He appointed Darby," said another. "Now he's running against him."

"Harry Darby has Eisenhower's endorsement," said the first.

They dispersed and headed in the same direction as the parade, continuing their conversation.

Kayla turned to head on. She wanted to return to the farmhouse before the rain arrived.

Pedestrian activity diminished as the end of the parade receded down Main Street along with vehicle traffic. Puffy clouds seemed to rush by overhead. By the time Kayla reached her street, she walked toward what would be her Victorian. It had peeling paint and wood rot around windows. She wondered if the inside was in less than good repair like the outside. It was in great shape in normal time when she bought it. West Hill Road was a different matter, looking better maintained here than in normal time. She hiked along it and came to the place where Mrs. Barlow's wreck would happen eleven years hence. Kayla continued the hike, veering over to the gravel drive up the hill to the barn. The contour of the hill allowed her to remain slightly hidden from the farmhouse. The older barn still stood up there, looking to be in good condition. She headed up to it. The old barn was classic 1800s style of barns. A shame Barlow would tear it down. But then, it was in the "wrong" orientation. When she reached it, she went to its south side where there was a good view of rolling hills to the horizon. The November grass was tall, mostly yellowish. Stepping out a bit from the barn gave her a good view to the western sky. Clouds gathered there and from her perch at the edge of the hill the wind whipped up to her, the hillside grass thrashing back and forth as the wind blew. She felt a chill and decided to go.

[141]

Eric T. Reynolds

A little girl who apparently was four-year-old Brenda answered the door. Kayla felt bad about rushing past someone so young, but she had no choice. Book in hand, she ran into the library and reshelved it.

* * *

Back in the present, she saw Kevin and filled him in on her jaunt, showing him pictures and playing audio.

"I wonder what happened with Mickey," she said.

"Dead," said Kevin. "I found his obit. He ran his convertible off the road north of town after graduation."

"He never made it to college. Poor kid, and poor Brenda."

"Are you going to tear this old place down?"

"No. I understand Brenda's gone through a lot in her life and she can use some understanding."

CHAPTER SIXTEEN
A Rainy Afternoon

KEVIN CHANGED INTO JEANS and a polo shirt and returned to the farmhouse.

"Where are you headed?" Kayla said as she met him in the foyer.

"1938."

"Something pulling you back?"

"Kevin shrugged. "1938 is."

"Leave a way to get back into the house."

"I will," he said. "I might be a while. And you said *Out of the Silent Planet* takes you to 1938?"

"I haven't verified that. You go ahead and try it. The story of art book takes you to the 1950 library, then pull out *Out of the Silent Planet.*

He shrugged, pulled out *The Story of Art,* faded to the nighttime house, grabbed *Out of the Silent Planet,* and faded to an earlier time.

It was raining outside. He reshelved and jumped his way back to normal time.

"That was quick," Kayla said.

"I need an overcoat and umbrella," he said, walking past her, heading out the door. An hour later, he returned wearing a new raincoat, twirling an umbrella.

"Take that tag off before you timeshift," Kayla said.

"Yeah, okay," he said while he pulled the tag off. "So I had to go buy this coat and umbrella."

"Coat looks good. You got clothes under it, right?"

[143]

"I won't be scaring anyone, but you be careful, too. I'm going to see this town, pre-World War Two."

"Good luck," she said. "Wait, you have money?"

"Not really."

She reached into her bag and pulled out some old silver certificates to hand to him.

He stashed them away and said, "Thanks a lot. Bye." He reached for the book.

"Bye-ee," she said.

He timeshifted his way back to the rainy day. The timeline replayed like Kayla had described it.

Mr. Nolan went to the foyer. A woman joined him. Kevin eavesdropped.

"I'm going to miss this house," she said.

"I feel ashamed," he said.

"Don't. It's not your fault. I read four million homes—"

"I know! That doesn't make it any easier. The economy's supposed to be better this year and I still don't have a job. We'll be next if I don't get work."

"What about that young couple, the Barlows, down the hill? Have you approached them to see if they'd be interested in our house?"

"How that whippersnapper was able to afford that big house, I'll never know."

"He married into money."

"I suppose that's it."

Mr. Nolan headed off the porch around the house and the two men left.

Kevin put the book safely into his attaché case and headed to the porch.

Out on the porch, Mrs. Nolan came up beside him.

"Are you with the movers? Looks like they left without you," she said.

"It's not the first time," Kevin said, pretending to be annoyed.

"I'll ask Mr. Nolan to give you a ride into town," she said.

"I'd be much obliged," Kevin said.

Nolan came back to the porch and Mrs. Nolan filled him in.

"Come on," Nolan said, and he headed down the steps toward a mid-to-late 1930s Chevy.

Kevin followed and stepped onto the passenger side running board after stamping his feet on the gravel. He slid onto the seat. Nolan was already settled in. He turned the key and stepped on the starter knob on the floor. He turned the windshield wipers on, which were clunky by modern standards.

As they went down the gravel lane, the ride was amazingly smooth, even on the rough gravel. Kevin forgot he wasn't wearing a seatbelt.

"This is sure a nice car, Mr. Nolan," Kevin said, gazing at the shiny dash that had a glove compartment where he would expect one and a clock in the middle of the dash. The windshield was split into two panes angled for streamlining.

"Used 1937," Nolan said. "Got it last summer when I still had a job, but it runs good and I'll sell it if I get hard up, which might be soon. You remember to look me up if you want an almost new Chevy."

"I will," Kevin said.

"Now, where do you need to go?"

"Please drop me off at Weber's Grocery."

"Weber's it is."

Kevin sighed in relief that Weber's was in business.

"The missus got you picking something up before you head home?"

"Yeah, we always need something."

"Ahhh."

Kevin decided to cut the small talk and the risk of saying something wrong. Minutes later, they pulled into a diagonal spot opposite Weber's. Kevin thanked Nolan and headed with umbrella to the end of the block and crossed to the other side. A smiling man in a raincoat and hat stood in front of a car dealership among several shiny new 1938 Chevys. Kevin accidently made eye contact.

The man approached Kevin and extended his hand. Kevin accepted it.

"Let's get in out of the rain, sir!" the man said during an uncomfortably firm handshake. He grabbed Kevin's elbow and started to lead him toward the entrance. "I'm Chester Brach. Just call me Chester!"

Chester maintained his grip on Kevin and took him into a well-lit showroom of more shiny cars sitting on a gleaming floor of alternating black and white tiles. The smell of new tires abounded along with the tangy aromas of oil and lubricants.

"And your name, sir?" Chester said.

"O'Brien."

He extended his arms in a gesture introducing the cars in the showroom. "Professor O'Brien?" Chester said.

Kevin looked away.

"That was forward of me, I realize. I was fooled by your impeccable look. Some professors have longer hair."

"It gives me away every time," said Kevin. "I don't usually let on what I do."

"Well then, Professor O'Brien, even on a nasty day like this, you could be enjoying the day in a new Chevy."

So I *can* fit in, Kevin thought.

"Well, Professor, look at these beauties. Go ahead, pick a car and sit in the driver's seat. See how it feels."

What the hell? thought Kevin. He picked a sleek maroon sedan with a brown interior, opened the driver side door and climbed in. Chester was right to be enthused by these cars. An unusual warmth surrounded Kevin with this 1938 version of new car smell long before his time, leathery and rubbery from the seats and floor with the faint aroma of oil and other scents thrown in. This warm feeling was probably how Kayla felt in past timelines, he figured, but for different reasons.

Chester got in the passenger side.

"These new models are very nice," Kevin said.

"You're looking at just the right time."

"Of course I am," Kevin said, chuckling. "How is business?"

"Well, Professor O'Brien, it's very good. We're seeing a lot of demand for these new Chevrolets."

"Are you experiencing any changes with the different economy this year?"

"Well, it's certainly helping," said Chester. "Now I won't go too deep into this with a college professor. I'm optimistic, though."

"Things will work out," said Kevin. "Let's talk about cars."

The dashboard and the feel of the seat had a craftsmanship Kevin had never experienced from a car before. He placed his hands on the oversized steering wheel.

He drove a friend's classic car a few years before in normal time, an early 1950s Chevy Bel Air. It also had a large steering wheel that took a lot of turns to steer the car. That was enough for him to appreciate modern steering technology, but the timeless beauty of a classic like this transcended its lack of modern technology.

Chester started to open the car door. Kevin took the cue and got out of the car.

"Well, Professor, the rain has let up. Why don't you take this beauty for a test drive?"

"No, thank you, but I'd welcome a ride in it if you'd drive me around town a little."

Chester nodded. "Now then, that's what we'll do." He waved to another person in the showroom who went to slide open the large door to the outside. Now that it was wide enough to drive through, Kevin slid across the bench seat to the passenger side and Chester climbed in the driver's side and started the engine. Its low rumble kicked in.

They drove out across the damp parking lot onto Main Street. Chester took Kevin down a side street where they passed by familiar houses that were still standing in normal time, craftsmans, bungalows, foursquares, Victorians, and other popular first half of the century styles. Then they drove to the vicinity of the college area. Kevin remembered it wouldn't be founded until the mid-1940s. Just an empty block here and the smaller white mansion toward one side of the block. They went by the high school which still looked the same, and turned back to Main Street. Like Nolan's car, the smooth ride impressed Kevin.

"This fine automobile could be yours," Chester said.

"Can I get it through a time portal?" Kevin said with a grin.

"You college men," Chester said.

Men? Kevin thought. We have women, too.

"I couldn't resist asking," Kevin said. "I've got my students working on research papers. But imagine if I came from the future and took this car back with me."

"I can't imagine you would," Chester said. "They'll have floating cars in the future."

"Well, this car feels like it's floating," Kevin said.

"That it does," Chester said, obviously excited about a looming possible sale.

Then Kevin saw her walking along the sidewalk when she stopped to look into Lenny's Café.

[148]

"Chester, please let me out here," Kevin said. "Sorry so sudden."

Chester pulled into a diagonal spot just down from Lenny's.

"Thank you for showing me the car and driving me around."

"Glad to," Chester said, handing printed material to Kevin. "Here, take this literature. Talk with the missus."

"Thanks, I'll do that. Good day, now."

Kevin stashed the brochure and hopped out of the car. As soon as he hit the sidewalk, he hurried down to Lenny's Café.

There she was. Sitting at a table along the wall. She looked up at him and smiled as he sat across from her.

"Well," Kayla said, "thanks for saving me from searching all day."

"You're spying on me?" he said.

"Checking on you."

"You saved me from buying a car." He pulled out the brochure and placed it in front of her. "This gem. It'd make a fine car for us. Plenty of room for the kids."

"You can't bring it with you anyway."

"I know, I asked the sales guy."

"You didn't."

"The look on his face was priceless. He thinks I'm a crackpot anyway and I'm working on my idea."

"The town's not just talking to me, it's also talking to you," she said.

"I'm feeling that."

She started gathering her things together. "Time to get back."

"I'm ready."

Out on the street, Kayla mumbled, "Looks familiar, just like I imagined it would."

[149]

"No doubt."

* * *

Chester returned the car to its place in the showroom. Andrew pulled the big door closed and wiped down the floor where the car had tracked in water.

Andrew met Chester by the car.

"How's business?" said Andrew.

"Looking up."

"How about that fella who took a ride in this car?"

"He's an odd one. Those professors usually are."

"That's no professor," Andrew said.

"Looks like one to me."

"Did he enjoy the ride around town?"

"He did. He went to meet a friend, or his wife, I'm not sure, afterwards."

"Did he enjoy the ride? Did it work?"

"We'll see."

* * *

Kayla and Kevin knocked on the farmhouse front door and waited.

Mr. Nolan answered.

"Oh, Mr. Nolan," Kevin said. "I believe I left my billfold here. May I look in the back room?"

"Yes, of course."

Nolan invited them in. "Follow me," he said.

"This is Mrs. O'Brien," Kevin said.

Nolan glanced at Kayla, nodded with a smile and led them to the library.

He stood next to the library as Kevin and Kayla pretended to look for his wallet.

Nolan turned away and walked around the living room.

"Trusting, isn't he?" Kayla said to Kevin.

Nolan's voice boomed behind them. "Any reason I shouldn't be?"

Kayla cringed and straightened to face him.

"Did you find your billfold?" he asked Kevin.

"Yes I did," Kevin said, pretending to push one into his pocket.

"Kayla pulled the book from her bag while Kevin retrieved his.

Both reached to reshelve their books.

"What are those extra books?" Nolan said. "We don't want those there."

"It's the only way to get back to our time," said Kayla.

"Then go."

Kayla faded, followed by Kevin.

They made their way through the maze and tumbled into the present.

"Whew!" Kayla let out the breath she'd been holding.

"The only way to get back to our time?" Kevin said laughing. "Listen to you. Good thing that timeline doesn't lead anywhere. And I still say we don't know for sure."

"Has to be," she said. "Besides, we tested it."

Kevin groaned.

"Okay," she said, "we're seeing some risks, but you got to observe 1938 anyway."

"Not like I'd have wanted. If I'd had more time, I'd have gone around more."

"And bought a house and a car," she said.

"No. I knew what I was doing. I was going to avoid you, but you found me. All is well. I think I'm feeling the message."

"And?"

"Just wait. I have a plan," he said.

CHAPTER SEVENTEEN
Kevin's Big Idea

THE MORNING SUN FILTERED DOWN THROUGH THE FOLIAGE and glinted off the shiny '37 coupe. Billy signed the title over and handed Kevin the key.

"Enjoy it," he said. "Change the oil often. This isn't like a modern car."

"Right."

Kevin took the key, climbed into the car, and started the engine.

He smiled. "Okay, take me to Kayla's."

* * *

Sitting on the sun-drenched porch of the Victorian that morning, Kayla opened her laptop and started writing while she waited for Kevin.

"Where is he?" she mumbled. She set the laptop aside and stood when an old maroon Chevy with large curvy fenders and chrome bumper pulled into the driveway.

"Now what has he done?"

Kevin stepped out of the old car and hopped up the porch steps.

"What are you doing with that?" she said.

"I've been wanting a classic car for years. Now I have a reason to have one."

"Is this part of your big idea?"

"It is. My historic tours company."

"Giving rides in an old car?"

"Not that simple."

"Did you figure out a way to get a car from the 1930s timeshifted to the present?"

"I got it here the old fashioned way through the normal passage of time. Somebody restored it. Pretty authentic. I sat in the real thing in 1938 when Mr. Nolan drove me to town in his used car. This is just like it."

"What are you going to do with it?"

"Cruise around for now. Make it a town fixture, drive it around."

"You can start by driving me to Weber's."

Kevin shrugged and they headed off the porch to the car.

They settled in, Kevin started the engine, and leaned toward the radio. "Take us downtown," he said.

"You talk to the car?" Kayla said. "I'm scared."

"Meh," he said.

"Okay, let's go."

When they reached Main Street, Kevin said, "Getting a lot of looks already."

She felt like ducking sometimes, feeling uncomfortable with that kind of attention.

"Relax," he said, "it's all good. This is a start."

"Okay, you like old cars, but not everyone's into them like you are. You need to keep in mind how different everyone is."

"It's not just about old cars. It's about antiques and history. This is just part of that. An intro. There's an old homestead up in Olathe called the Mahaffie Farmstead, which was a stagecoach stop out of Kansas City. In addition to tours of the old colonial house, they have stagecoach rides as part of the whole experience. We could do that with Sycamore Falls."

"Okay. Take a historical tour of Sycamore Falls."

"Right. Part of the experience of visiting Sycamore Falls' past, a way to experience its history. Bring the past to the people. Historic sites are big draws. With my idea, let people

[153]

experience the past. We could also offer covered wagon rides in the Flint Hills. All kinds of possibilities. Start with one thing, then build on it."

"Okay, so your classic car is a trial run."

"It is."

She rubbed her eyes. "Okay this mimicking the past is making me need to go up to the farmhouse."

"You're addicted."

"Maybe, but I'm experimenting until I figure out the why of it; it's calling to me again," she said. She rubbed her eyes again thinking she saw a 1920s Ford Model T in an oncoming lane.

"The town wants me to go back now," she said.

"Okay," he said, "let me know what you need from Weber's."

"Look at the historic architecture of these downtown buildings," she said.

He steered the old Chevy toward Kayla's street.

"The buildings go back to the late 1800s."

They reached her street and pulled into her driveway.

"That thing is pulling us both back," Kayla said. "I'm glad it's not just me. I've got to get to the library up there really soon."

"I feel it, too. The urge is almost uncontrollable," he said. "The town is speaking to us both."

"The town or the house?" she said.

"I've been debating that in my mind. I want to say, both."

"Okay," he said, "you head on up first and we meet up there later."

CHAPTER EIGHTEEN
To the Polling Place

ON A HIGH SHELF, KAYLA NOTICED *Jailed for Freedom: American Women Win the Vote* by Doris Stevens, Edith Mayo. She pulled the book out, felt the familiar breeze swirl, and timeshifted to morning in the library. She smelled remnants of breakfast: scrambled eggs and toast with a hint of coffee. The book had an old Voter ID Card sticking out of its pages. The card was issued to Maureen Brown, born in Madison, Kansas, May 22, 1887, registered to vote by the city of Sycamore Falls, on September 8, 1920. A blaze of color from autumn trees outside filtered into the room. She looked out the window. A Ford Model A sat on the gravel drive. A youngish woman in a loose, straight dress and bobbed hairstyle with a hat negotiated the gravel in T-strap heels. She climbed into the car while another woman turned the hand crank on the front of the car. The engine almost started, but the crank lurched backward, nearly knocking her over. She grabbed the handle and cranked it again. Finally, the car started and she got in the driver side. They drove away.

Some activity in the front rooms startled Kayla. She sat out of the way in one of the chairs next to the library window and eavesdropped on the start of a conversation in the foyer.

"She went with Alice to the poll," said one woman. "She's excited to vote."

Kayla realized it was 1920 Election Day.

"And you?" said another woman.

"I voted already this morning first thing when the poll opened. I think half the women in town were there. It's so exciting."

"What was voting like?"

"I showed them my voter ID card before they had a chance to ask me for it and they gave me a ballot. I made my choices and put it through the slot in the ballot box. The box was wooden, not metal like I wondered it might be."

"I mean, how did it feel?"

"Wonderful! Empowering. We have a say. You know, one reason given for not allowing us to vote was that we might choose the more attractive man. But I couldn't care less about that."

"Me, either."

"Well, we have it now at long last."

"I'm going soon."

"I'll go with you!"

"I would like that."

Kayla waited in her somewhat hidden place until they left. She got up and headed to the foyer then stepped out to the porch. She didn't think she had a lot of time so she gazed for a moment down at the Victorian. Here in 1920, her house was thirty years old. She skipped down the steps and went down past her future house and walked to downtown.

She checked her bag for silver dollars. If she found a coat she could afford, she'd buy it.

Main Street's pavement and curbs looked almost identical in 1920 to that of normal time and there was no shortage of Model A, Model T Fords, and their competitors cruising up and down Main Street and occupying diagonal parking spaces. A lot of women headed to the polling place where there was a line. Some wore sweater jackets over dresses. Perhaps Kayla didn't need a coat after all. It wasn't that cold and she generally liked cool fall weather.

Kayla happened by a store called Cook's Electric Store after passing a couple of tire stores. She went into Cook's. It was like an antique shop except the items were brand new with hundreds of table and floor style lamps, a toaster or two, irons, electric fans, and a floor appliance she couldn't identify with a painted General Electric logo on a board leaning against the appliance. The same logo as in normal time. An Electric Floor Master vacuum cleaner stood near a couple of space heaters. A large console radio stood at the back, where the high-dollar items were. One wall had an ad banner showing an iron with caption about how it held its heat. The banner included illustrations of smiling women ironing. A man stood in the back next to the large radio. A woman approached Kayla.

"May I show you any appliance, miss?" she said.

"No, thank you. I am just browsing. It's very busy outside."

"Yes, with the election today."

The man joined them. "Yes, and many men are still certainly opposed to women's suffrage, but not me."

"This is Mr. Cook," the woman said, introducing him to Kayla. "I'm Mrs. Cook and I voted."

"And I am Kayla."

"Glad to know you, Kayla," said Mr. Cook. "Did you vote?"

"Yes."

"I'm glad," he said. He smiled, excused himself, and returned to the back of the store.

Two middle-aged women entered the store, one gathering her sweater jacket about her shoulders. Both women were quite attractive in their 1920 fashions—too bad Kevin missed this, Kayla thought, smiling to herself. One wore a light-colored hat with the brim turned up in the front revealing a hint of bangs beneath; the other wore a similar though darker hat over short-cropped hair.

[157]

"Much better," the woman in the light hat said.

"Boy wasn't that a mad house?" said the one in the dark hat.

"It sure was. I wish Mary could have experienced voting."

"She certainly would have enjoyed it," said the one in the dark hat, suppressing a tear.

The other consoled her with a hand on her shoulder. "That awful influenza. She helped all those returning soldiers, many of them still around now because of her sacrifice and generosity."

"I know," said the other through bleary eyes. "Mary Dodd will be remembered."

Kayla went to them. "I don't mean to eavesdrop," she said.

"Of course you didn't," said the one in the light hat, extending her hand. "I am Florence."

Kayla accepted her hand. "I am Kayla. Nice to meet you."

"I am Sarah," said the other. "Glad to know you, Kayla."

"Oh. Kayla, would you join us for lunch?" said Florence. "We have a restaurant in town. It's new, called Main Street Coffee House. Let's celebrate voting."

"I would love to join you," Kayla said.

"You can eat for sixty cents if you keep your order small," said Sarah.

Kayla looked in her bag. She didn't use her silver dollars for a sweater so she still had two dollars.

"Let's treat Kayla," Florence said to Sarah.

"Sarah nodded.

"That's not necessary, ladies. I can pay for my meal," Kayla said, feeling embarrassed.

"Let's go," Florence said, turning toward the door.

The three of them exited the store and headed up Main.

Half a block along, Florence stopped, took Sarah and Kayla by their arms, and pointed across the street. "Oh, how long I've wished to see that."

Workers were removing a sign that read: "National Association Opposed to Woman Suffrage" from over an entrance to a building.

"Oh, my," said Sarah. "It's so good to see that go."

In the next block, the three women arrived at Main Street Coffee House.

It was dark inside with square wooden tables lined up and a counter to the side where men and a couple of women sat.

A group of men occupied a fairly large table along the wall beyond the counter, complete with a small cloud of smoke above them.

Florence led Kayla and Sarah to a table in the middle, not too close to the men but within earshot.

The three of them sat, regarded the menu, and a young man came by to take their order.

Florence leaned toward Sarah and Kayla. "Listen to what they're saying," she said.

"It's a threat to womanhood," said one man.

"Not only that, most women didn't even want it," said another.

"Some of their votes will cancel their husbands'."

"What do women know of business and national issues?"

"There is no benefit realized that will justify the expense."

The waiter brought their orders. He tilted his head toward the group of men and asked, "Would you ladies prefer a quieter table?"

Florence looked at Kayla and Sarah.

"Yes," said Sarah, "that would be nice."

They relocated to a table near a window, settled in, and didn't seem to attract attention except for admiring stares at Florence and Sarah by some of the male patrons.

"Well," said Florence, "those men aren't of the same opinions as some men. For example, Mr. Cook."

"They were hard to listen to," Kayla said.

"Interestingly put, Kayla," said Florence.

They finished lunch, paid, and headed out. A few seconds after they started down Main: the skid of tires and a crash a half block ahead at Brook Street and Main startled them.

Kayla had never imagined what a crash between two 1920 vehicles would look like. She saw twisted fenders over sideways wheels, a bent frame, and dented in side of the car's body. A westbound pickup truck had t-boned a northbound car. It looked to Kayla as though the car had pulled out in front of the pickup which appeared to have the right of way. The pickup's front end retained its shape with a crumpled grill. Its driver leaned in the car's open window on the passenger's side. He had opened the door to reach in and assist the driver. Several people stood in a semicircle around the wreck. An ambulance, a modified Model A with enclosed back end displaying a red cross with white background on the side arrived. As responders jumped out of the back and rushed to the car's driver side, they waved the small crowd away Two men had what Kayla figured were extraction tools working on the bent dashboard that had folded around the driver.

Kayla didn't want to watch too closely and looked away as they got closer to the intersection. She and the other two women crossed to the other side of Main. Sarah and Florence excused themselves and went on their way. Kayla wanted to see more of 1920 Sycamore Falls. An abbreviated repeat of her walk around with Kevin in 1961 would be adequate for today. She found a much needed sweater jacket to buy and decided that a walk around could be informative.

Now comfortable, Kayla headed north on Main. She passed a gas station. It had a sign that said, "Notice – All our gasoline is Filtered before going into these tanks. Positively no chance for dirt or water." Next to that, a sign, "30 cents a gallon." If only she could bring her car back and fill up. At least the gas was filtered and as far as she knew, lead wouldn't be introduced to gasoline for years.

Enough crazy thinking for now. She continued north and reached the corner of Third and Main.

The hotel was being renovated like Kevin said. She headed east on Third and walked past familiar houses. A few pics for Kevin, this 1920 street was picturesque with some fall leaves still hanging on. A maple leaf tapped down the street as it skipped along in the breeze and the smell of autumn abounded.

She continued along Third then made her way to the high school. It looked the same, but had a fresher look. The lawn was less manicured, but still green and the school looked nice. Class was apparently in session, no kids out and around.

A couple emerged from a side street, walking toward her. The man dressed in a dark suit with tie pushed a wicker baby carriage and the woman cradled the baby in her arms. They turned toward downtown. Going to vote, certainly as Kayla overheard them discussing Warren G. Harding and James Cox.

Kayla stopped for a while, took in her surroundings, and drew a deep breath. The town was healthy here at the beginning of the Roaring Twenties. She checked her bag. No suitable money for shopping. She wasn't about to repeat her mistake from 1950 Cattlemen's Day, so she'd have to forget spending any money.

She returned to Main Street. It was all there. The shops, the restaurant, the banks, the line outside of the polling place. The anti-suffrage sign was gone and moving out activity continued at that office.

Eric T. Reynolds

Kayla picked up the pace and headed back to the farmhouse.

* * *

An elderly woman opened the farmhouse front door.

"May I help you?" she said.

"Hello, my name is Kayla. I just voted and I think I'm supposed to meet my friends here."

"I'm afraid you may have the wrong house, but please come in. I am Ida."

"I don't want to impose," Kayla said.

"It's no bother, come in for a while and make yourself at home."

She led Kayla to the living room. "Have a seat and I'll make us some tea."

Ida excused herself and Kayla wandered around the room past a table along the wall with a wood-encased radio. A few feet away along the same wall was a console table that held a bookstand with an opened book, *The Portrait of a Lady* by Henry James, a picture of a middle-aged woman, probably from the mid-1910s displayed next to it.

Kayla sneaked a peek at the inside cover. Not the book with the birthday inscription.

Ida entered and said, "This display is for sentimental reasons, the book and the lady's portrait," she said.

"Interesting arrangement, that book title with the picture next to the book," Kayla said.

"She was a dear friend," said Ida.

"I am so sorry."

"I am blessed, as were others, just to have known her." Ida gestured to the sofa. Please sit, Kayla."

"Thank you, Ida, but I wonder if you would show me that room with the bookshelves."

Ida smiled and started for the library. "This is my favorite room."

[162]

Kayla stepped into the library with her. "I certainly understand that. It would be mine, too."

Ida stood next to the bookcase and Kayla reached into her bag and reinserted the voter ID card back into the *Jailed for Freedom* book. Ida stood in front of where Kayla needed to reshelve the book. Kayla went to the shelf.

"Is there anything you'd like to see?" Ida said.

"No, thank you," Kayla said, trying to think of a way to distract Ida from her position. She pulled the book from her bag and pushed past Ida to slide the book into its place, returning her to normal time. She felt ashamed at her rudeness.

CHAPTER NINETEEN
Book Club

BACK IN THE VICTORIAN, Kayla caught up on her article, thinking through things while she wrote. Common sense told her she should resist timeshifting sometimes, but she feared losing the anomaly if anyone else learned about it, more so if a lot of people did. And if Sheriff Rick decided it needed to be off limits, then it'd be gone. So she needed to explore it as much as she could.

* * *

Kevin joined her at the farmhouse the next day. She stood in the middle of the library.

"Okay, here goes," she said.

She pulled *The Story of Art* off the shelf and timeshifted to 1950, then timeshifted back from there with *Out of the Silent Planet* to 1938.

A copy of *The Prince and the Pauper* by Mark Twain sat slanted against another book on a lower shelf. She hadn't been to the 1938 library much so she didn't notice it before.

She reached down and grabbed the book.

A breeze swirled around her.

It was high noon. The still and quiet house was nicely adorned with nineteenth century furnishings. The little corner table was gone. Sashes held back green floor-to-ceiling drapes that were suspended on rings, allowing in plenty of light. A pedestal writing table with a wooden chair sat in the center of the room. On the table was a feather quill with ink well. Kayla went to the table, careful not to touch or brush against anything.

[164]

Also on the table, a bookstand propped up *The Portrait of a Lady* by Henry James.

Writing paper next to the quill had something written in neat cursive.

May the First, 1885

The First Meeting of the Sycamore Falls Ladies Book Club

Hosted by Ida
With—
Emma
Mary
Anna
Elizabeth
Margarete
Florence
Alice
Sarah

Kayla looked around and felt the essence of 1885, the décor, and the scent of resins used to make the shellac finish of the time greeted her. Jennifer would love this. So would Kevin. She retrieved her phone and snapped a picture. The area rug in the adjoining living room covered most of the floor. A long red leather sofa sat with its back to the south windows.

She snapped another picture and took video around the living room then listened for a moment and as she peeked around to the foyer, she saw no one and decided to sneak out. She tiptoed past the fireplace, next to it a simple chair and spinning wheel with a half full bobbin. Down the hallway was a drop leaf table with kerosene lamp. The front door was ajar so she went out onto the porch.

[165]

No one around. An intact barn sat where the ruined barn was in normal time. She stepped off the porch and walked around the house, past a bed of jonquils sprouting bright yellow flowers. A few small trees were taking root in the backyard. There was no shed or woods. Grass mostly where the wooded area was in normal time but with a line of encroaching trees a ways down the back of the hill.

The wind whipped through the tallgrass here in 1885 like in normal time, singing as the breeze pushed past, giving her a feeling of continuity through time. The house was missing the kitchen area; the back of the house was expanded later. Commonly done when homeowners wanted more space, she had heard: add on rather than move up to a bigger house. She wished she could stay here for a while, but had to move on, so she hurried around to the front porch.

From there, she had another look out over 1885 Sycamore Falls in the valley. A few of its houses down there were still around in normal time. At the bottom of the hill where her Victorian would be was the vineyard for the winery of this property's past. It'd be nice to sit up here and feel the 1885 breeze for a while.

"I would love to taste wine from the vineyards here," she muttered.

She went back inside to the living room. Realizing she was getting caught up in the moment, she hurried into the library.

A light knock at the front door.

She gasped, kneeled next to the bookcase, and held on to the Mark Twain book.

Someone opened the front door. Several subdued female voices came from the foyer.

The Book Club!

Kayla wanted to stay for a while as the women settled into the living room. Several sat on the sofa and engaged in

[166]

quiet conversation while Kayla listened. She took a few seconds of video.

Their conversation focused an upcoming vote in November. One woman, the hostess, Kayla assumed, walked into the living room.

"Oh, Ida," said one woman in a hushed tone, "how are you and Lewis doing since voters ratified Prohibition in Kansas?"

She appeared ready to answer, but stepped toward the library. Kayla gripped the book and froze.

Ida stepped through the entrance. "Oh my!" she said, staring down at Kayla. "Who are you and where are your clothes!"

Kayla was tempted to reply, but decided against it.

Three other women joined Ida. A couple of them held their hands over their mouths, one shielded her eyes.

"I've never seen such a thing!" said one.

Kayla smiled up at them, reshelved the Mark Twain book, and jumped through the nodes back to the present.

Kevin stood there, noticing the smirk on her face.

He smiled. "What's going on? Okay, you look guilty."

"As charged. It was wonderful! I was in 1885! May first. A beautiful spring day and the house was like a museum setting where you tour a historic house. I'm going back there again."

Kevin sighed. "You're wearing me out with worry," he said.

"I need to run down to the Victorian first, use the bathroom, and change."

"Change? Why?"

"Shorts weren't in fashion in 1885," she said, trying to contain a laugh.

"Did anyone see you?"

"Several women."

Eric T. Reynolds

"You shouldn't play with people you encounter like that."

"It wasn't on purpose. It's not like they're real after we timeshift back to the present."

"We don't really know," he said.

"You keep saying that," she said.

"Even if the timeline resets the next time, that first timeline might continue on its own course indefinitely for all we know, even if we can't get back to that timeline. Good thing no one else saw you. You could have been arrested. Did you see any more possible artifacts, for going to an earlier time?"

"Nothing definite," she said and left to go down to the Victorian to change.

CHAPTER TWENTY
Join?

KAYLA RETURNED TO THE FARMHOUSE LATER to find Kevin was poking around upstairs.

"I'm about to go back to 1885 again!" she shouted up from the foyer before she went into the library.

Kevin came down to the library and noticed her outfit, a plain long off-white dress that reached the floor.

"I had this dress already," she said. "I'm wearing comfortable shoes. Can you see them?"

Kevin looked her up and down. "It's okay. Do you need a corset?"

"I don't need one," she said.

"I'm just thinking of the times and undergarments that squeeze the hell out of you."

"Common women didn't dress that way. All I need to do is pass for the times. My research shows most women wore simple long dresses around that time. Flats might have looked funny, so I want to make sure they're concealed."

"I can't see them," Kevin said.

She fanned the dress out and let the hem fall to the floor.

"I think you're good to go," he said.

She stuffed a tiny envelope under the neckline of her dress.

"What's that?" Kevin said.

"An 1870 dime." She pulled it out and removed it from the envelope. "Here, look. I've had this for years. And other coins from that time."

Kevin took the coin. "Wow—you're sacrificing this? Looks in good condition."

"For a chance to journey back to 1885, I'd sacrifice thousands of them. It's a Philadelphia mint, not rare for that year. I have several coins from the 1870s through 1900. This one is in good condition. I probably won't use it, but just in case." She put the coin back into its envelope and tucked it away. "Okay, I'm going now."

"Be careful," he said.

She told him the sequence of timeshifters to 1885 in case he needed to go back after her, then she grabbed *The Story of Art,* and jumped back through the nodes to the 1885 library.

As before, the house was quiet. She glanced at *The Portrait of a Lady* on the pedestal table.

Wait—it had bookmarks this time.

She eased the book open to the first bookmarked page 32. No pencil underlines this time. The bookmark sat sideways on the page beneath the line: <u>for her love of knowledge and her imagination was strong</u>.

"What?" Kayla whispered.

She took a picture and opened to the next bookmark, also sideways on page 133 where it marked:

<u>I'm very glad they're such good friends.</u>

She needed to get to her task, but two more bookmarks: On page 172, the end of one marked <u>give it back</u>. On 211 marked: <u>universally intelligent and unprecedentedly virtuous</u>.

Kayla shrugged, went to the front door, and stepped onto the porch to wait for Ida. She sat on one of the wooden porch chairs and took in the view and breeze. She almost dozed, stirred to alertness by the arrival of a man and a woman pulling up in a horse-drawn buggy to the side of the house. The man helped the woman down, unhitched the horse, and led it away.

Kayla stood as the woman came up onto the porch. Kayla assumed she was Ida, the hostess of the Book Club.

"Oh, how do you do?" the woman said.

Kayla nodded and repeated the greeting.

"You must be Sarah," the woman said.

"My name is Kathryn Wolfe," Kayla said.

"I beg your pardon, Kathryn," Ida said. "The other ladies will be along presently. I am Ida, your hostess today and I welcome you to our first meeting of the Sycamore Falls Ladies Book Club. We start this week and I'll give everyone the rotation order to borrow the book."

She has this well structured thought Kayla.

Ida led Kayla in through the foyer to the living room and offered to her to sit on one of the chairs or the sofa.

"I usually wait for all the guests, but I have something special to offer to you." She left the room.

Kayla sat on the sofa and drummed her fingers on the seat in anticipation until Ida returned with a tray holding a carafe of wine and glasses, placing the tray on a serving table she had wheeled in earlier.

Kayla gasped.

"I didn't know if you partake of wine, Kathryn. Our current vintage. Forgive me if I've been presumptuous. Especially in these days."

"I would love to taste it," Kayla said.

"Oh, that's nice. We don't know how much longer we'll be able to enjoy a nice glass of wine like this, do we?"

Kayla nodded.

A knock prompted Ida to head to the front door. She invited several women in and poked her head outside to look around.

Kayla stood as the women entered the living room and took their seats around.

Ida introduced everyone. "And Kathryn, are you from out of town?"

So the replay is affected by my entry into it, thought Kayla. But then, why wouldn't it be?

"Why yes, I just moved here," Kayla said.

Ida handed each guest a glass of red wine. Sarah giggled at the offer of forbidden wine.

"Welcome to our village, Kathryn," Ida said as she handed a glass to Kayla.

Kayla waited until the others started sipping and noticed their glances toward her until she took a sip. She rolled it on her tongue and let it sit for a moment before swallowing. She'd never tasted wine like this.

"It's wonderful," she said.

"We are pleased with this vintage, Lewis and I," said Ida. "I'm so glad you're enjoying it. After all, as prevalent as the Temperance movement is, I assumed you wouldn't partake if you were a Prohibitionist."

"No," Kayla said, "That is, I am not a Prohibitionist."

Kayla realized what a gift this opportunity was and couldn't help wondering if a bottle might have survived to the present hidden on the property somewhere.

"Oh, Ida," said Sarah, "how are you and Lewis doing now since the voters ratified Prohibition in Kansas?"

Ah! thought Kayla, this segment of the timeline is an exact repeat of my previous visit except Ida didn't step over to the library this time like before when she saw me.

"No one has come calling to demand we stop," Ida replied. "We're allowed to provide wine to churches that use it for communion."

"West Hill Vineyard will be safe," Florence said.

"This will all be over before you know it," Anna said. "Only for a few years. It'll change back."

[172]

Ida regarded Kayla. "You certainly have taken a liking to our reds, Kathryn."

Kayla smiled. "Yes, I have! It melts in your mouth."

"Well that's something I've never heard," Ida said, smiling.

Ida rose, excused herself, and went into another room. The other women smiled at Kayla, displaying looks of anticipation. Kayla tapped the book in her bag with her fingers, trying not to allow any urgent thoughts about having to timeshift away intrude into this moment.

Ida returned with a still-corked bottle of red. "A gift to welcome you to our little group, Kathryn," she said. "Keep it stowed away. But please enjoy it when you can if your husband will allow it."

Kayla drew in a deep breath. "Oh, Ida! I must pay you for this."

"I won't hear of it."

Mumbles of "of course not" accompanied smiles from the other women.

Kayla decided she needed to accept it graciously and said, "Thank you, Ida. I'm not yet married. I'll enjoy it on my own time."

"Pardon me," Ida said, holding her fingertips to her mouth. "That's a very special vintage. Relish it."

Kayla cradled the bottle. When Ida turned to step out again, Kayla stood.

"Ida," Kayla whispered, "May I please buy another bottle of red from you? Please forgive me for my bluntness."

"Oh, Kathryn, you have such a manner of speech. Of course you may have another bottle. It's something you won't be able to get as the years pass."

You've got that correct, Kayla thought.

"Thank you, Ida," she said.

Kayla returned to her seat and smiled at the others.

[173]

"I have three bottles," said Mary with a hint of guilt in her tone.

"I have two," said Emma.

Ida returned with several bottles and handed two to Kayla. "Our 1876 vintage."

"Wonderful," said Kayla.

Kayla cradled all three bottles in her lap. The other women each took a bottle amidst smiles and giggles.

"Shall we get along with business?" Ida said. She sat and held up the book, *The Portrait of a Lady*. "I finished reading this book yesterday." It's wonderful, about a quite independent woman. I have a list for our rotation. Kathryn, you may borrow the book first."

"Oh, thank you, but if you will believe it, I've already read it. I was fortunate enough to borrow it from the Kansas City library before I moved."

"Oh, ladies," said Ida, "we have a city girl among us." The other women gathered around Kayla and welcomed her.

Kayla tried her best guess of 1885 embarrassed modesty and smiled, continuing to cradle her treasured wine bottles in her bag.

"Everyone," said Ida, "I have a question."

The guests perked up and focused on her.

"Suppose you came into some money and are very independent. Would you give up that independence for marriage?"

Anna tapped her head and said, "Depends on the man, doesn't it?"

"It certainly does," said Alice.

"Depends on both," said Elizabeth.

"What do you think, Kathryn?" said Ida.

"It depends on where and when they're living," said Kayla. "For instance, how are things for women where she lives? Can she be happy there living independently? How much freedom would she have?"

"I agree, Kathryn," said Mary. "Why, if we women could vote, we might have more freedom. We certainly would by having our say in government with our vote."

"If we ever get that right," said Anna.

"I think we will," said Kayla. "I've heard they're close to getting it in Colorado."

"And if women get the right to vote in Colorado, Kansas might be right behind," Anna said.

"Each state is different," Mary said, "but let's hope we are successful."

"It might take a while," Kayla said. "Maybe we'll have it not long after the turn of the century."

Mary nodded and smiled at Kayla.

"Yes, I think we should be optimistic," said Mary. "I believe it will happen. Maybe an answer to the question isn't just where she lives but when she lives."

After about an hour or two of conversation, and sipping of precious wine, the meeting wound down. Kayla had to use the bathroom, but how does one ask that in 1885, and where does one *go*? Kayla had seen chamber pots when touring historic houses. She might have to improvise, but she *had* to go. Fortunately, Anna stood and headed to the hallway. Perhaps. . .

Kayla stood as well.

"Oh," Ida said to Kayla. "I haven't shown you the water closet. We have an indoor one."

After Anna emerged, Ida led Kayla to a small room that smelled like a port-a-potty. A full pitcher of water provided means for flushing the surprisingly modern-shaped toilet. She finished and used a tissue from her own bag and poured some of the water down the toilet, then cleansed her hands in the wash basin bowl. She used one of the coarse beige hand towels stacked next to the wash basin.

She returned to the living room and the women were all standing, ready to disperse. It was a sad time for her. She had gotten to know these women and knew she'd never see them and Ida again.

She reached into her bag and grabbed the book. It and the story of art book were safely there.

"May I see your room with the books?" she asked Ida.

Ida nodded and led her in. Kayla went to the bookcase, reshelved *The Prince and the Pauper,* and jumped through the nodes to the present.

Back to the present through tears in her eyes, she spotted a blurry Kevin on the couch in the living room doing something on his phone.

"Well, welcome back," he said. "You're not as perky this time."

Kayla sniffed and said, "Oh, Kevin! I have new friends I'll never see again." She wiped her eyes. "*Had* new friends."

Kevin came over and hugged her. "Tell me about it when you're ready."

"Oh, but look!" she said with a quick sigh while pulling out a bottle of wine.

"What! Where'd you get that? You know that we can't—" She slapped her hand against his mouth.

"It's a gift from Ida. She gave me three bottles. I'll cherish these forever."

"You're not going to drink them?"

"Well, maybe one. Don't worry, I'll share," she said.

"And remember, you can go back and retrace your actions and get more bottles if you want more."

"What I *want* is to see my new friends again!"

"Okay, okay—it's so hard to figure this."

"And they're dead and gone now," she said, sobbing.

Kevin took her hand. "Let's go for a walk and head into town."

Kayla took a deep breath. "Sounds good."

They headed to the Victorian first where Kayla put her wine bottles in a wine rack in the dining room, setting one on its side in a special area in her china cabinet where she kept family heirlooms.

"I'll be back down in a minute," she said to Kevin, then headed up to her bedroom.

She flopped onto her bed in a brief soft cry.

After a moment, she changed out of her long dress and into a comfortable skirt and top then stood in front of her dresser mirror, pulled her hair back, and gathered it into a ponytail.

She headed down the stairs to rejoin Kevin.

"Let's head out," she said.

"Downtown?"

"Sounds good. See it in normal time. I want to compare it with its pasts that I've visited recently."

As they went out the front door, Rick pulled up.

"Damn," said Kayla.

Kevin took her hand and they started toward the street.

Rick got out of the car and joined them.

"Kayla," he said, "That thing in the farmhouse is a hazard. I don't want anyone near it until we figure out whether it's safe to be around so a deputy will be posted to restrict access."

"How do you explain restricting access?" Kayla asked.

"The deputy won't have details. He just won't allow anyone in that room."

"How soon?"

"In a couple of hours. I'll let you know. I'll call you."

"Okay, Rick," she said.

"Let's go on downtown for a while," Kevin said.

They walked down to Main Street and headed north.

"Seems like I've been in the past here more than in the present," she said. "But I didn't make it out of the house in 1885."

"You spend a lot of time in the past."

"Many people do," she said.

"Not like you."

"What if I went back to 1885 for a while and spent more time there. I've got to sort this out if I can convince Rick not to deny me access."

"Can't get enough of the past?"

"I have to go while I still have a chance. How much longer will I be able to do this with Rick closing in?"

"What would you do back in 1885?"

"Spend time with my new friends, Mary, Ida, Sarah, and several others. I felt a connection with Mary. We think alike, even though separated by time."

"Would you find a room to rent, like in an old style boarding house?"

"Everything's old style in 1885. Ida might be able to recommend a place to stay. I've got some old coins, quite a bit for 1885. I could live well for two or three weeks."

"You would get attached to your new friends."

Kayla looked down. "I know. Kevin, I already am, even after a short time. What is it that's making me have to go back?"

"You're obsessed," he said.

"A natural force pulling me. You felt it, too."

"Not anymore," Kevin said. "Like I said before, going back makes me nervous. That 1938 trip was a fluke. Something I enjoyed."

"You did some research," she said.

"You need to be careful," he said.

"I want you to keep watch on the bookcase if I manage to slip into the library when the deputy's there and timeshift. Rescue me if I don't come back."

They reached the block with Weber's and noticed Hank Weber arranging apples in a wooded display box outside the store.

Both laughed with high fives.

"That's what I call continuity," Kayla said. "Oh, man, I want to show him the picture I took of him in 1961."

"If the timeshifting becomes known, then you should."

"Assuming we still have timeshifting," she said.

Kayla got a call from Rick.

"Rick's posting a deputy," she said. "Deputy's heading up there in a few hours. I'll need to get there and figure out a way to timeshift again."

"The deputy won't let you timeshift."

"He's going to be in my house so I want to meet him."

CHAPTER TWENTY-ONE
What Are You Trying to Say?

KAYLA HEADED UP TO THE FARMHOUSE later and went inside.

"Hello?" she said as she headed into the foyer.

No one answered. She stepped into the living room. He wasn't there.

"Hello!" she said.

No answer.

Kayla called Kevin.

"He's not here. Come up here."

After Kevin arrived, they ran outside, checked the shed, the barn, all around the property, and throughout the house.

"He must have timeshifted," Kayla said.

"Maybe stranded."

"Oh, God. I hope not." She paced around. Out to her car, she popped the trunk.

"We need to rescue him," Kevin said, following her out.

"Should we? Or should the sheriff? I'm not surprised the deputy got curious," she said.

"He didn't know about it."

"But he would have seen the sheriff's tape blocking the entrance to the library."

"He's not going to disturb anything if he's not supposed to," he said.

"There's still a possibility that he grabbed a book," she said.

"Maybe Rick could check. Then he can see why you and I still need access when he finds out what it's really like."

"The sheriff isn't skilled at navigating the timeline nodes like we are. We need to look for the deputy ourselves," she said.

Kevin rubbed his chin. "But where?"

"Back to 1961 to start yet again. You want to go?" she said. "If he's not there, we'll keep looking."

"I'm not sure. I'm getting more nervous every time we go back. Don't you think we've risked enough?"

"I don't know, something always pulls me back. If you don't want to go, just wait for me in the living room, make sure I return, and promise to push past the deputy if he's here and rescue me if I'm not back soon."

He shook his head, "Okay, I'll keep watch."

"I'll risk it, Kevin." She pulled her early sixties outfit from the trunk of her car, then threw the car keys to Kevin. "Your suit's in there if you have to go back."

They went back inside and she changed into her outfit and they headed into the library.

"See you in a while," she said, pulling out *Stranger in a Strange Land.*

She timeshifted to the sunny fall day and explored, sneaked around the property, then searched for the deputy around Sycamore Falls. She went to the courthouse and looked around the halls before looking all over the town.

When she exhausted all ideas for where to look, she returned to the farmhouse, looked around the barn and shed, dashed into the library.

Back in the present, Kevin was in the living room, reading.

She joined him, sighing as she settled onto a chair across from him.

"Well?" he said.

She shook her head. "No sign of the deputy. But I felt like the town was speaking to me. It's the town that's drawing me to go back, even though I was there to look for the deputy, but I don't know. I have to keep going. It's all I think of, each trip satisfying that urge more, leaving me wanting to go back to a new place. Could be something else, maybe this is part of it."

"Could be, maybe the town is asking for help," he said.

"Notice how well the town looked and functioned back in 1961," she said. "I'm talking about the town itself as an organism."

"So like the town is alive?" he said.

Kayla nodded. "It is and it's asking for our help."

"We're trying to do our part to help the town," he said. "Many people are."

"Maybe it knows that," she said, "and knows I can influence you as I learn from its past selves."

Kevin wasn't sure.

She shrugged. "Or maybe the house is what's pulling me back. Those books. Are they a plea not to tear the house down?"

"Or a plea *to* tear it down."

"While making the timeshifting addictive? I don't think whatever it is wants me to tear the house down. I need a real reason."

"Maybe you'll get one."

"So is the town speaking to you with your trips to 1938 and to 1961?"

"I don't know," he said. "The 1938 trip certainly opened my eyes, and 1961 did as well."

Kayla sighed. "1961 opened mine, too. As did 1920, 1950, and 1954. I want to see the 1885 town near its beginning. I'll know more about 1885 Sycamore Falls by going back there again and getting out."

She sighed again, closed her eyes, and napped for about an hour.

* * *

She woke and Kevin was still on the couch asleep.

She stood and went over to him.

"Hey," she said.

He opened his eyes and looked up at her. "No," he said.

"I have to. It's pulling me back."

"The town?"

"I don't know, the town, the house, even the hill for all I know. I just have to timeshift back."

She tapped him on the shoulder. "You hungry? Want to go into town and grab lunch first?"

He yawned and stretched his limbs. "Do you get hungry after your timeshift fixes?"

"Shut up, get off your butt, and let's go."

Kevin stretched and stood, then stretched again. "Where?"

"So it's good to go see the town now while the past ones are fresh in my mind, but first, I need to change. Meet me at the Victorian."

Kayla went home and changed into shorts and flip-flops and sat out the porch to wait for Kevin.

He pulled up, hopped out onto her driveway and went to her.

"I'm almost not used to twenty-first century clothes," said Kayla.

"People dressed up a lot in the past," Kevin said.

"And covered up. Let's go."

They walked to Main Street, and retraced their 1961 walks.

"Well, a little traffic, but not like in sixty-one," she said.

"We can develop tours of the past, people will come for them," he said. "Visit the past. – Come to Sycamore Falls."

"Have you done a market study? Researched other towns that have historical attractions?"

[183]

"I will. Still in the creative stage. It's a gradual thing. Start with one aspect of it, build on it as it takes hold."

"Vintage cars, right?"

"Vintage cars. Part of the atmosphere. Take people around and hit the historic spots, old architecture, the old hotel, City Hall."

"I've seen that old building! Impressive."

"And go by the oldest house in town."

"My farmhouse?"

"Noooo."

"Whatever. Continue. . ."

"Tours in comfortable shiny old cars. Go by the old college. Stories about it as we drive around it. "

"Did you get pictures of it in 1961?"

"I did."

They looked for some of the places they saw in 1961 and came across an abandoned store they thought used to be Lenny's Café. There was a plate glass window there still and they could see inside. Outside light penetrated the dark toward the back wall. Remnants of an old countertop still stood. The faded green walls had peeling paint and old chipped flooring covered the floor. Tables and chairs gone.

"How long has this place been abandoned?" Kayla said.

"I think Lenny's was there until about thirty years ago."

"That long, it's been empty? Hard to imagine a place not occupied that long."

"The town went through hard times."

"Who owns it?"

"Wendy might know. Interested?"

"Ha, no. I don't know anything about setting up a retail establishment or a restaurant."

"Retro diner. I know a place where you could get some design ideas."

Kayla smiled. "But not me."

[184]

Kevin pointed across the street at Nonstandard Artifacts Gallery.

"Mara has new work displayed there today, I think," he said.

"Let's go see," said Kayla.

Inside the gallery, Mara stood beside a large landscape and turned to greet Kayla and Kevin when they entered.

"What do you think?" she said, waving a hand toward the painting.

"Nice! That's the view. And you stuck my shed in it."

"I've been dabbling in photorealism."

Other paintings of a hill and people on top by Mara hung on the opposite wall. One had an indigenous woman standing on the grassy hilltop talking to a non-indigenous woman.

Kevin went up to the painting and looked closely.

"Kayla, look," he said, still standing next to the painting. "One of those women looks like you. Like Mara's doing that as a metaphor. Think about it."

Mara smiled at him from across the room while Kayla joined him next to the painting.

Mara gathered her things and left the gallery.

Kayla grew fidgety. "We need to check with Rick after lunch and ask him where the deputy is," she said. "If he's still supposed to be guarding the library, then. . ."

* * *

They skipped lunch and headed back to the farmhouse.

She sat in one of the chairs in the library. "I'm going back again and see what the town wants," she said.

"You're still convinced the town is pulling you back?" said Kevin.

"Something is," she said, "and it's trying to reveal things about its past."

[185]

"They're pretty pronounced from your point of view, I guess."

"You saw the town back in time, too," she said.

"So what's the town trying to tell you?"

"I don't know!" she said. "I just don't! I think I'm getting a message, but I feel like I'm missing something that I have to go back for and the urge stays."

"So, all the things that pulled us back: the missing kids, the murder, the town difference, now something else?"

"Yeah! No, I mean, I don't know."

"Where do you have an urge to go to now?"

"1885."

"Again?"

"Yes! Again. This time I'm going out, into town."

CHAPTER TWENTY-TWO
Out and About

"I NEED THE DRESS I WORE TO BOOK CLUB."

"1885 again?"

"I only experienced the inside this house. I told you I need to go out, into town."

"Okay, you go and I'll check with Rick about the deputy."

"Thank you!"

"What about money?"

"Got it. I have some 1880s silver dollars."

Kayla went to the Victorian and changed into her long, drab white, mostly straight, not tight dress with long sleeves. She threw a few granola bars and bottled water into her bag and she was ready. She felt the adrenaline as she started to head up to the farmhouse.

She decided she would resist replaying the Book Club timeline and making friends again, to make time to head out.

She followed the timeshifting path back to the 1885 library with the writing table and the living room waiting for the book club.

The timeline started its replay with the quiet house and midday spring warmth. She double checked inside her bag and headed out the front door, down the road past the empty lot where her Victorian would be and into 1885 Sycamore Falls. She reached the wide dirt Main Street. It had some of the same ornately crowned buildings that survived to normal time.

"I'm here," she said aloud. "Do you have more to say to me?"

Horse-drawn buggies and wagons filled Main Street. One side of the street was lined mostly by stone and brick buildings with tall, narrow windows on their upper floors, a few with simple wood post-supported overhangs sheltering porches occupied by men in dark pants and coats, with matching dark hats, derbies, and slightly wide-brimmed hats. A horse-drawn enclosed wagon that said "Goods" on the side rolled by. Among the men hanging around the store fronts were some in overalls wearing light-colored wider-brimmed hats. Kayla noticed occasional stares from the men as she made her way along. "No cowboy hats," she mumbled.

The building that would sport the Rock Cola ad was already there. She stood out from it and snapped a pic of the blank wall. She wanted to go up to the wall, but figured she was already conspicuous. She walked on.

A fair number of houses similar in style to her farmhouse flanked side streets. No bungalows yet.

Downtown looked functional with businesses serving many needs of this period of time. The newly built grand courthouse of native limestone stood in the central square. Some pedestrians milled about, most of them attending to their horses or sitting in their buggies, perhaps waiting for someone to return.

"Okay, I understand," said Kayla. "You're showing me your beginnings, how you became a community, all the hard work from generations of people who built you up and how that would be in vain if the town declines in my time. I walk your early streets and I know you are crying out. You don't want to fade like some of your contemporaries. Is that it?"

She walked down one of the covered boardwalks in front of the shops. Men tipped their hats as she passed by. A few women were out, but Kayla noticed some tended to go directly from stores to their buggies where male drivers waited.

[188]

Other women walked in and out of stores holding black sunshade umbrellas as they got ready to cross the street.

Kayla knew she couldn't spend too much time here, but she decided to venture into a residential area. As she started to turn down a side street, a man came up to her.

"Good afternoon, miss," he said, tipping his hat. Kayla nodded to him.

"May I be of any assistance, miss?"

"No, thank you," she said.

He tipped his hat again and turned back. She walked on with a quick glance back and passed by the location where Mara's bungalow would be. In 1885, it was empty ground. She continued on the short road that dead ended with countryside beyond the end.

A two-story house under construction a ways down the block caught her attention. She hurried to it.

When she got there, she snapped a picture. The construction looked surprisingly similar to that of normal time. The frame was up. Men worked about on the first and second floors. One man was working with a handsaw that could just as well have come from Kayla's favorite hardware store in normal time. The subflooring was down. No plywood in the 1800s, the subfloor consisting of planks installed diagonally across the floor joists. Kayla gazed at the workers up there. She noticed a diversity of carpenters at the site. Native Americans, African Americans, and white. No one person was obviously in charge. She figured each man knew his job and skill and they worked together. She snapped another picture showing the temporary cross-bracing on the wall studs, then turned and headed back downtown.

Just like building a house in our time, she thought. Maybe better. They built houses well in the 1800s. And that house was still there in normal time.

She reached Main Street and noticed how pedestrians stepped around piles of manure as they crossed the street while avoiding horse-drawn traffic.

"Good to know," she muttered. She managed to avoid any mess and once across the street, stepped onto the boardwalk there and walked along new store fronts.

She mumbled to the town, "I know it's not your fault or your townspeople's that the economic trends of the future changed."

She stopped when a Native American man stepped out of a store and she almost ran into him.

"Oh, pardon me," she said. She realized she was walking her usual fast pace, which probably wasn't appropriate or "ladylike" for this time. She figured she didn't need to draw attention to herself. The man nodded, smiled, and turned back to the door.

The shopkeeper emerged. He walked up to the man and placed his hand on his shoulder. "I can't do anything about it, Bob," he said. "I wish I could. Maybe the Board of Indian Affairs can help."

Kayla wanted to ask the man what he needed, but he headed away. She wondered if there was some way she could help whatever the issue was. No, she mustn't interfere, even in a temporary timeline like this.

She then walked toward two women talking in front of a shop and almost gasped: Anna and Mary from Book Club. Kayla tried not to make eye contact or display a look of recognition, but Mary flashed a bashful smile at her. She hardly seemed like the bashful type when they met at Book Club in Kayla's journey to that timeline.

The two women watched the Native American man walk away amidst a quiet giggle and discrete pointing by Anna. Mary looked away from Anna and started to walk away herself.

[190]

"So much for whatever high opinion I had of you, dear Anna," Kayla mumbled.

A moment later, Mary passed by Kayla and smiled at her again.

"Pardon me," Kayla said. "Is that man all right?"

"Oh, you mean Bob? He has been quite affected by the resettlement. I am so disheartened to see him so sad."

"Anna doesn't seem to care," Kayla said, quieting down quickly, realizing her verbal slip.

"She will understand one day. Are you acquainted with Anna?"

"Only slightly," Kayla said.

Mary flashed an embarrassed smile. "Oh my, where are my manners? I am Mary Dodd."

"And I am Kathryn Wolfe."

A ways down, Bob took a seat on a chair outside the shopkeeper's door. The shopkeeper stepped out and sat next to him. They conversed for a while.

"Barlow's Yarn Shop has the best selection of yarn," Mary said. "If you haven't patronized his shop, I recommend you do. Anna won't set foot in there."

"Didn't you say she will understand one day?"

"Anna is a good person, and a fine lady, but she isn't as worldly as you seem to be if I may say so. Her upbringing and all," Mary said.

Don't make excuses for her, thought Kayla.

"A pleasure meeting you, Kathryn," said Mary.

She offered Kayla a polite handshake and turned to leave.

Kayla accepted it, smiled, continued on her way, and looked for Weber's. It wasn't established yet, but a store that sold timepieces occupied the same spot. She stepped into the long, narrow shop. Wood floor planks ran the length of the store along the counter and display case from here to the shadowy back. The display case held pocket watches and small timepieces on pendants. Larger mantle clocks sat on shelves that lined the wall the length of the store. The shopkeeper was helping a woman at a counter in the back. They went to the front counter and finished their business. She glanced up and down at Kayla's dress as she left the store.

The shopkeeper greeted Kayla.

"Good afternoon, miss," he said. Then he smiled and lowered his voice. "You can buy much less expensive watches at the train depot. The telegraph operator has some fine timepieces for sale."

Must be my dress, she thought. He thinks I can't afford anything here.

"Yes, of course," she said. "Thank you. I shall consider it."

She stepped over to the window and peered out to the street at some commotion causing a gathering.

She then went to the door to get a different view. An 1885 sheriff's deputy was escorting a distraught man by his arm—Sheriff Rick!—down middle of the street.

Rick kept trying to shake free. Kayla giggled. "Oh!" she said with her hand to her mouth, then she started to head out the door.

"Too dangerous for a lady, miss," the shopkeeper said. "That stranger has been milling around the street all day and yesterday, too. Seems they didn't find anything to arrest him for, but those funny clothes and that strange-looking gun can mean he's likely up to no good. I haven't seen a man wear a holster and gun in years. He can do that, of course, but it certainly looks strange. The sheriff's got the deputy on him now. You best get with your husband if you have one or to your home until the matter is resolved."

"What will the sheriff do with him?"

[192]

"Don't worry. You're safe. He's probably harmless, but he's making people nervous and they want him out of town and the sheriff didn't take to him wearing the phony badge and those funny clothes." As the shopkeeper said that, he looked Kayla up and down; she realized her outfit wasn't quite as authentic as she had hoped. Were her shoes showing? Then again, she had once heard it wasn't proper for a man to gaze at a woman down there in the 1800s to get a peek at her ankles.

"You be careful, miss," he said.

She nodded and headed out to the street. The 1885 deputy continued to lead Rick down the middle of the street as gawkers looked on and laughed and when they reached the corner, the 1885 deputy waved his arms, shouted, and kicked dust onto Rick who tried to step way, but the deputy grabbed hold of him again.

Kayla wanted to go to him, but knew she had to be careful since she was also a stranger and if found in the company of Rick, the 1885 deputy could consider her suspicious, so she followed but kept her distance. They headed toward the courthouse. Kayla followed and when the deputy led Rick inside, she picked up her pace.

The deputy was quick and by the time she got into the courthouse, Rick was already behind bars. She walked to the sheriff's desk. There were several cells in the back. Rick's boots were just in view, but she couldn't quite see all of him. The 1885 sheriff sat behind a desk and he and the deputy who brought Rick in looked up as she entered the room.

"What can I do for you, miss?" the 1885 sheriff said.

Kayla cleared her throat. "I understand my no good brother came to town, Sheriff, have you seen him? He's about this tall, and he's wearing. . ."

"Well, miss," the deputy said, "we just might know of his whereabouts."

"Oh, is he here? I knew it. He's harmless, sir, but just a little. . ."

The 1885 sheriff and deputy chuckled.

"Well," the 1885 sheriff said, "I don't want a crazy man stirring up trouble. Best to keep him locked up for now."

"May I see him?" she asked.

The 1885 sheriff glanced at the deputy who went back and brought Sheriff Rick out.

Rick started to speak, but Kayla interrupted him with a discrete shh gesture.

Kayla burst out laughing. "You best keep quiet, brother!"

Rick remained stunned to see her, then got an angry look on his face.

"Kayla. . ." he started.

Kayla shook her head. "I told you not to go wandering around wearing that. If I were sheriff, I'd lock you up, too." Rick looked at the 1885 sheriff, then at Kayla.

"Well, what did you expect, wearing your costume around town?"

He caught on and nodded.

Kayla turned to 1885 sheriff. "Sheriff, if you'll release him to me, I'll make sure he doesn't come back."

"Where are you from, miss?"

"We're from Kansas City. We were on our way to Wichita for a performance when he had a bit too much to drink." She turned to Rick. "But you're sober now, aren't you?"

Rick nodded. "I'm sorry, Kayla. Please don't tell Pa about this."

"I just might. You don't need to be getting in trouble with the law. We'll kick you out if this happens again." She looked at 1885 sheriff.

"Sheriff, I'll take him now, if you please. And he won't set foot in town again." The 1885 sheriff looked at his paperwork for a moment then nodded to the deputy who released Rick. "I don't want to see you around here, you understand?"

Rick nodded.

"I'm releasing him to you, miss," the 1885 sheriff said. "Keep him out of trouble."

"Thank you. I shall."

The deputy showed Kayla and Rick to the door.

Once outside, Kayla led Rick down Main Street to a dirt road, to the farmhouse.

"Sheriff Rick," she said on the way, It's okay, we'll get back."

"But he has my gun! What's he going to do with it? What's that going to do to their future and how's that going to affect us? I've got to get that back and my badge, too."

"No, it's okay, this timeline ends as soon as we return to our present. This is a dead end."

"How do you know that?"

"Because each of these timelines resets itself every time we return to them. It's just a fragment. Your gun is trapped here. It's possible it's still here if we return to it, just like you were here when I returned to this timeline after you did, but it is its own thing, nothing that leads to us."

"How do we get back?"

Kayla pulled *The Prince and the Pauper* from her bag. "This is our way back."

They had to wait until dark and fumble their way back to the farmhouse. The window was unlocked. They slipped into the library and jumped their way through the nodes to the present.

Kevin was there nodding and smiling.

"Sheriff," Kevin said, "where's your deputy?"

"He hung around here for a few hours. I decided to send him away before I went back in time. And I can see that we definitely need to condemn this place."

Kayla stepped a little closer to the bookcase. "You can't condemn it. This place is structurally sound and there's been no crime committed here, except maybe you crossing your own line."

Kevin started laughing.

"That's enough," Rick said. "I've had enough of that for today. I didn't think I was going to get stranded. It was part of my investigation into this thing."

Rick turned to leave. "Still need to think this through," he said as he headed to the front door.

[196]

CHAPTER TWENTY-THREE
Who Are You Talking To?

"HOW WAS 1885 THIS TIME?" Kevin asked while staring at the floor.

"So how was your adventure, Kevin?"

"*My* adventure?"

"You can't fool me," she said. "Where'd you go while I was in 1885 this time?"

"1961," he said.

"1961?"

"I'm familiar with it and most comfortable there. I went into town. I couldn't help it. I had to go. More research."

"Aha!" she said. "You've caught the fever, if maybe you're less adventurous. So I think you realized we won't have these opportunities much longer."

"It's not that. It's something else. And it's not a 'fever'."

"Then what?" she said, folding her arms.

"Don't you understand?" he said.

She put her hands on her hips. "Well, yeah, it's been me all along and now you're catching it."

"It's not just you," he said. "The town wants my help, too. It's using you to get to me. And nothing personal, but I'm better positioned to help the town. The things I saw this time in 1961 and 1938. The town's like a sentient being like you said. It consumes, it thinks, it expels waste."

"Thanks for the mental picture," she said.

"It's true and it doesn't do all that as well as it used to."

"Exactly!" she said. "That's what I noticed."

"And you finally convinced me of it."

"So my job is done," she said.

Kevin held his hands up. "Whoa there, pardner."

"Good, because I really need to timeshift again."

"Something else has its hook on you," said Kevin.

"If not the town, then what?"

"You'll have to go back and find out."

"I'm taking Jennifer back before Rick forbids it after his bad experience, then I'm going back again."

"Better get started," he said. "I've got more timeshifting to do, as well."

Kayla went to the Victorian to rest up while Kevin headed to the Artists Loft.

CHAPTER TWENTY-FOUR
Kayla's Dilemma

KAYLA JUMPED UP FROM THE SOFA when the doorbell chimed and Jennifer appeared at the door.

"It's so lovely in here," Jennifer said upon entering.

"When I'm here I spend most of my time writing," Kayla said. "I'll do a lot more decorating when I get over my timeshifting addiction."

"Oh?"

"I'm spending a lot of time in the past."

"I suppose I do, too."

"Intellectually, maybe, but how about jumping back to the past for real with me?"

"I've been waiting for an opportunity. If it's for a long time, I'll have to have someone stay with Megan and Caleb. I'm so glad Sheriff Rick cleared up the mystery for people around town. We're giving the donations back that were collected from Mara's fundraiser."

"We don't need long for a timeshift I have in mind."

"Ooooo. What do you have in mind?"

"Book club."

Jennifer displayed a puzzled look. "Book club? Which book club?"

"How about the First Sycamore Falls Ladies Book Club of 1885?"

Jennifer's happy shriek nearly broke glass.

* * *

When Kayla and Jennifer timeshifted back to the 1885 library, Kayla stepped over to the writing table and pointed to the stationary with the names and waved Jennifer over to look closely.

"Here is the list of book club members," Kayla whispered.

Jennifer smiled and nodded in a "that's nice" way.

"Jennifer, did you have a direct ancestor or great-great aunt named Mary Dodd who was from around here?"

"I did! Great-Great Aunt Mary Dodd. She was my great grandfather's sister."

"I met her. She was a wonderful person," said Kayla. "How long did she live?"

"She died in 1919 during the Influenza epidemic. She was a nurse and traveled to St. Louis in 1918 to assist with the Red Cross efforts. My mother said she was also very outspoken opposing the resistance against black nurses joining the Red Cross. She was a feisty one and raised hell, pointing out the illogic of discriminating against qualified nurses."

"I am so *not* surprised," said Kayla. "I got to know her a little."

"Sadly, she got exposed while caring for a soldier returning from World War One and she died at age 59. Far too young." Do you think I could meet her?"

"We would need an hour or two and you'd want to wear something close to period clothes. You'll see some dresses shortly when the women start arriving."

Kayla showed Jennifer around the 1885 living room into the foyer, keeping careful track of time to avoid the two of them being seen.

Jennifer went to an open window and drew in the scent of outside. "Ahh, smell the lilacs. Spring in 1885. Is there anything better than this?"

"I've noticed before. It stirs those spring feelings inside."

"I think it's more pronounced at this time long before ours," said Jennifer.

"It's pure and real," said Kayla.

Noises came from outside.

They went back to the library. Moments later, women's voices came from the foyer.

"They're here," Kayla whispered.

Kayla led Jennifer to the bookcase to wait just out of sight of the women who entered the living room. After a couple of minutes, the women took seats, and engaged in quiet conversation. Kayla pointed out Mary and gave Jennifer a moment to listen to her voice. Jennifer retrieved a tissue from her bag.

Great-Great Aunt Mary's voice. Jennifer had never heard it.

She wiped her eyes then took a video.

Kayla put a hand on Jennifer's shoulder.

Ida entered the living room. The women discussed the prohibition vote again.

Jennifer gasped as Ida stepped into the library.

"Hello," Ida said. "Come join us."

Kayla looked at Jennifer. Jennifer nodded discretely.

"Thank you," said Kayla.

Ida led them to the group.

"Ladies, somebody brought two stowaways," Ida said with a smile.

She turned to Kayla and Jennifer. "Please introduce yourselves, ladies," she said.

"Kathryn."

"Jennifer."

The others greeted them with "welcomes."

"Do you want to stay?" Kayla whispered.

"Of course I do."

Mary and Anna made room for them to sit on the sofa.

Kayla waited for Jennifer to choose a spot next to Mary and then Kayla took a seat next to Anna.

To Jennifer's delight, Ida offered wine.

The conversation replayed minus Kayla's previous entry into the conversation. Mary started discussing women gaining the right to vote in response to comments about marriage, and time and place favorable for an independent woman. Jennifer mostly listened.

When the meeting wound down, Kayla and Jennifer excused themselves to the library.

"I would think you came from there, Kathryn and Jennifer," said Ida, smiling.

Kayla smiled and they reshelved the books.

CHAPTER TWENTY-FIVE
Kayla's Finding

KAYLA AND JENNIFER RETURNED to the present, left the farmhouse, and went to the Victorian. Kevin was waiting on the porch and greeted them when they arrived.

"Well?" he said.

"It was wonderful. Jennifer got to see her great-great aunt at the Book Club."

"I got a little bashful," Jennifer said.

"So what have you been up to, Kevin?" Kayla said.

"Rick came by here while you guys were in 1885."

"Oh, dear."

"He talked about sealing the library off."

"No!"

"Wait—hold on. I talked him out of doing it right away."

"Phew!"

"He's worried about the potential hazards."

"If he restricts access, won't that get around?"

"We talked about that and that's why he's not doing it right now. I'd still like to set up guided tours of the past."

Kayla shook her head. "No. We need to keep it secret if Rick stays away. The past still has something to tell me or needs some kind of help. I need to find out first. I don't want anyone interfering."

* * *

Jennifer stood in front of her full-length mirror checking the fit of her new dress again when Megan appeared at her door.

"Are you going out?" Megan said.

"Going back," replied Jennifer.

"To where?"

"1885. With Kayla."

"Oh! Can I go?"

"No, it's too risky."

"Aw, I'd love to see 1885. I'll stay right with you and not stray."

"You don't have anything to wear."

"I'll find something. Please?"

"I have to check with Kayla. I don't know how many can go at once. And what about Caleb? Is he going to want to go, too?"

"He won't. He doesn't want to go near that thing."

"Help me with my hair, please, with that clasp while I think about it," Jennifer said. Megan pulled Jennifer's long, straight hair back, combed through it, and fastened the wide clasp just above the shoulders. Jennifer stepped away from the mirror, grabbed her phone off the dresser, and contacted Kayla.

"I just got message from her. She says you can go back and observe Book Club for a few minutes."

"Thank you, Mom!" She threw her arms around her.

"Careful!" Jennifer said with a chuckle. "Okay—go change into one of your long dresses, then let's go."

* * *

Kayla met Jennifer and Megan at the front door of the farmhouse and led them to the library.

"Well," Kayla said, "Ready to visit a new century, Megan?"

"I am!"

Kevin was sitting on one of the chairs in the library, frowning.

"We'll be right back," Kayla said to him.

Kevin sat up and gave her a salute gesture, then went into the living room at stretched out on the sofa.

"He's mad because I'm hogging all the timeshifting time and Rick's threatened to restrict this thing to make it off limits. Okay, ready?"

Kayla, Jennifer, and Megan jumped their way back to the 1885 library.

Kayla showed Megan the writing table.

"Oh! Can I have that piece of paper with the writing?"

"We really shouldn't pilfer from the past," Jennifer said.

"It's okay," Kayla said, "this timeline deadends after we exit back to our time. So go ahead, Megan."

Megan picked up the paper with the names and the pen.

Jennifer frowned at her. Megan went and looked out the window.

Kayla waited so Megan could look around the library, outside, and into the living room, then motioned them both back to the bookcase when people started gathering out front.

"We can stay for another minute, and Megan, you can have a peek at people in the 1800s," whispered Kayla.

Megan relished the opportunity.

When Ida entered the living room, all three jumped back to the present.

Back in the present, Kayla went into the living room and stood in front of Kevin.

Jennifer and Megan left.

"I want to go somewhere else."

"No!"

"Not the past, you grungy beatnik. Come on. Get in your car and follow me."

She went to the front door and Kevin followed. Moments later, they each pulled away from the farmhouse, Kayla leading.

* * *

Eric T. Reynolds

Under a big sky, Kayla and Kevin stood among old worn headstones. Kayla let the wind blow her hair back as she turned her face toward the breeze. She wandered through the grassy medians. Many headstones had barely readable chiseled inscriptions. The readable ones showed typical lifespans from around 1820 to 1895 or 1830 to 1899, with occasional longer ones and others showing shorter lives ending during the Civil War. The really worn ones, she found fascinating and tried to decipher them.

Kevin stood bent over a tombstone. "Want to see this one?"

"Did you find Mrs. Barlow's?"

"No. It goes farther back."

Kayla strolled over and leaned toward it.

In Memory of
Mary Dodd
1860 - 1919
For her love of knowledge and her imagination was
strong
—Henry James

Kayla brought a tissue to her eyes.

"I'm, sorry. It's hard. She was my friend. It's like I just saw her. Will I ever see her again? Can I?"

Kevin put a hand on her shoulder. "Maybe you could go back again."

"And start all over with her friendship?"

"Take a longer trip."

"Thanks for understanding."

"You know I always will."

She dried her eyes and looked back at the inscription. "There's something. . ."

Kevin hugged her. "Something?"

[206]

"About that inscription." She looked through recent pictures on her phone.

"Look!" She showed him the picture of one of the bookmarked pages in *The Portrait of a Lady*. "There's the inscription! That's definitely Mary."

Kayla shrugged and they went back to their cars and drove to their homes.

CHAPTER TWENTY-SIX
Extended Stay

KAYLA WANTED TO SPEND MORE TIME with her friend, Mary Dodd.

"I'll keep watch," Kevin said, "and I'll let Rick know you've timeshifted for a while so he doesn't do anything."

"Don't tell him where I'm going. I don't want him looking for me."

"I'll pretend I don't know anything."

"That'll be easy, won't it?"

"Careful or I'll end up in your blog."

"You got it backwards, silly."

He hugged her and whispered, "Shut up and be careful."

"She reached for the book. "See you in a couple or three weeks."

She pulled out the book and timeshifted her way back to the 1885 spring day.

Later, after going through the replay of joining the Book Club, she stood at the end of Sycamore Falls' dirt Main Street and went to find the rooming house Ida recommended.

She decided she would go as Kathryn.

It was especially nice out today.

A rooming house on a side street had a sign that said "Single Men Only." She walked past it and came to the one Ida recommended, a large white house with clapboard siding and covered porch similar to her foursquare farmhouse but bigger. Several women sat there in wooden chairs enjoying the weather.

Kayla headed up the porch steps. Among the women there sat Mary who flashed a smile.

Kayla wanted to greet her twenty-first century style, but remained reserved like the other women. She smiled at Mary and headed up through the front door into a large reception room. Several women sat in chairs around the room and the boarding manager was at a small table toward the back next to a window. She stood and approached Kayla.

She arranged a room for her and explained the house rules.

Kayla took the key and visited her room.

The chamber pot on the floor beneath the edge of her wooden twin-size bed reminded her of when this was and what that part of life would be like for however long she stayed. Across from her was a writing table with kerosene lamp next to a small chest of drawers with wash basin and water pitcher. The room had a very slight ammonia-like smell from the tallow and lye soap used in those days to wash the linens and other laundry. It was a fresh, pleasant smell.

Kayla relaxed the rest of the day and joined the other boarders for dinner at the long table in the dining room. She perked up when Mary sat across from her.

"Good evening," Mary said.

"And to you," replied Kayla, maintaining the low key manner.

Kayla appreciated the variety of food including cornbread, vegetables, and cheese. There was plenty of meat, but she opted for a lighter diet. No one paid attention to her food preferences.

After dinner, Mary took Kayla aside to the living room where they sat on a sofa against the wall and talked.

"I'm reading *The Portrait of a Lady* said Mary, "and I think I'll be finished by next book club meeting, although I'm not a fast reader."

"Oh," said Kayla, "neither am I. I had plenty of time to read it when I lived in Kansas City."

"You must tell me what it's like there."

"Yes, of course. There's much to tell." And Kayla thought: Shall I tell you about rush hour traffic and the new airport? "There are many fascinating things there."

"How does a single woman make it there by herself?" asked Mary.

"I was born in Kansas City and I have some family there, cousins and such. I know my way around the city."

"You must show me around there someday!"

"That would be so much fun."

Mary smiled and gazed through a window. "Say, if it's beautiful out tomorrow, let's go on a picnic lunch!"

"I'd love to," said Kayla.

* * *

The next morning, when she met Mary in the expansive kitchen, Mary said, "They have everything here." She pointed around to skillets, pans, and copper pots hanging on one wall. Wash basins and a pitcher sat on a workbench-like counter against a wall next to a cast iron wood-burning stove with venting pipe that curved up and out through the wall.

"I rose early and prepared some things," Mary said, standing over an open book on the counter.

"What is that?" Kayla asked.

"It's *Science in the Kitchen* by Ella Eaton Kellogg. I'm reading the chapter on Picnic Dinners."

"What does it suggest?"

"Sandwiches are in order. We have several choices. Would a beef tongue sandwich suit you?"

"I should like to know some other choices."

"Yes, of course. We aren't a large party with a crowd to impress. We shall make it simple. Bread with knife for slicing, cheese, jellies, and pound cake, which was made yesterday, and pickles."

"That will do nicely," Kayla said.

Mary said, "I am familiar with everything and I can do the final preparation. You may wish to relax in the living room."

"I'll resist falling asleep," Kayla said. "A lot of activity in the home early this morning around six o'clock woke me. Decent people are in bed at that hour."

Mary suppressed a giggle. "Oh, Kathryn, you are so funny."

"Where shall we go?" asked Kayla.

"My grandfather has a ranch we could walk to if you're of a mind to. It has a pasture up on the hill next to it."

"Yes, that sounds perfect."

Mary went over to a table and opened a small crock, smiled, and looked at Kayla. "Cheese, fresh from the farm," she said. Grabbing a small metal bucket with lid, she cut off some cheese and placed it inside along with the other items: bread from the breadbox and two apples from a fruit basket completing today's fixings for lunch.

"How convenient," Kayla said.

"A lunch bucket is always available," said Mary. "And we're always welcome to take food if we have plans for lunch outside the home."

Mary picked up a canteen and handed it to Kayla. "A stop by the well outside and we're on our way," she said carrying the lunch bucket as they left the kitchen.

They went down a cross street and got to a road that ran along the edge of town.

As they turned onto the road, Mary said, "Grandfather has an Indian man working for him. He lives in Grandfather's house. He doesn't get out much and I want to invite him to go with us. Do you mind?"

"No, of course not. It'll be fun. What's his name?"

"George Crow. Grandfather hired him several years ago."

They walked a minute more and Mary said, "Kansas City must be exciting. I do hope we can go sometime."

Kayla didn't think she wanted to travel that far from the farmhouse library. Then again, it'd be a chance to see 1880s Kansas City that she'd never have again. But to risk it was beyond what she considered safe.

They walked for another half hour and came to a dirt road that led to a big Victorian house nestled in a grove of trees surrounded by prairie and some low hills.

Mary led Kayla into the house.

Kayla thought her own Victorian was grand, but Mary's grandfather's house was everything it could be.

"Grandfather should be around in a moment," Mary said.

Kayla took in the decor, admiring the paintings on the walls: Western mountain scenes, portraits of men and women.

Someone entered the room, interrupting Kayla's concentration.

"Oh, hello, George," Mary said.

"Hello, Mary," said George.

Mary introduced Kayla and George to each other.

"George, will you join us for a picnic lunch?" Mary said.

"I will ask Mr. Dodd," said George, turning to head into a side hallway.

After a few moments, Mary's Grandfather and George returned together. George stepped over toward the women and smiled.

Grandfather Dodd nodded. "Enjoy your lunch and bon appetit, and watch for cattle," he said as George and the women left.

They ascended the small hill and reached its crest. Sycamore Falls of 1885 was in view to their north. Kayla recognized a few of the brick buildings along Main Street and a couple of houses. The grand courthouse dominated the

[212]

scene. Grandfather Dodd's herd roamed the valley below this hill while ranch hands on horseback circled the cattle and an enthusiastic dog herded the perimeter, mostly staying out of the way.

The pooch might better serve if Grandfather Dodd decides to raise sheep, thought Kayla, but she was no expert.

She and Mary halted when George stopped and pointed to the west. A higher hill with a few trees near its base dominated the landscape over there. Near its top stood a small structure, Ida's farmhouse.

George made a sweeping gesture with his hand. "This was my people's land."

Mary placed her hand on his shoulder.

"I'm so sorry your people were forced to move," she said.

He looked to the sky and smiled.

Kayla smiled, too. "It's a beautiful area," she said.

Mary looked to her feet, standing on a large flat imbedded rock.

"Maybe this is a good place to have lunch," she said.

She placed the lunch bucket onto the rock slab and sat while George crouched next to her.

Kayla sat crossed legged and helped Mary retrieve their lunch.

George said a quiet prayer to the spirit of the animal that provided the meat in two of the sandwiches.

Kayla gazed skyward. Puffy clouds floated across the afternoon sky, casting shadows that draped across the grassy hills.

One of the shadows reached the three of them on their hilltop perch bringing a momentary cool breeze.

"How refreshing," said Kayla. She looked out across the rippling sea of green, the shadows spotting the land to the distant horizon. She wanted to stay up here forever with her new friends, and tried not to think about having to leave them eventually.

George closed his eyes and faced the breeze.

After a while he opened them and looked around.

Mary broke the silence. "Kathryn, you must bring a hat next time."

"I need to buy one," Kayla said, combing her windblown hair back with her fingers.

"Tomorrow we go find you a hat." Mary sighed and smiled.

Shopping for a hat in 1885 Kansas, a rare opportunity.

After a while, George began to stir. "Are you ladies ready to go?" he said.

Mary sat forward and took hold of the bucket. "Yes, it is time."

All three stood together.

Kayla shielded her eyes. One last gaze around to take in the view and compare to its modern equivalent from her memory. But first, she stepped aside, snapped a couple of pictures, and took a short video.

The hike and picnic wasn't at all strenuous but for the slight sunburn on her cheeks and nose. Back in her room, she tossed her shoes onto the floor, crashed onto the bed, and slept the rest of the afternoon to a breeze flowing from her window until the slam of her door startled her awake. She should have used a doorstop.

Then with the door latched, she dozed again. She woke later to curtains sailing inward. It was almost time for supper. She freshened up using her 1885 facilities.

That was interrupted by a knock at the door.

"Kathryn?"

"Yes?"

"Are you coming to dinner?"

"Yes—I'll be ready in a moment."

"I'll wait then."

Kayla didn't recognize the voice. It wasn't Mary or the house manager. She fixed her hair quickly and answered the door. A middle aged woman with strawberry blonde hair stood there with a slight smile. "Mrs. Marshall sent me up, not wanting you to miss dinner. Most everyone is seated."

"Oh, then let's not keep them waiting," Kayla said, trying to mask her embarrassment.

Supper was uneventful and Mary and Kayla exchanged a few whispers about going shopping the next day.

* * *

Kayla hoped she wasn't conspicuous in her makeshift period dress. Maybe Mary taking her hat shopping was just the start of righting her wardrobe for visits to this time, which she hoped she could do again. At least she would have a "local" to assist in selection. She couldn't ask for a better way to ramp up an 1885 wardrobe.

They walked along Main Street. It looked much the same as in the previous 1885 visits. Nothing like old Hollywood portrayals. People went about their business and the town seemed healthy.

"There we are," Mary said, pointing to a sign that said "Millinery" extending overhead from a storefront.

"We'll find you a nice hat here, one of the new styles."

"Oh, nothing fancy," Kayla said.

They stepped in and the smell of fabrics and old wooden fixtures greeted them. She found a plain hat. Its modest brim slanted forward and the hat resembled a fedora with a bow on the side.

* * *

Kayla eventually abandoned her reluctance to consider a train trip with Mary to Kansas City. A few days after the picnic, they were purchasing tickets for the next train scheduled to depart around mid-morning.

[215]

"The price is less than it was last year when my sister went on her trip to Kansas City," Mary said.

Kayla spent $3.52 on two tickets, insisting she pay for both.

"My treat. It's my pleasure to show you where I came from," she said, not taking no for a response. Where she came from, indeed. Would it be possible to run into Great Grandma Gayle? She doubted that, as fascinating as that would be.

She clutched her bag and patted the book inside.

"There's a ladies' car if you prefer that," said the man behind the counter.

Kayla declined that option and Mary agreed.

"How fast does the train go?" Kayla asked.

"This is a fast one," he said with some pride. "It can go forty or fifty miles an hour, but you won't be going that fast. Probably around thirty. The tracks are in good condition, but thirty miles an hour is safe for passengers. You'll be in Kansas City late today with some stops along the way for coal and water, Buffalo Creek, Topeka, Lawrence, and others. And there's a Fred Harvey Restaurant at the Topeka depot stop."

"Oh," Kayla said, turning to Mary, "we won't go hungry then. I also insist buying you a nice meal there."

"I must worry about taking advantage of your generosity."

"I won't hear of it."

After the conductor shouted "All aboard!" Kayla and Mary got onto their car and chose their seats. The seats were leather-padded bench style. Men, already seated, looked them up and down and Kayla was careful not to make eye contact although there was one interesting-looking man wearing spectacles who sat in the back, holding an open book. He was Kayla's image of a stereotypical nineteenth century man. She tried not to stare and stood aside in case Mary wanted a window seat. Mary declined and Kayla sat next to the window, followed onto the seat by Mary. Scanning around the car, Kayla was happy to see a sign next to a door at the forward section that said "Ladies Closet." She pointed discretely and whispered to Mary, "Is that?"

"The ladies toilet, yes," Mary whispered back.

"Good to know." Kayla nodded her approval and made herself comfortable with the partially open window allowing in a breeze. Steam hissed from the giant locomotive. Mary stashed her bag in the long whicker-like basket mounted above the window. Kayla had no intention of physically parting from her own bag.

She stole a quick glance at the studious man. He didn't look up.

The chug-chug, hiss of the locomotive started and Sycamore Falls slowly passed behind.

After a while, rolling countryside slid by.

"I've never gone so fast," said Mary.

It was a snail's pace to Kayla, but an experience unmatched in normal time. She dozed as the rolling woodlands eased by. The Flint Hills were a ways behind them now. She'd seen landscape like this from Interstate-35 between Kansas City and Emporia, but now there were no modern farms or roads or water towers in the distance. It was as close to pristine land that she ever expected to see. This is what she figured Mara imagined of her people's land before white settlers.

She assumed they were headed straight toward Topeka, but she knew not how close.

If she had a better idea, she'd look for familiar landmarks to see if any existed yet.

A stop must have been coming up. The train slowed.

The conductor announced: "Next stop, Buffalo Creek with stage connection."

Kayla figured there'd be a stage coach connection since a stage in the distance had been traveling along a course parallel to the train at times.

The landscape crawled by now as they eased to a stop. The depot was a lonely little building along the tracks with aging board and batten siding covered by fading whitewash. A ratty cloth awning flapped in the breeze. The window beneath it had an empty space where a pane had fallen out, a box of glass shards sat on the ground below the window.

Kayla couldn't take her eyes off the old place: an "old" building in 1885, a structure already in decay so long ago. Kayla tried to put that in perspective.

A woman and boy emerged through a rickety door from the building's dark interior and were escorted onto a train car ahead. The massive engine started to pull the train forward and Kayla could just make out a distant carriage with its team of horses racing across the land leaving a wake of dust.

The train gradually picked up speed and the smooth ride lulled Kayla into a drowsy state; she was out in a minute.

She took a long nap and woke when Mary stirred.

Moments later, the conductor announced, "Topeka. Next stop, Topeka."

They entered the outskirts of the 1885 Capital City, finally slowed, and pulled alongside the depot.

"One hour," the conductor said. "Board in one hour or be left."

"Oooh," said Mary, "let's go." They headed off the car and it felt good to stretch one's legs. Inside the depot, they found Harvey's Restaurant.

"How fancy," said Mary, "table linens and fine china. Can we afford this?"

Kayla convinced Mary they should get a table quickly. The wait staff brought menus, which had a variety of items.

"Please order anything you like," Kayla said.

[218]

The Artifacts: A Flint Hills Story

The hash browns hit the spot for Kayla while Mary enjoyed a steak. They dined until the conductor stepped in and announced boarding time was in fifteen minutes. After a visit to the ladies closet, Kayla and Mary went out and boarded their car. The mid-afternoon sun was hot and Kayla was thankful for the cross breeze through the car.

"Tell me about Anna," Kayla said.

"What do you mean? What would you like to know?"

"How long have you known her?"

"A long time, since we were little girls. Her father owns a saw mill on the north end of town. We see them in church every Sunday. I spent most of my days on our ranch and didn't get into town much. I saw her in school, which was a long walk for me. Ma and Pa took me into town to for church and to visit other kids my age sometimes, but that's most of my time with Anna."

"Do you think she's very nice?"

"Usually, but she made fun of the some kids and I didn't like that."

"Why did she do that?"

"Who knows what drives people to hurt others. One day, I went to the saw mill with her and Old Tom, an old Indian man, was sitting by the stream that ran next to the mill and Anna's father started yelling at him to get out, then kicked him. Old Tom protested and Anna's father ran inside and got his shotgun, fired into the air, and threatened him. He said he'd shoot him if he ever came around there anymore and that he didn't want him near his girls."

"*His* girls? How terrible. Was there a problem?"

"No, I loved Old Tom and he told me many stories when I saw him in town. He never did anything bad to Anna, me, or to anyone."

"I'm afraid Anna picked up some of her father's attitudes and many of his cynical ways."

[219]

"Is Old Tom still living?"

Mary lowered her gaze. "No, he died about ten years ago. A group of men from Mound Grove accused him of looking at a woman a certain way. The men found him in front of one of the stores where he was working one of his odd jobs, dragged him onto the street and beat him terribly. They hurt him so much, he died from that."

Mary clutched her stomach, bent forward, and moaned. "It makes me sick every time I think of it."

Kayla put her arm around Mary's shoulder. "I'm sorry! We don't have to talk about it."

Mary dried her tears and said. "It was awful. I saw the whole thing. I was only fourteen years of age."

Kayla reached into her bag and fumbled for a roll of Tums. She retrieved a tablet and handed it to Mary. "This will help you feel better. I got these in Kansas City."

Mary took the Tums and consumed it. "Oh, that's much better. Thank you."

Mary removed her hat and fanned her face with it, closed her eyes and let the breeze from the window blow through her hair.

Kayla wanted to offer the rest of the roll to Mary to keep, but decided she couldn't.

She reached into her bag and felt for the timeshifting book.

Mary interrupted Kayla's thoughts. "Oh, what's that ahead?"

Kayla leaned toward the window. Men on horses rode alongside the engine.

"Oh, no," Kayla said. "Are we going to be robbed?"

Mary stood and poked her head through the window.

"Those are lawmen."

The train slowed.

"Slowing down reminds me of one of those math problems," Kayla said. "If one train leaves the station at 10:00 AM and travels 60 miles per hour, and a second train leaves one hour later and travels 80 miles per hour, what time will the second train overtake the first? Oh, I hate problems like that."

"May I borrow your fancy writing pen?" said Mary.

Kayla retrieved it from her bag and a piece a paper.

"Thank you," said Mary. "Well, you find how long it takes each train to travel the same distance and you go from there." She did some figuring on paper. "You find the second train will overtake the first at 2:00PM." She smiled and returned the pen and paper to Kayla.

"I am impressed, Mary," said Kayla.

She's an avid reader and a math whiz. I hope she's able to utilize her talents, if she desires to.

Kayla finally noticed the dark clouds to the south.

A few minutes later, the conductor stood at the front of the car.

"Ladies and gentlemen, they just got a telegraph message in Ottawa warning that a tornado is spinning its way on a path in front of us. We're going to wait it out here."

"Oh, dear," said Mary.

An 1885 early warning system, Kayla thought. "My that's smart thinking to send the deputies up to warn us," she said.

"They do think of everything," said Mary. "Do you ever wonder how people years ago managed to avoid disasters like we do now? We have so many things now they didn't used to have. I am grateful to live in these times. What did they do before the telegraph?"

"Yes, indeed," said Kayla.

The conductor added, "You may step off the train while we're stopped if you like."

Kayla and Mary opted to hop off.

Kayla recognized the landscape, rolling woodland and prairie like around Lawrence. Beyond the farthest hill to the south, dark clouds dominated the sky.

She reached into her bag for her camera and pulled it out, keeping it hidden with both hands. If a tornado appeared, she wanted to get a photo. The closer still-sundrenched landscape stood stark against the dark clouds that formed a contrasting backdrop.

She and Mary walked over to where the lawmen were talking to the engineer and conductor.

Kayla mimicked Mary by smiling and nodding to the men tipping their hats.

"You ladies needn't worry," said one of the lawmen, "that ole tornado won't likely backtrack once it's passed on by. You see, a tornado is just ferocious swirling wind and it has a typical pattern that can be predicted, but sometimes it can double cross you." He tipped his hat, nodded, and smiled.

Kayla chuckled at his effort to mansplain it, my how times haven't changed, she thought. She and Mary turned to walk back to their car. Kayla stepped away from the line of cars to savor the breezy air and gaze at the approaching dark clouds. The breeze cooled her. Around beyond the front of the train, the dark clouds started their slow roll to the north. Kayla figured that was ground zero for the tornado.

"All aboard!" yelled the conductor while the lawmen disbanded and got on their horses.

Menacing clouds from the southwest drew nearer.

"Let's go!" said Mary, starting to trot back to their car. She reached for Kayla's hand. Kayla lunged for it and tripped as she started to run.

Mary stopped to help her up as did the man with spectacles.

Kayla quickly brushed off the front of her dress and rubbed her stinging hands on the skirt, then ran toward the car with the others. She heard shouts of "There!" and "It's on the ground!" They were in the path of it now. The train would have to get them out of the way. Move at right angles, Kayla had heard before, so that seemed like the best thing. After they settled into their seats, the train started chugging, gradually building up speed over the next minute or two until they were rolling across the land faster than before. Kayla hoped the ticket taker was right that this train could go faster. It appeared the tracks were mostly straight up ahead.

Mary seemed to be enjoying the ride, if a bit nervous.

Kayla reached into her bag to fumble for the book, sighed when she took hold of it. It didn't spill out during her fall.

A sudden shake threw her shoulder toward the window. The gust front just passed overhead. A ragged squall line slid over. Turbulent clouds rolled up behind and inside it. Behind the dark front, green clouds indicated the worst of it to come. Mary grabbed Kayla's arm. Kayla hugged her, which seemed to reassure both. She glanced around at the other passengers. Two men were looking out a window toward the incoming storm, mumbling. The spectacled man stood and waddled his way up toward Kayla and Mary and sat across from them. "Are you ladies all right?" He crouched to view out their window.

"Oh, yes, thank you," said Mary.

"Yes," repeated Kayla. "That's some storm."

The man nodded. "If you'd like company, I'm happy to oblige."

"Thank you," Kayla said. At least he's not pushy, she thought.

"Good day, then." He nodded and stood to go to another seat a ways toward the front of the car.

Kayla returned her attention to the storm. Rain marched toward them. She slid the upper window up a ways before rain started tapping against the glass. Following that, hail pelted the roof with a racket loud enough to make her ears ring. Hail littered the ground outside. Soon it was so thick, that the ground looked snow covered.

They continued to race along the track. Kayla kept her fingers crossed.

"You are so calm, Kathryn," Mary said.

I must be putting up a good front, thought Kayla.

"When I get nervous, I like to sing."

"I'd like to hear you sing," said Mary.

"This is a song about being on a train," Kayla said. "I first heard this when I was little."

"It's called 'Five Hundred Miles'."

Kayla sang softly.

"If you missed the train I'm on
You will know that I am gone
You can hear the whistle blow a hundred miles
A hundred miles, a hundred miles,
A hundred miles, a hundred miles
You can hear the whistle blow a hundred miles. . ."

Kayla smiled. "I wish I had my guitar."

"That's beautiful," said Mary. "I must have the music for it."

Kayla thought: It won't be written until 1961, but maybe I can help.

"I've never seen the music for sale, but I'll write it down for you."

She retrieved some paper and wrote the lyrics with annotations showing the chords throughout, then drew a crude treble clef with the melody score. She double checked it silently and gave it to Mary.

"Thank you. I'll practice this. Kathryn, are you enjoying our time?"

Fear shot through Kayla. She looked at Mary. Oh my God! Does she know about my timeshifting and is she in on it?

"Oh my," said Mary. "You look like you've seen a ghost. I do hope you are enjoying our time together."

"Oh, Mary," Kayla said, embarrassed, "yes, I love the time we've spent. Such an adventure!"

"I'm so glad you are. Thank you for the song. I'm thrilled to have it."

Mary sat back and sighed. She looked at the music Kayla sketched out for her and sang it softly. Kayla noted another talent and added that to Mary's list. Her voice was far more beautiful than Kayla's.

"Mary, your voice is beautiful," Kayla said.

"Please sing with me," Mary said.

They sang the song together and attracted several passengers who moved to nearby seats.

Kayla reached down to check on her bag sitting on the floor.

As she started to reach inside it, she slammed into the back of the next seat, the bag ripping from her hand. Mary toppled over. Kayla grabbed hold of the seat. The impact knocked the wind out of her. Chaos filled the car as the train skidded to a stop. Mary put her hand to a bleeding cut on her chin, then held her knee and groaned

"Are you all right?" asked Kayla.

"I think so."

The spectacled man minus his glasses stood and turned to face everyone.

"Here comes the conductor," he said. He bent down to check on his things. Kayla leaned down and looked for her bag under the seat in front of them. There it was, several rows ahead, its contents scattered about, and *no book*.

Please! No!

She stood up. "Excuse me, Mary." She scooted by her and searched under the seats ahead.

What if I get trapped in 1885? Can I get back without the book? Can I survive here? She thought about it while crawling on the floor. I do have new friends. It would be fun to consider, living in this time but could she live in this time?

"Ladies and gentlemen," said the conductor.

She realized it wasn't "ladylike" for her to be on the floor like this in 1885. Whatever—she didn't care.

"We have stopped the train hard," the conductor continued, "to avoid the tornado where it is now crossing the tracks ahead. We barely missed it. Now we ask everyone to move to the car ahead of us. This car is derailed and must be unhitched from the train along with the car behind it."

"If you please, sir," Kayla said, standing. "I've lost some things. May I look for them?"

"Make haste," he said.

Others continued gathering objects from their seats and the floor. The formerly spectacled man continued to look around his area. Kayla continued to look.

"Everyone off the car right away," said the conductor. Kayla dashed from seat to seat in a panic looking for her book. The conductor waved everyone to the exit and ushered them off the car. Kayla started to hyperventilate as she started to follow Mary out. The spectacled man had found his glasses. He gave a polite nod to Kayla and Mary as they approached the exit. The conductor made his way to him and started to take his arm to usher him out.

"Time to go," he said.

"Just a moment," the man said shaking free while he ducked into the men's closet for a moment. He left the door open and fumbled around with his bag. "Time to go," the conductor insisted. The man joined the line to exit after he found a spot.

[226]

Kayla and Mary stepped off the car, followed the line to the next car, and entered. There were still some seats. They found a place at the back. The spectacled man tried to enter, but the conductor waved him away, gesturing to him to get in the car in front of the one Kayla and Mary boarded.

"Oh, that's too bad," Kayla said. "He is so friendly."

"That he is," said Mary. "He is from Sycamore Falls, you know."

"I didn't know that."

"He's a school teacher. George Fielding."

"He seems the knowledgeable type," said Kayla.

"He is very much," said Mary.

"He also seems like a nice person."

"He has advanced things at the local school."

"Too bad he isn't in our book club."

"Ida decided ladies only, but she might have him join us sometime as a guest."

Kayla realized she might be around for that now and tried to remain positive and accept the possibility.

Clanking noises outside.

The car shook as the engineer outside unhitched the car behind them. After the engine started chugging, they pulled away and Kayla got a view of the unhitched car stalled on the track, her book trapped inside it—her way back to the present.

There must be a way to retrieve it!

The engine chugged faster and they started on their way.

Kayla patted her abdomen to check her money pouch. Still snug and safe. At least she had that. But no amount of money would get her back to her time.

Mary tapped Kayla's arm. "What's the matter, Kathryn?"

"I lost my book and diary, and I want them back; I had some other things in my bag that spilled out."

[227]

"Don't worry. I think the lawmen will be back to search the car or send people up from Ottawa to do that to prevent losing things to bandits."

Mary leaned over Kayla toward the window. "Look at those trees damaged by the tornado," she said.

Kayla glanced at the swath of uprooted trees that ran into the distance. She strained to see the tracks ahead where the tornado had plowed over there. Mostly clear from what she could see. Large limbs strewn around and a wagon wheel tangled in limbs. A couple of small limbs up against the side of the tracks, hopefully not close enough to cause any worry. The engineer evidently decided to be cautious for the train slowed to what Kayla guessed was about fifteen miles per hour as they closed in on the tornado crossing. That was an idea. In normal time, they should put up "Tornado Crossing" signs on I-35 and 70.

The massive steam engine built up speed as it hauled them across the eastern Kansas countryside.

Kayla usually couldn't sleep in a moving vehicle, but managed to drift off again. She dreamed about nineteenth century book clubs, nineteenth century sensibilities, and tornadoes.

* * *

It was mostly a long, fitful sleep and she woke to late evening sun glittering off the Kansas River out to their left. Neighborhoods of small houses in Kansas City, Kansas, some brick, some wooden, dominated the view on the hillsides, with brick industrial buildings closer to the river, and spanning the Kansas and Missouri Rivers, a steel bridge or two.

The conductor announced, "Atchison, Topeka, and Santa Fe Depot, Kansas City, Missouri." If you are missing any items from the tornado avoidance stop, the good people of Ottawa searched the car brought what they could by horseback to the depot. You may claim your property there after you disembark. Thank you from Atchison Topeka and Santa Fe Railroad."

Kayla sighed. "Oh, how wonderful," she said to Mary.

* * *

Inside the depot, ATSF had set up a table full of small items, mostly pocket watches, pendants, brooches, hair combs, and other personal items. Kayla and Mary queued up at the end of a line of passengers, some she recognized, where ARSF workers sifted through the items as passengers reached the table.

Kayla felt the anticipation of receiving her book. The other items, she could do without. She planned to suppress any loud woohoo! when she received the book.

But when she reached the front, after searching through the items, the ARSF worker produced no book.

Kayla's knees almost gave out.

She pleaded with the worker to do a more thorough search. He complied, but came up with nothing.

"Could the book have been given to someone else?" she said.

The man shook his head. "No book. There were no books among the items."

Kayla broke down and Mary rushed to console her.

"Let's go eat, dear Kathryn," she said. "We'll figure out a way to find your book."

Kayla lowered her head. "All right."

"There's a Harvey's Restaurant here, too. Let's go."

They made their way through the small crowd.

Kayla was looking down as she walked and bumped into someone.

"Oh! Excuse me," she said. She looked up.

"My fault," said George Fielding.

"Mary stepped over. "Hello, Mr. Fielding."

"Good evening, ladies. Are you planning on dining at Harvey's? If so, will you do me the honor of letting me join you?"

"Yes, of course," Kayla said.

"Yes," echoed Mary.

George offered each arm to them.

Mary took one. Kayla took the other.

How quaint, Kayla thought as they found a table.

Linen and fine place settings just like the other Harvey's.

They ordered their meals. As they waited, George reached into his satchel.

"Does this belong to either of you?" he said, pulling a book from his bag.

"Oh!" Kayla almost screamed, but retained her composure. "Yes! Thank you, Mr. Fielding!"

"It got mixed up with my things all thrown into the men's closet. I beg your pardon for that."

"Mr. Fielding, it makes no difference where you found it. I'm so thankful." She cradled the book for a moment and let out a sigh that seemed like she'd been holding for hours.

"I wanted to return it at once," he said, "but after they separated us, I kept it safe with some other things that I believe are yours."

"I can get those whenever it's convenient," she said.

"And I also would like to ask you both something. I am here in Kansas City by invitation of Professor Schwartz of Westport College where I earned my degree. I haven't seen him since I graduated ten years ago and I'm going to his house." He pulled out his pocket watch. "He will have a carriage waiting for me in an hour. I am sure you ladies are most welcome to come with me if that's your fancy. I will be staying the night in his large house. Perhaps you could board there, too, if you've no other plans. I'm sure you'd be most welcome." George pulled an envelope from his satchel, opened it. Here's his letter."

Dear Mr. Fielding:

As several years have passed since you completed your studies here at Westport College, Mrs. Schwartz and I would take this opportunity to extend an invitation to you and your colleagues for a visit to our home here in Kansas City. I endeavor to stay current with my former students. I expect after your exemplary performance here at Westport College that you are settling into a productive and rewarding career, and I would appreciate some time for good conversation with you and your colleagues should anyone accompany you. We offer our home to all of you for lodging and the fine cooking of our live-in chef.

Best regards,

Professor John Schwartz
Westport College

"That would be lovely," said Mary. She glanced at Kayla. "Kathryn?"
"Yes, I'd love to go."

* * *

When nightfall started to settle in, a horse-drawn carriage arrived outside the depot. They climbed onto the luxurious facing seats and rode through the streets of Kansas City. They had a bit of a hill to scale from the depot area and were soon among the relatively tall buildings, monoliths in the twilight. "I wonder if we'll see that tall building going up, the highest west of the Mississippi River," said Mary. "I saw an illustration of it in a magazine."

The driver was listening. "We'll go by it if you wish," he said. "It's called the New England Life building. Since night is

[231]

settling in, it might be hard to see all of it. The gas street lights might show it; the city will start testing electric street lights in a couple of years. A few homes west of Main Street here have electric lights, but no one else has them yet. So by then, this area will be lit up like day during the night.

They rounded several blocks. When they reached 9th Street, there it was, a seven-story metal skeleton under construction just visible.

Mary moaned with awe. "I've never seen anything like that."

The building still stood in Kayla's time. So fascinating to see it being built in a way that it will stand for over a century.

They went to 11th Street and turned east. Clothing shops, a millinery, a shoe store, and women's "undergarment" shops beneath awnings lined the street.

The driver pretended to whisper. "I've heard people suggest a nickname for this street."

"Petticoat Lane," said Kayla.

Mary smiled.

"You've heard mention of that?" the driver said.

"I'm from Kansas City," said Kayla proudly.

* * *

Professor and Mrs. Schwartz greeted and welcomed them into the tastefully-adorned parlor of their large home.

Professor and Mrs. Schwartz offered them to sit and went to a butler's table that held a carafe of wine, five glasses, and a small block of cheese then moved the table to the guests.

They all spent a few minutes sipping wine and chatting.

"Is this West Hill Vineyard's 1876 vintage?" Mary said. She looked at Kayla.

"It certainly is," said Schwartz. "I'd buy the whole inventory if I could with the upcoming ban on its way here from over in Kansas. No telling how soon Missouri will follow suit."

[232]

They spent a while discussing that and Mary finally stood and went over to the square piano in the corner.

"Professor Schwartz, what kind of piano is this?" she asked him.

"That is a pianoforte. Would you like a demonstration?"

"Wonderful."

The others agreed. Schwartz rose and spoke to Mrs. Schwartz.

"Would you ask Diana to come in, please?"

She nodded and left. A minute later, a young woman entered the parlor with Mrs. Schwartz. After introductions, Diana sat at the pianoforte and played some scales. Mary waited for Diana to nod approval before standing over her to watch. Diana opened a compartment to the left of the keyboard and adjusted some knobs.

"These change the tone and sound of the instrument," she said. "I can also adjust the keys in pitch and I can also make the instrument sound like a harp in different ways."

"Thank you," said Mary. She returned to her place on the sofa. Diana played a familiar Beethoven piece much to the delight of the guests. The evening passed by, Diana stood to light applause, excused herself, and left.

"Now," said Schwartz, "Mr. Fielding, "I'd like to hear about your post-college life." Schwartz turned to Mary. "Ladies, you are welcome to stay if you wish. You might be tired from your trip. Mrs. Schwartz will show you to your rooms whenever you'd like to turn in."

We're being politely dismissed so they can talk, thought Kayla. She could understand if they wanted to simply catch up on things. "Yes, of course, Professor. Your hospitality is most appreciated."

Mary nodded and they followed Mrs. Schwartz who led them from the parlor, up the panel-lined curved stairway.

Kayla's room presented a fireplace, canopied bed, writing table. There was no wash basin or chamber pot.

Mrs. Schwartz stepped in and gestured down the hall. "The toilet and bath are down this hall." Please join us for breakfast in the morning. Diana will knock around eight-thirty." She smiled and left.

"Thank you." Not too terribly early, but earlier than she liked on vacation. After a moment, Mary knocked quietly and cracked open the door.

"Goodnight, Kathryn," she whispered.

"I was tempted to stay up with the men for a short while," Kayla whispered back.

"I was, too," whispered Mary as she left.

As she settled onto bed, Kayla knew it'd never be this quiet outside in normal time. Up here on the bluff above the Missouri River in what would one day be called Kansas City's Northeast neighborhoods. She would have to see if this smaller mansion still stood in normal time. Typically, she'd be able to hear distant highway noise and river activity. Here in 1885, noise pollution was minimal. Even in normal time Sycamore Falls, there was noise at night. The steady thump-thump of the oil wells actually had a lulling effect in the middle of the night. But here in a city, the quiet was strangely beautiful.

Sitting on the edge of the bed, she grabbed her bag and felt the book in inside, which was reassuring. She felt relaxed now, a welcomed feeling after that earlier stressful time.

Sobbing in a nearby room broke the silence.

Mary!

She jumped up and went out into the hall. The sobbing came from the room diagonally across from her own. The other bedroom doors were cracked or wide open so she assumed Mary didn't occupy those. Kayla tapped her fingernail against the door.

[234]

"Come in," said Mary, her voice quivering.

Kayla entered and sat next to Mary on the edge of the bed.

She put her arm around her. "What's the matter, my friend?"

"I was thinking about Old Tom and what those men did to him. It was a long time ago, but it still hurts."

"They should have been tried for murder." Kayla realized her comment wasn't consoling.

"Some people in town wanted the sheriff to arrest them, but he wouldn't. He said there weren't any witnesses and the men weren't around since they came over from Mound Grove."

"What about you?"

"I was too young. I went to the sheriff and he didn't take me seriously. I just wanted justice for Old Tom and for the sheriff to pursue them in Mound Grove."

"What a tragedy!"

"All along, I wanted Old Tom to be happy. His people were forced to move to Oklahoma and I know he was sad and angry about that. People were nice to him like the yarn shopkeeper. I had other friends my age, but I don't think he had any friends in town besides me."

Mary dried her eyes. "I think I'll go to bed now."

Kayla sighed. "I'm so sorry for you. Yes, it's time for bed. Good night."

* * *

Kayla slept reasonably well that night, considering Mary's sadness and how quiet it was. It wasn't much different from the boarding house and she could get used to the quiet. The full moon spilled its ghostly radiance onto her face in the middle of the night. She gazed at it for a while and let her eyes adjust to its brilliance. She could make out the dark "seas" and found what she believed was the Sea of Tranquility where Neil

Armstrong would first step onto the Moon in 1969, and she knew she was looking at a lonely, pristine world free of human footprints. A quick mental calculation told her humans would first arrive there 84 years from this time, and for now in 1885, the entire Moon was completely mysterious.

* * *

She sat with Mary at breakfast.

"Do you have plans," said Professor Schwartz.

"Kathryn is showing me around," said Mary, "She's from Kansas City."

"Oh?"

"I didn't know you are a city girl," said George.

"I was born here."

"You must have been a little girl during the Battle of Westport."

"It was before my time."

"I beg your pardon. That's none of my business."

"It's perfectly all right." Kayla realized his estimate was accurate and she shouldn't have said that. "It was before my memory. Yes I was very young during the War."

"Of course."

"You must be familiar with the new cable car here about to start operation." the professor said to her.

"Oh, yes, they were building it before I left."

"Well then, you must have left about three or five years ago."

Whew, thought Kayla, that was close. I'll research that when I get back to the present.

"I knew I would miss my chance to ride it when I moved away."

"Then I will ask my driver to take you ladies so you can ride the new cable car. You're welcome to stay here again tonight at our home."

"Thank you for your generosity," Mary said.

"Very well then. When you're ready, my driver will take you to the cable car stop. At its end you can get a taxicab. I will arrange for my driver to meet the taxicab there and pay the fare for wherever you'd like to go around the city."

"Wonderful," Kayla said.

Kayla and Mary rose to go freshen up before their day's outing.

They all convened in the parlor where a small picnic basket provided by the Schwartz's sat waiting.

Mary picked it up. "Lovely," she said.

"Would you care to join us, Mr. Fielding?" said Kayla.

"No, thank you, the professor and I will be leaving to visit the college when the driver returns with the buggy."

Kayla smiled, nodded, and they left.

* * *

Kayla and Mary boarded the cable car and rode around corners with "tall" buildings. Kayla thought it fascinating to see these buildings in their newer state. Many of them were gone in her time, except the so-called New England Life Building that was now under construction. Interesting to see nineteenth century building methods at work during the day with scaffolding. Kayla didn't consider herself an expert on building materials, metal or otherwise. The skeleton frame's load-bearing columns appeared be cast iron, not steel. She sneaked her camera out and stole a shot of the construction.

She and Mary had to grab hold of their seats when they whipped around a curve.

"Oh my!" said Mary. "That almost threw me out the window." She looked around at other passengers, a bit embarrassed.

The cable car took them on a route with a view between the sparse buildings where they could see out across the "bottoms," across the Kansas River to the Kansas side of the border.

They reached the end of the line and met the horse-drawn taxicab hired by Professor Schwartz.

The open air was nice and Kayla took it upon herself to direct the driver. They rounded a few more blocks toward the what would be the Crossroads arts district in normal time. They drove down a street that had a couple restaurants and saloons. A few people milled about, most looking "respectable" to Kayla's twenty-first century eyes.

They drove by a saloon. Kayla leaned out toward it and listened.

"Driver, stop, please," she said.

"What is it, Kathryn?" asked Mary.

Kayla cupped her ear. "Listen."

"I hear piano music from inside," Mary said.

"Yes!"

She driver pulled the carriage over. Kayla gave him a half dollar and he agreed to come back by in an hour.

Kayla hopped out and started for the swing-doors.

Mary got out of the carriage. "Kathryn, wait!"

Kayla stopped in front of the swing-doors and turned to Mary. "It's fine, let's go in!"

Mary gestured to a side door. "The ladies entrance," she said.

"Of course! I'm sorry. I missed that."

Mary took Kayla's hand and led her through the door into the large room. Men in neat coats, collars, some wearing hats, occupied a few tables, one of which had a card game going. The proprietor and a couple of men stood attention-like behind the bar. The only African-American person in the saloon was a well-dressed man at the piano filling the room with fast, happy music.

Kayla and Mary found a table not far from the bar.

[238]

Kayla leaned toward Mary. "Do you like this music?"

"Yes, it's happy music."

Kayla was confused: This kind of music wasn't played in Kansas City yet in 1885. She had to find out who that pianist was. There was something familiar about him. As she took Mary with her to the bar, men throughout the place looked them up and down.

They stepped up to the bar together. One of the men tending bar asked, "What can we do for you ladies?"

Kayla listened to the music. "My husband owns a saloon in Kansas. I want to tell him about that pianist. What is his name?"

"You can ask him yourself in a minute," the bartender said.

The music stopped and the pianist stepped up to the bar, a few feet from Kayla and Mary.

Kayla nodded and turned toward him. He leaned onto the bar.

"Excuse me, sir," Kayla said, "my husband owns a saloon in Kansas. May I know your name?"

Oh please, please let it be.

"Yes, ma'am. My name is Joplin. Scott Joplin."

Kayla almost screamed and jumped ten feet. "I love your music," she said.

"I'm on my way to St. Louis," he said. "I wasn't supposed to come through Kansas City, but the train had to take a detour through Kansas when the weather got bad in Arkansas and since my stop here was for a couple of days, I looked for a place where I could play my music. I'm sorry I won't be able to play in your husband's saloon."

"Oh, pardon my presumptuousness."

"That's fine, miss. Thank you for the compliment. I'm glad you like it."

Kayla pretended her phone in its case was a compact, held it up, and took a picture of him.

She and Mary returned to their table and listened to him play. Kayla relished every note, bar, chord, and melody. She took a short video.

After a while, they decided to leave.

Out front, they waited for the carriage.

"I think you'll like where we go next, Mary."

After a few minutes, the carriage pulled up and they climbed aboard.

Kayla directed the driver to take them down to Penn Valley Park where a road split off and went around a hill. The driver took them to a path that led to the top and they got out. The hillside was mostly grassy with shady trees here and there. Picnickers sat scattered across the hillside. There was no World War One Liberty Memorial tower on the hill nor the eighteen-story building that also occupied the hill in normal time. It looked strange to Kayla.

"If you ladies would like to enjoy a picnic, I'll wait here," the driver said, smiling at Kayla. She retrieved a quarter this time and handed it to him. He seemed satisfied.

Kayla and Mary eagerly took to the path up to a shady spot where they sat and gazed at the view.

"What a wonderful place Kansas City is," Mary said. "You can see all around from up here, the river, the bridges, and look, there's a steam ship rolling along. I wonder where it's going."

"St. Louis, perhaps," said Kayla, "which is where that pianist is headed."

"I want to find his music for sale."

Wait till you hear "The Entertainer," thought Kayla. "I think you will find his music sometime soon," she said.

The driver walked to the front of the horse and fed it something. Kayla and Mary gathered the picnic items into the basket.

[240]

"I must go behind the bushes," Mary said.

So that's what you do when you have to go at the park, thought Kayla.

When Mary emerged, Kayla found a place and relieved herself behind some shrubs then she rejoined Mary. They headed down the hill to the carriage.

"I wonder how long Mr. Fielding will be staying with the professor," Kayla said.

"I'm afraid I don't know, but I think I would like to go back to Sycamore Falls tomorrow."

Kayla agreed.

* * *

That evening, Professor and Mrs. Schwartz provided a lavish dinner.

The dinner came in several courses. They started with savory soup, then roast turkey with dressing and the chef's specialty potatoes, dinner rolls with sweet cream butter, and assorted jams and jellies followed by cake and preserved fruit. Beverages included coffee or water.

Kayla never ate so much on a non-holiday.

After supper, Kayla decided to turn in early rather than sit up with the professor and Mr. Fielding. Mary deferred to an early bedtime as well.

On the way upstairs, Mary whispered, "Better to get to bed early, so we get plenty of sleep in the morning like decent people." She tried to suppress a giggle.

"Now where did you hear an expression like that?" Kayla whispered back.

"Why I can't imagine."

They snickered softly as they went to their rooms.

Kayla made sure her bag was ready for morning and double-checked the book. She was glad to be going back to Sycamore Falls; she was starting to feel homesick. And then she would have to avoid hazards and deal with saying goodbye to Mary before timeshifting to normal time, not to mention parting with her other new friends, perhaps forever. As for hazards, she had gotten over the scare on the train with the excitement of seeing KC and taking Mary around town. Mary was getting to be a really good friend and she would miss her terribly when she exited this timeline. She had much to do back in the present and now she missed Kevin and her new friend, Jennifer. But wow, did she have stories to tell, and videos to show. She looked forward to that, but now she had to avoid hazards or never be able to tell her stories. Stop worrying, she told herself.

The next morning, Professor Schwartz had his driver take Kayla and Mary to the depot along with George who had also decided to go back home. The train ride this time was uneventful, at least to start. The ride out of Kansas City past Lawrence to Topeka was normal enough. At the Topeka stop, a maintenance person and the engineer had to work on a problem with the engine, something with the steam locomotive's boiler. They said the problem made it unsafe and the passengers had to spend the night in their train car after dinner at Harvey's. Kayla tried slumping back on the seat as did Mary. Sleep for both was difficult.

Another day later, the Flint Hills were a welcome sight as they chugged toward Sycamore Falls. From the east, the hills were like a front range. Kayla and Mary arrived at the hometown depot late, weary, and ready to rest for a month.

* * *

At the rooming house, Mary took hold of Kayla's wrist. "What's wrong, Kathryn? You don't seem happy."

"I am unsure what to do. Stay here or go back home. If I go, I'll miss my new friends here."

"It's not my place to say, but sometimes you do seem out of place. I know life in the city is much more exciting, but you'll love it here and we would all miss you if you left."

Kayla gave Mary a quick hug. "I know, thank you. And I would miss all of you if I went back."

"Perhaps if you had a gentleman friend here."

"Perhaps," Kayla said with a shrug. She nodded and smiled. She thought of Kevin. Some of the old feelings persisted. The romance wasn't there anymore, but she valued his friendship and they got along well.

Mary smiled and nodded.

"I think it's you I would really miss if I go back," Kayla said. "We're like sisters."

"I feel the same way about you. We share so much in common; we understand each other."

"We do." Kayla sighed. She'd have to go back to the present and think about it. And if she razed the house, then she would be stuck with her decision forever.

"Thank you, Mary, you've given me much to think about."

"I hope you decide to stay," Mary said.

* * *

Back at the rooming house, Kayla went to her room to prepare for her exit back to normal time. Book Club was in a day. Until then, she'd hang out with Mary. She attended Book Cub with her on Friday. After Ida and the others welcomed them back, Kayla forced herself to get it over with: go into the library, and return to the present.

[243]

CHAPTER TWENTY-SEVEN
Sacred Hill

A TEARFUL KAYLA reacquainted herself with the normal time library and shabby house, that musty smell she had almost forgotten. She went to the Victorian and took a shower and crashed. Her own bed was wonderful after sleeping on a train seat.

The next morning, she texted Kevin and Jennifer. They came by soon after.

Jennifer talked Kayla into going back to the farmhouse. The anomaly still tugged at her anyway even after her extended stay.

* * *

Kayla and Jennifer stood in front of the bookcase.

"Is there a way to an earlier time?" Jennifer said.

"I've been looking for a way." Kayla said. "1920 and 1885 are the earliest I've found so far."

"Any other ideas?"

"Actually, I had thought of going back to 1885 and checking the basement below the library."

"Let's go," Jennifer said. "Is there time?"

"If we head right down. We have to access the basement from outside."

They timeshifted. During the quiet time in the 1885 replay, they ran outside to a narrow sidewalk that led to the cellar door and heaved it open. Down the steps, they stood on the basement dirt floor and looked around. The coal shoot was in active use.

"How fascinating," said Jennifer. "Their primary means of warmth, a modern convenience back then."

"There's a pile of rocks," Kayla said. "Kevin said they placed rocks like that for footers. She pointed to a support beam supported by a rock that had been partially buried, then pointed to some rocks under the library. "The one on top is too loose to support anything." She stepped over to the rocks and hoisted the larger one off the top of the pile.

The house above vanished along with Jennifer. Kayla stood in a large rectangular hole with dirt walls.

Without haste, she put the rock back.

The house above was back and Jennifer stood there with a puzzled look.

"I went back to an earlier time!" Kayla said.

Jennifer came over to her.

"Shall we both go back?" Kayla said.

Jennifer agreed and they timeshifted to the center of the rectangular dirt hole.

Kayla went over to a wall and clambered her way up to the ground. A horse-drawn wagon pulled away, leaving stacks of lumber. No one remained. The trees were gone, just a grassy hilltop here.

Kayla got on her hands and knees next to the edge and reached out.

"Jennifer, I'll pull you up."

Jennifer stepped over and reached up to take Kayla's hand.

She made her way up and joined Kayla.

Jennifer stood next to Kayla and gazed around at the pre-1885 Flint Hills. "No Sycamore Falls yet," she said.

"Amazing to see the land without farms, grain bins, and all the other modern structures," said Kayla.

"The beauty of it—whenever this is," said Jennifer. "How wonderful to witness."

[245]

Kayla noticed a flat embedded rock along the ridgetop with a heavy stone on it. She went and lifted the stone, revealing a large arrowhead. She picked up the arrowhead and a strong breeze nearly knocked her down as she timeshifted to an earlier time. Jennifer vanished. The large dug hole was gone, as if filled in and sodded. There was no wagon, no trail of wagon wheel ruts and no lumber: only the grassy hill on which she stood.

In the setting sun, long shadows stretched over the pristine hills. A herd of bison blanketed a distant mound. A cool breeze blew through Kayla's hair, giving her chills. She looked toward the location where Sycamore Falls would be, to a valley with a tree-lined creek meandering between the hills. The trees were budding, indicating spring. Across on a nearby hill stood a woman in indigenous clothes gazing at Kayla. Kayla clutched the arrowhead and hiked over to the hill, stopping a few feet from her.

"Hello, Kayla," said Mara. "Welcome to long ago. You are the only non-indigenous person on this continent, indeed in the whole New World as you call it." She gestured to where the farmhouse would be built.

"This hill is the highest in the area of what you call the Flint Hills and you remember I told you this hill is sacred to Indigenous People. As I've said, up here, the Tribes come together. The farmhouse will be built on the top of this hill. Return to your own time. Consider arranging to have the farmhouse removed and contact tribal leaders. We can help each other. You can sell the hilltop to the Tribe and we can reclaim this hill. We will partner with Sycamore Falls and bring visitors and commerce to town. Seek out Kevin. He has other good ideas. Set up a meeting with him and tribal leaders."

CHAPTER TWENTY-EIGHT
A Sip of Wine

KAYLA AND JENNIFER RETURNED TO the present.

Kayla went home and got ready to head down to the Historical Society.

In the Historical Society front room, she looked at the portraits on the wall. Now that Mary was fresh on her mind, she found the portrait resembled her closely. Even though Mary and the Georges lived over a century before, to her, she saw them only recently.

Kevin appeared next to her and put his arm around her shoulder.

"Hey," she said quietly.

"Hey."

"The farmhouse goes tomorrow," she said.

"You've decided to get rid of it then."

"I want you and Jennifer to meet me there this afternoon for one last visit."

"No, you're not going—"

"I'm not. The timeshifting is over; it's done its job. I doubt it even works now."

"Any idea what caused it?"

"A joint effort by the Tribe and town entities for their mutual benefit. We might figure it out one day, but that's what strikes me, the thought slapping me across the face."

"Then we've been given a great gift," he said.

"Now we must give back to the town and the Tribe. But I really miss my friends from 1885."

"You have memories of your friendships with people who lived over a hundred years ago. That's priceless."

"It is. Okay, meet me at the farmhouse at 5:30 this afternoon. I'll contact Jennifer. See if Sheriff Rick is free for a while."

Kevin nodded and retreated to the Loft. Kayla exited and emerged out to the sidewalk to behold present-day Sycamore Falls.

"My how you've changed," she said. "But you're looking better, really." She was about to head to her car but walked to The Niche instead.

"Oh, hello, Kayla," said Ronnie.

"I think I'll bring some of the old books Brenda left," Kayla said.

"Do consider it."

"I will. I'm getting ready to raze the old farmhouse."

"Oh, that's interesting."

"It's a money pit."

Ronnie nodded, giving a look that she understood.

* * *

Kevin and Jennifer arrived at the farmhouse along with Sheriff Rick in the late afternoon.

"I want to sell some of these books to The Niche," said Kayla, "but I don't really know if the timeshifting is still there with some of them."

"Probably not, like you said," said Kevin.

"Only one way to find out," said Jennifer who stepped into the library and pulled *The Story of Art* from the bookcase.

"Nothing," she said. "Here's one you can sell." She handed the book to Kayla. "Actually, "Jennifer continued, "I think Caleb would like it."

Kayla handed the book back to Jennifer. "With my compliments. He earned it."

[248]

Kayla motioned to Jennifer, Rick, and Kevin to sit with her in the living room. She sat on the old couch and retrieved Ida's special vintage 1885 bottle of wine, a corkscrew, and glasses from her bag. She opened the bottle and poured herself a small amount.

"If you'll indulge me in taking the first sip," she said.

She then started to pour more glasses. Let's drink a toast to Ida and all my friends in the 1885 Book Club and others. To Mary, to Anna, to Emma, to the Georges, to Elizabeth, to Margarete, to Florence, Alice, and to Sarah. How I would love to see you all again, share conversation and ideas. Especially Mary Dodd—oh, how I'll miss you, my friend." She nodded at Jennifer.

Kayla lost it and pulled out a tissue. Kevin and Jennifer went and embraced her on the couch. Rick kneeled next to her. She regained her composure and sat forward.

"I need to be careful not to spill this," Kayla said as she held her glass out.

"Again, to my friends past and present."

"To everyone," said Kevin.

"To you, Kayla," said Jennifer.

"Hear, hear," said Rick, holding up his glass.

"And now," Kayla said as she took the first sip.

But before she could savor the wine, a breeze swirled around her.

Lilacs. The aroma wafted in through a window. She recognized the nineteenth century sofa on which she sat while holding the wine bottle. Ida, Mary, Anna, and the other women in Book Club sat around the room as they did in her 1885 visits.

"Oh, my!" said Kayla.

"Welcome back," Kathryn," said Ida.

Mary smiled at her with a puzzled look as did the others although they did seem to recognize her.

[249]

Kayla didn't know what to do, how to get back to normal time. And this—this—she thought this could no longer happen.

She glanced into the library. No change since her last jaunt to 1885. The familiar timeline wasn't replaying this time. After a moment, a terrifying thought: she didn't have a book to reshelve. Was she in this time to stay? The other timelines were real in a sense, but she had a door into and out of them. How would she return to normal time now?

In a moment of temporary clarity, she pulled a nail file from her bag and pretended to use it as one would expect, then pretended to drop it onto the floor drawing a glance from the others.

She faked embarrassment and leaned forward to grab the file. As discretely as she could, she scratched a "K" into the wood floor board as hard as she could. She sat up and filed one of her nails then smiled and put the file away.

"Well, ladies," said Ida, "I think we'll adjourn our meeting for today." "We're glad to have you back, Kathryn."

Several utterances of "Oh, yes." followed.

The women rose and prepared to leave. Mary went to Kayla.

"I'm so glad you came back," she said. "I was afraid you moved back to Kansas City."

Kayla held out her hand to Mary's. "Oh, no. I love it here in Sycamore Falls."

"I thought maybe our trip to there reminded you of home and your feelings for it."

"No, this is my home now."

"I'm so glad." Mary wiped a tear away. That started Kayla welling up.

Mary remembers me, and our times together! Definitely not a timeline replay.

What did my reappearance look like? she wondered. Did I just pop into their midst? Maybe they were suspended during my entrance.

She didn't know.

"Be careful with your wine bottle," Mary said, "you don't want to accidently spill it."

"Oh, yes." Kayla went to the sofa, sat and carefully recorked the bottle.

The room faded to the shabby version in normal time.

"You left," Kevin said along with mumbles by Jennifer and Rick.

"I went back to 1885 Book Club!"

"You said—" started Kevin.

"I didn't know!"

She leaned forward and looked at the floor.

"What're you looking for?" said Jennifer.

"Permanence."

Kayla got up and onto her knees so she could turn up the old area rug in front of the couch. "It's there!"

"There's a 'K' there," Kevin said.

"As I expected, or wondered. I scratched the floor during that quick jaunt to 1885 with the sip of wine."

"Unlike the timeshifting with the library artifacts," he said.

"Right. It wasn't a temporary timeline like with the timeshifting books. I figured since I was there, I'd try."

"And there's the risk of a time paradox," Kevin said. Good thing we didn't end up losing World War Two."

"World War?" said Kayla. "There was a World War?"

"Shut up!"

"Okay, haha, I was careful."

CHAPTER TWENTY-NINE
Cultural Center

KAYLA DIDN'T SELL THE HOUSE and land to the Tribe, but gave it back to them.

A few months later, she leaned back in the chair and took in the familiar view.

Mara sat next to her.

"Do you miss the farmhouse?" she said.

"Not at all. I love what the Tribe has done up here."

Mara smiled.

"I'm glad we came to an agreement, and not to diminish my enthusiasm for the Tribe's new visitor center and museum up here, but I couldn't afford to fix the house up anyway."

A cooling breeze sent both women's hair floating out.

"It's so nice up here," Kayla said.

"You're always welcome here, Kayla," said Mara.

As the afternoon wore on, Kayla noticed the time and headed down to the Victorian to get ready to go meet Kevin down at the Historical Society for something new he wanted to demonstrate.

* * *

He was sitting in a chair next to the brochure table when Kayla entered.

"What's so important you wanted to demonstrate?" she said.

"Follow me." He led her outside to his vintage car.

"Okay, it's nice, but I've seen and ridden in it before," she said.

"Let's go."

"Where?"

"You'll see."

She settled into the old Chevy and they pulled out onto Main. They went a ways and turned onto a side street that was lined with old bungalows, some being restored.

"Some renovation going on?" she said. "That's exciting to see these houses being fixed up."

"You've missed a lot with your head stuck in the past," he said, ducking a potential slap.

"Hey, I've been in the present since the Tribe reclaimed the land up there and built their visitor center."

He pointed at a couple of houses under renovation. "Mara and other artists have been holding online fundraisers where the perks for big contributors include paintings."

"Fantastic."

They pulled around, turning back the other direction, then headed toward downtown and turned onto Main, passing Weber's and slowed to pass a somewhat familiar place.

"Lenny's!" she said.

"Bernice restored it to its past. I gave her some photos I took inside in the past, converted them to black and white, printed them, and told her they're scans of old photos we acquired at the Historical Society. She's convinced they're authentic."

"They *are* authentic."

"So she restored the place to be as close to the original as possible and avoid cliché-ish décor. Got with some old-timers for pointers who remember it when it was open."

They stopped, went in, and sat at the counter.

"This is so authentic," Kayla said to Bernice.

Bernice smiled. "Now, what can I get you all?"

"I'll have the deluxe cheeseburger with fries and a Coke," Kevin said. "No, make that a Cherry Coke."

[253]

"I'll just have a salad, fries, and water and some apple pie," Kayla said.

"With ice cream?"

"No, thanks."

"You're really splurging," Kevin said.

"Shut up. I'm looking forward to the pie."

Bernice set two rough textured plastic glasses of water out, and brought their orders.

"She nailed it," said Kevin after he started devouring his food.

"She did."

* * *

After their meal, back in the car, Kayla said, "Glad to see Lenny's restored."

"One step of several. We want to capture the feeling of the past."

Kayla thanked Kevin for the short tour and said, "I need to talk to you. Can you drop me off at home and come in for a bit?"

"I can." He drove the old car down Main to Kayla's street and drove up to her driveway.

They went into the parlor.

"Is something bothering you?" he said.

"Sit down."

He complied and she sat across from him.

She almost had to hold back tears. I miss my 1885 friends dearly."

"I was afraid of that."

"I like what you're doing with the new business and what the Tribe's doing. And the new businesses that are starting in town."

"Like Lenny's."

"Right. And I feel there's a positive attitude around town, a new optimism about Sycamore Falls that wasn't here when I arrived."

"We can't take credit for that. People here have worked hard to get some things going. Bernice, Ronnie, Marsha, Mara, and others."

"No, but I think we helped start something."

"Yes?"

"I'm confused. I'm excited about Sycamore Falls' resurgence."

"What're you saying? Why are you confused?"

"Sometimes I'm tempted."

"Kansas City?"

"No, Sycamore Falls is my home now."

Kevin sighed.

CHAPTER THIRTY
Pow Wow—Old Friends and New

KAYLA STOOD IN A LINE OF PEOPLE ON THE HILLTOP as Indigenous People performed traditional dances to beating drums. The drumming came from a circle of people near the dances. Turnout was heavy with a lot of people from out of town. She looked around for Kevin and saw him in a line across from her. A little while later, she went over to some vendors beneath canopies, a short walk along the ridgeline. One vendor representing several Tribes had a variety of pottery. The next vendor was Mara displaying some of her paintings showing scenes on this hilltop, including the one she painted when her artist group had set up on the hillside that one weekend. Kayla contemplated one of the paintings and got lost in the scene as only she could. Mara came next to her.

"Follow your heart, Kayla," she said.

Kayla smiled, shrugged, and headed out from the vendor area. She caught Kevin's attention. He was walking with a group of people who had just dispersed from the dancing. He smiled at her and looked happy, among friends.

Kayla paused and searched for familiar Sycamore Falls landmarks from the past. The roof of the rooming house that still stood rose from some trees. And she looked over to the hill where she, Mary, and George had their picnic over a century before. She focused on the spot where she thought they had been and sat down in the grass to relive those moments in the warm sun and gaze out across the same distant hills like during the picnic. A wave of peace flowed over her, remembering her friends. She could come up here anytime and relive that picnic. But she couldn't see Mary and the Georges again, nor Ida, nor the others.

CHAPTER THIRTY-ONE
Another Sip?

DURING AN EVENING IN THE VICTORIAN, KAYLA SETTLED INTO HER COMFY CHAIR IN THE DEN with her laptop and started updating her blog with her latest observations in Sycamore Falls and Kevin's progress with the business. She portrayed Sycamore Falls as a destination worthy of any daytrip or from farther away and included photos of historical places around town.

She got up and glanced out a back window. The hill was missing the farmhouse now with the silhouette of the cultural center in the house's place. She headed into the parlor.

The wine rack was mostly decorative. She bought it to hold the precious gifts from Ida. With a smile, she ran her hand over two of the ancient bottles that sat on the top rack and took hold of the bottle she had opened that last day of the farmhouse and held it up to the light. The magic liquid—for she knew of no other way to think of it—from more than a hundred years in the past displayed gorgeous backlit burgundy color. She eased the bottle upright and regarded the level at its top, just an inch or so below the cork. She ran her fingers over the simple black and white label that displayed "West Hill Vineyards" and 1885 below an illustration of a hill with a house on top.

"I'm sorry, Ida, razing the farmhouse was the right thing to do."

She dusted off the bottle with her sleeve and returned the bottle to the rack, palming it as she rotated it into place. "Maybe someday for a very special occasion, I'll share some glasses of 1876 vintage with a friend or two." As she started to head to the sofa, she retrieved the 1885 bottle again and sat on the sofa with it. The setting sun cast light across the parlor floor. She cradled the wine bottle and thought about how it seemed Ida had just recently given it to her rather than over a century ago. She settled back and dozed for a few minutes then woke and put the wine bottle back. She walked around, deciding whether the parlor needed more decorating or any changes. It'd be nice to make the room like an art gallery.

There was no point in mourning the farmhouse. This house had everything she wanted. Beautiful woodwork from a time when it was done well. All the things about this house that lured her to buy the property in the first place helped her forget about what the farmhouse could have been if she'd renovated it. She liked what the Tribe did on the hilltop, so she had no regrets about tearing the old house down. Brenda got what she wanted and needed. Seeing Brenda around town would be weird now after witnessing what she had done in 1961.

Kayla would see about acquiring some of Mara's art and a painting by Caleb to display here on the parlor's walls. She spent the rest of the evening working on her article. There was a lot to update about the town's progress. She didn't shy away from inserting her opinions on things or masking editorial aspects in her articles. Kevin's contribution to "progress" here was going to be making things like the past, not what is usually called "progress" or "improvements," which she found to be contradictions to what was really happening like in suburban Kansas City where surrounding countryside was being eaten up by metro sprawl as it was around many cities. She looked forward to what Kevin and others had in the works.

* * *

The next morning, Kayla headed out on foot during the cool of the morning and walked downtown where she was met by heavier than normal traffic. She called Kevin.

He answered. "Hey," he said, "the art festival starts today."

"It does? "So I've been busy!"

"Okay, okay. You want to meet me at the courthouse lawn if you're close?"

"No, I just started out," she said.

"Then how about Nonstandard Artifacts? Twenty minutes."

"See you there," she said, picking up the pace.

Nonstandard Artifacts was busy with a milling crowd that filled the gallery.

Mara was there. She went to Kayla. "I just sold a painting," she said.

"Fantastic! I want to acquire one of your works for my house."

"I didn't sell that one you were eyeing at the pow wow, the one of the hill before the farmhouse. I'll give you that one."

Kayla threw her arms around Mara.

Mara jumped back, regaining her balance. She laughed. "Careful!"

CHAPTER THIRTY-TWO
Visitors

AMY AND ANTHONY DROVE INTO SYCAMORE FALLS.

Amy looked at her phone. "Three blocks ahead, turn right."

"Don't you want to see the downtown first? The art fair is going on."

"I do, but, let's get to the B&B and get checked in. There's a tour in an hour. How about we do that and go to lunch? The fair goes all weekend."

"Okay, that works."

They turned onto the street.

"I like these old houses," she said. "Look at those bungalows."

"I'm a Victorian guy myself."

"You don't have to clean one."

"Hey, I do my share. I would if I lived in it."

"The bungalows are cool."

They drove a block and turned onto another street.

More old houses greeted them. Halfway down the block, a bungalow had an old 1940s car in the driveway.

"Wow, look at that," Anthony said.

"There's another," she said, pointing to the end of the block where a 1930s car sat in front of a fairly large house. The house's roof sloped from the roof line down to the front, forming the top of the porch.

"Oh, what style of house is that? I've seen those," Amy said.

"Craftsman style. They built a lot of those in the early 1900s. A lot of them in the twenties and thirties."

"Go slow. I'm getting a picture."

"Get the car in it."

"And there's another interesting house, no old car there."

"That style's called arts and crafts."

"Well, aren't you the expert?"

They turned left at the next intersection and drove by a ranch style house with a tour sign in the front yard and a mid-1950s car in the drive. Another ranch had a tour sign out front with a mid-1960s Pontiac parked in the driveway.

"Nice!" she said. "Mom wants a ranch like these when she retires. She grew up in one. She wants to go 'home' when she retires, she says."

They reached the end of the block and a sign on the corner said: "Sycamore Falls Historic Tour: 1880s to 1980s."

"I've never seen an all-encompassing tour like that. Usually just older homes."

She pulled up the site on her phone. "They take you through time driving you in a 1920s Model A Ford to an early twentieth century home that you can go in and tour, then a 1940s car picks you up and takes you to a house paired with it, and so on. Someday, it says, the tour will start with a horse and buggy ride to an 1800s house, then switch to cars."

They went to the B&B, a large foursquare house with wraparound porch, a couple of blocks from downtown. A 1938 Chevy sat out front. They pulled up and went to check in.

They were met by a young woman wearing a badge that said, "Michaela – University of Pennsylvania." She greeted them and led them to the registration desk, an antique table with a seated young man wearing a badge that said, "Devin – University of North Carolina, Chapel Hill."

CHAPTER THIRTY-THREE
Preparation

KAYLA SPENT PART OF THE DAY IN TOWN RUNNING ERRANDS.

"Thanks for meeting me down here," Kayla said later as she and Kevin walked along Main Street past Second.

"Of course. You sound as if I needed convincing to meet you."

"I know. I'm just a little out of it lately," she said.

"I mean, what's up? I've noticed you a little down. A new place takes a while to adjust to. I want you to be happy here and I hope you aren't actually thinking of moving back to Kansas City."

"Don't worry," she said, "Like I said, Sycamore Falls is my town now, where I belong."

"Good. Let's walk around, then let's see what Jennifer's up to."

"That works."

He put his hand on her shoulder. "Whenever you need me, let me know."

"Thanks, Kev."

They walked half a block more and Kayla stopped. "Here's where the hat shop was that Mary and I went in to buy my hat."

Kevin looked at the abandoned store entrance. "That's changed who knows how many times over the years."

Kayla grew quiet. "Everything from then is gone," she mumbled, "including my friends."

"I'm sorry," he said. "I shouldn't put you through that."

"I miss them."

They reached the end of the street. Kayla pointed across to an empty store front near Weber's. "That's where the yarn shop was."

"What about Weber's?" he said.

"It wasn't established until a few years later."

"Are you ready to head over to Jennifer's? I'm afraid this is tough on you."

"Thanks, that'd be great."

* * *

Later at Jennifer's, Kayla sat holding her phone on the couch with Kevin and Jennifer on either side. She paged through her pictures and videos.

"That really is Scott Joplin," said Jennifer.

"It is," Kayla said. "I mean, was. I couldn't believe it. So I'm sending some of these pics to you guys."

"I appreciate that," said Kevin.

"Me, too," said Jennifer.

"Might as well have backups," Kayla said. "Although I do have them copied to my laptop."

They looked at more pictures of 1885 Sycamore Falls and of her friend Mary and other 1885 friends.

After a while, Kayla stood. "Well," she said, "I'm a bit tired. Thank you, Jennifer, for having us over and thanks, Kev, for the walk today."

Kevin and Jennifer also stood. Kayla hugged Jennifer then threw her arms around Kevin and held back tears as she hugged him tightly.

"Well, you guys, I'm going home." She headed out the door.

* * *

After Kayla left, Jennifer said, "Is she okay?"

"She's been down a lot lately," he said. "I'm a little worried about her. She'll need our support."

"She's got it."

* * *

When Kayla got home she grabbed a waiting package off her porch, took it into the parlor and opened it. All was there. She spent a lot.

She gazed at Mara's painting on her parlor wall—Mara on the hill.

"I did the right thing with the farmhouse," she affirmed.

She hesitated for a moment then grabbed a box of tissues and tossed it onto the sofa.

She sat and hand wrote a note to Kevin and Jennifer, sealed it in an envelope, and propped the envelope up on the mantle.

She went through the box of tissues in less than half an hour.

CHAPTER THIRTY-FOUR
Gratitude

KAYLA SAT ON THE FRONT PORCH of Ida's house gazing out at the Flint Hills of 1885. Ida emerged from inside with a tray that held a pitcher of tea and a couple of glasses. She set the tray on a little table in front of the matching wicker chair on which Kayla relaxed.

The grassy hills rolled from horizon to horizon. Missing were farms and other modern effects. Also missing was her Victorian house and there was not an airplane to be seen nor heard, the clear blue skies absent flying machines and contrails.

* * *

Ida handed Kayla a glass. "I'm so glad you came back, Kathryn."

"I missed you and the others, Ida," said Kayla.

"Mary will be over soon."

"Wonderful."

A cool breeze wafted along the porch. She looked down at nineteenth century Sycamore Falls and sighed. "You're welcome and thanks," she said.

"I beg your pardon?" said Ida.

"Nothing. Just acknowledging a gift."

Kayla didn't expect the reality of 1885 to match her romanticizing of the time as she viewed it from her twenty-first century perspective, but so far she was living it.

It was the Gratitude of Mara, her Tribe, and Sycamore Falls. She wasn't sure she deserved gratitude.

EPILOGUE

MEMORIAL DAY, A YEAR LATER IN NORMAL TIME.
Jennifer and Kevin strolled around the headstones.
Jennifer leaned toward one. "Is this our Kayla?" she said.
"She took control," he said. "She owned her life. She must have had a long, full, happy life."

In Memory of
Kathryn Wolfe
Died 1955
Universally intelligent and unprecedentedly virtuous
—Henry James

Jennifer reached into her bag and pulled a book out.
"What's that?" he said.
"Surprise," she said.
"Where did you find that!"
"At the library."
Kevin held his hand to his mouth.
The title was:

My Life and Times: An Autobiography
by Kayla Ramsey

Jennifer opened the book.
"Look at the dedication."
To Kevin, Jennifer, and Mara,
And to Mary, who, sadly, left us far too early
With friends like these, I am fine.

[268]

* * *

"Thanks for letting us know, sweet Kayla," Kevin said softly, rubbing his eyes.

They both wiped away tears and hugged for minutes, kissed, and went home.

APPENDIX – THE BOOKS

Next Door Neighbors by Josephine Lawrence
The House of the Seven Gables by Nathaniel Hawthorne
Daddy-Long-Legs by Jean Webster
Little Women by Louisa May Alcott
The Best Short Stories of 1915, Edward J. O'Brien, ed. Published 1916
Destination Unknown by Agatha Christie (Published 1954)
The Story of Art by Ernst Gombrich (Published 1950)
Out of the Silent Planet by C.S. Lewis (Published (1938)
Stranger in a Strange Land by by Robert A. Heinlein (Published 1961)
The Witness Stand by Hugo Münsterberg (Published 1915)
Jailed for Freedom: American Women Win the Vote by Doris Stevens, Edith Mayo (Published 1920)
The Portrait of a Lady by Henry James
The Prince and the Pauper by Mark Twain (Published 1885)

ABOUT THE AUTHOR

Photo credit: Nancy Reynolds

Eric T. Reynolds is Editor/Publisher with Hadley Rille Books (hrbpress.com). He was born in the Flint Hills town, Eureka, Kansas, has also lived elsewhere in Kansas, and on the US East Coast. His fiction has appeared in the magazines *Mythic Circle, Galaxy's Edge,* and *Sci Phi Journal,* and in several indie press publications, and he had several non-fiction science articles published in an encyclopedia about the history of space exploration. *The Artifacts* is his first novel. Contact him at erictreynolds@gmail.com and on Facebook as Eric T. Reynolds.

www.ingramcontent.com/pod-product-compliance
Lightning Source LLC
Chambersburg PA
CBHW010837250626
47157CB00011B/3297